No Lady

No Lady

SASKIA HOPE

First published in 1993 by
Black Lace
332 Ladbroke Grove
London W10 5AH

Copyright © Saskia Hope 1993

Typeset by CentraCet, Cambridge
Printed and bound by
Cox & Wyman Ltd, Reading Berks

ISBN 0 352 32857 6

Black Lace novels are sexual fantasies. In real life,
always practise safe sex.

Chapter One

'*A*re you afraid?' he had asked.
   'Go to hell.'
He never let go of the gun all the time he was inside her.

'Romance,' said Sadie, 'is dead.'
   'You really think so?'
   'We're dumb to want it. If we do. We're told we want it, but who wants holding hands in the park and looking goopily into someone's eyes when you can have too much gin, a good screw and wake up in decent privacy the next morning.'
   'I certainly look like hell in the morning,' Kate agreed.
   'You've got it right. You go with a married man. No problems with him trying to take over your life.'
   Kate looked at her friend consideringly. She never knew quite how facetious Sadie was, or how serious, when she made these outrageous statements. 'That business with Paul is shit,' she said.
   'Because you expect too much. Honey, you don't really want him to leave her. I mean, the man's a bastard by definition.'
   'Because he goes with me?'
   'Of course because he goes with you. Look, adultery

1

is fine when it's a nice healthy abandonment to temptation. But Paul isn't tempted any more. He might have been the first four or five times, but three years with the same mistress is having your cake and eating it. The man is polygamous, ducky. You're just playing along with him. You have a lousy social life and you feel perennially guilty. Really, you are a cheap second wife. You're not sin, you're an institution. You're so stupid I guess you love him.'

'I guess I do,' Kate said bleakly.

'Dump the selfish bastard. Pack your handbag full of rubbers and go on the prowl. Get laid, Kate. That's what you need. You don't get enough sex. Go out and get laid. It's very healthy. I do it all the time.'

There was a silence. Sadie put her head on one side, looking like an amused sparrow. No, a starling. Vulgar, tough Sadie with short black spiky hair and big green eyes. No wonder they lay down in rows when she went looking. 'I bet you never went with anyone even on that dumb holiday you took alone.'

'I did, actually,' Kate said.

'Good for you. What was he like? Young, tanned, gorgeous from Bletchley? Reading lager-lout, all mouth and no staying power? Recently widowed millionaire sophisticate, New York Metropolitan culture-style? C'mon, give baby. The best bet for quality humping on a Greek island has to be a local. Am I right or am I wrong?'

'You won't believe me.'

'Try me.'

'He was a thief. He had a gun. He used me to shield him from the police. As a hostage, I mean.'

There was a silence. 'If you're not putting me on,' Sadie said, 'are you telling me you were raped?'

'I'm not putting you on and I wasn't raped.'

'He was very good-looking?'

'He stank of sweat and fear. He was grubby, not to say dirty. He was using me to stop the police shooting him. I was a tourist. It doesn't do for the police to shoot

2

holidaymakers in Corfu. Gives the tourist trade a bad name.'

'What had he stolen?'

'I don't know. He had it in a knapsack.'

'How did you get away from him?'

'He walked out on me in Paris.'

'Paris! Is this a joke?'

'I'm crazy, Sadie. I'm thirty years old, I've just walked out of my job, I've dumped my lover and I'm still in love with him and I went with a man who held a gun on me because I couldn't keep my hands off him.'

Sadie blinked. 'I know you're thirty; hence the fancy bath oil I bought you for your birthday. I'm glad you're shot of Paul, though I'm sorry you're sad for him still. Not your job, Kate. For Christ's sake.'

'I didn't get the promotion. When John told me I told him he was a chauvinist pig; I would have been the best group manager their lousy company would ever have had; he and his stuffy pals stank; I was sick of office harassment and he could puke over his computerisation programme for all I cared.'

'Really?' Sadie's eyes danced. 'The world of insurance has never been so exciting.'

'I made sure his cubicle door was open when I did it and I did it at full volume. The checkers clapped. Poor underpaid bitches.'

'Are you going to apologise and get your job back? I ask merely because of that trivial thing, money.'

Kate smirked. 'He phoned up, actually, and offered me my job, if I wanted to take a little extra leave first to get over the bad time I was having.'

'Thank God.'

'When I realised the schmuck thought I had early menopause rather than being authentically bad-tempered, I repeated everything I'd said before, with knobs on.'

Sadie gave a guilty giggle. 'You really are out of work, then?'

'I am. Unless I get something fast I'll have to sell this place.'

'How fast?'

Kate shrugged. 'Six months. One thing going with Paul meant was that I spent damn-all going out. We never went out, in case we were seen. Very economical, having someone else's man. My bank balance reflects it.'

She was tired and sad and winter-pale so she took a week in late spring to sun herself alone in Corfu. She was alone because her man was married to someone else and took his holidays with his family. She went to Corfu because it was cheap and easy and there was no point in making any more effort when she was just herself. She wanted to swim, sunbathe and sleep. Spain or Greece, it made no difference. It was the furthest south she could get on the money she was prepared to spend. She went in spring because it was an unpopular holiday time in the office and it suited the company that she took some leave then. The married ones with families had to go in the school holidays. Kate was senior enough to leave in charge as they all took July and August away.

Not senior enough to be promoted, as it happened, though that was still in the future.

Romance. Unlike Sadie, who had delicious and bizarre adventures with extraordinary men and seemed to feel no shame for her horny lifestyle, Kate had a lingering affection for romance. It depended on how you defined it, of course. She couldn't go for all the soupy stuff with the tough hunky male and the pale silly cow who ended up gazing adoringly into his tough hunky eyes. But she wanted her sex nicely served, as it were, with the trimmings. Prettified. If you just went out to get bonked, surely it was like having an uncooked steak slapped solo on to a dirty table. It might be the basis of a good meal, but the way it came was raw and unattractive.

4

The trouble was, she didn't know what she wanted. She liked smooth good-looking men who treated her intelligently, who were fun, and who didn't shower her with their hang-ups. Only, where were they? Mostly, they were married to her friends.

Occasionally she met one on the loose, but somehow, after an alarmingly short time, he became boring sexually. Intellectually he might be great. He might be really nice as a companion, asexual like a brother. But apart from Paul-the-bastard, she found herself simulating orgasms in a matter of weeks. Or less.

She didn't lack a sexual drive. On the contrary, she thought she was oversexed and it embarrassed her. Of all her female acquaintances only Sadie admitted honestly to an unslakable thirst for new cock, but Kate had got scared way back. In the days before Paul she had been as footloose as Sadie recommended. She had exerted herself to pick up men. She had played some very saucy games with them; she even liked them to specialise a little, so that if she felt like a particular item on the sexual agenda, she knew who to go to.

She still wasn't sure what had gone wrong. She had been scared once or twice; a man had gone almost over the top. She had got a little older and the risks she ran suddenly seemed more significant. She had felt an onset of romanticism; she had wanted her sex softer, sweeter, kinder. All the trimmings.

That was hopeless, of course. If she got tender, men ran away: they thought she wanted commitment. The result had been an increasingly lousy sex life followed up by Paul, who was so gallant, so sweet, so tender and so very married.

You have to grow up sometime, was how she put it to herself. You have to settle. You can't screw around like a teenager overdosing on hormones.

Can't you? Sadie did, if she told the truth.

Was the attraction of Paul-the-bastard that it was in the nature of their relationship that she could never get

5

enough of him? Or was it that he was a bastard? Now, there was a sick thought.

She had rented a self-catering unit in an apartment block – she couldn't stand cheap hotels – and she lay on her terrace turning pale gold. Then she lay on the beach and let her boobs tan along with all the other Brits. She went scuba-diving; she ate in little restaurants with clutches of black-dressed elderly locals eating fish soup. She avoided human contact. On her fifth day, she took a bus to Paleokastrítsa up the north end to look over the five beaches and the monastery. On the way back down the coast, she got off the bus to to walk up through the olive groves and lemon trees on the slopes of Mount Pantokrátor, intending to come back to the road and take a bus a couple of hours later. She wore a little shirt, a wrap-over skirt tied sarong-style at her waist, and she carried a bag with her swimming things in it. Her salty damp hair was tied back off her face and she wore big sunglasses. She thought of nothing in particular as she slowly climbed a dusty track, enjoying the warm sun through her thin clothes, enjoying her lightly-dressed body and feeling pleasantly stretched from easy exercise.

She heard a gun go off somewhere. She took no notice. She knew nothing of seasons and game shooting but she vaguely thought that must be a local out after a duck. It was funny how quickly you could escape other tourists, she thought idly, standing still and watching a lizard on a rock. The foreigers all stayed on the coast. The interior seemed untouched, even on this comparatively small island.

He came out of the undergrowth beside her all at once, landing with a thump on the track. The lizard vanished and for a moment white dust floated, disturbed by his violent arrival.

A gun went off with a crack, very close. He ducked his head and looked over his shoulder. Kate could hear noises now, crashing towards them. She stood still, dumbfounded. Was she on a film set?

The man grabbed her, and the pain as he held her upper arm brought her back to reality. He pulled her in front of him and, facing the direction he had arrived from, he began to shout.

He shouted in Greek, so she didn't understand. She tried to pull free but he shook her and held her against his body, backed against him, so that she was facing his pursuers.

The first one erupted out of the bush. He was dark and in uniform and he held a gun in his hand.

The man at her back spoke urgently and Kate felt something cold and hard press against her temple.

She had a gun at her head. She didn't believe it. She was Kate Matheson, insurance assessor, west London. This was Corfu, not South America. 'Stop this,' she said sharply. She meant it. The game had to stop. It wasn't nice.

In front of her the policeman looked over his shoulder and shouted. Then he looked back at Kate and the man holding her, warily.

The man began to back away pulling Kate with him. She could smell him, smell his sweat, smell the dust on him. Curiously he smelled faintly of mimosa.

He was rattling in Greek at the policeman. The gun jabbed her head. It was perfectly clear what he was saying.

'Stop this,' said Kate again.

There were three policemen now. They stood looking at their quarry and his hostage. Kate. 'Help me,' she said.

'Let her go,' said one of the policemen.

'The hell I will.' Her captor spoke in English.

'She is nothing to do with this.' The policeman's English was very good.

'She is now.' He kept backing away. 'You're not going to get me,' he added. 'Go away. You are risking her life.'

'We will get you. It will be worse for this.'

He moved his gun arm so he held her with it across

7

her breast, the gun pointing up under her chin. With his other hand he found a knife. He ran the point down Kate's bare arm. She saw the thread of red appear. A drop like a jewel gathered. The pain began, a faint stinging.

'Jump me, and I'll kill her. Follow me and I'll slice her up, piece by piece.'

The policemen argued rapidly among themselves. They began to back off.

'Don't go,' Kate screamed. The shrill of insects momentarily stopped, and then restarted.

The man cut her arm again. There was a cross now. It began to hurt properly.

The first policeman held up his hands in a gesture of defeat and the three of them moved further off.

The man at her back got her arm in a ferocious grip. He began to push her up the track ahead of him. The gun was pointed at her all the time though the knife had disappeared.

They ran up the track in the late afternoon drowsy heat. Siesta time. Kate's feet, bare in open sandals, were white with dust. Her raffia bag scraped her shoulder. Her heart thumped. She felt her blood pounding.

'Let me go now,' she gasped. 'You'll be quicker without me.'

'They're not far,' he said. 'I'll need you to help me get off this damned island now. Do as I say and you'll be fine.'

She stopped, pulling him round. 'You're English,' she said. 'Stop this. My arm hurts.'

He hit her, quite lightly, a cuff across her head. 'I haven't got time to play around,' he said. 'I won't hurt you unless you're difficult.'

'Or the police get too close.'

'Or the police get too close,' he agreed.

They struck out across country and for a long time Kate was force-marched across a rough empty terrain. They came high above the cultivated land into a country of loose scree, burnt white rocks, scrubby prickly bushes and a sky draining of colour as evening came on. Above them a bird hung. Even the insects were quieter. Kate could hear the man's rasping breath, feel his bruising grip on her right upper arm. The two thin shallow cuts on her left forearm nagged and stung.

The land tilted. They dropped into stony valleys and came up out of them again. She had had no idea the island was so big, though she could see the sea ahead of them quite often, and the mainland. They were up on a backbone of bare rock and Kate was dirty, tired and thirsty. Fear and anger were somewhere close by, when she had the energy for them, but just now she didn't.

'We're going to rest here,' he said abruptly. Sweat was rank on him. They faced a small cliff of big tumbled boulders. Little scraggy trees feathered the naked cliff and the air was softer. There must be water close by. Some flowers grew. It was even pretty.

There was a cave. He knew about it; it had a blanket on the floor and some stores piled against one wall. It was cool and dark inside. He pushed her in ahead of him and let her go.

She sat down and rubbed her arm. Tiredness rushed over her and she felt suddenly close to weeping. She heard water gargle and saw he was drinking from a bottle hung at his waist. Her eyes were adjusting to the gloom. He handed the bottle to her and squatted, watching her, the gun loose in his hand.

She wiped the rim and drank greedily. Water spilled on her chin and she let it. She spilled some into her hand and splashed her face. Her bag was beside her and she pulled at her towel and rubbed her face with it.

He took his plastic bottle back. He had another bottle now, taken from a cache in the cave. He upended it at his mouth and she saw his throat work. He handed it over to her.

She could smell it was whisky even though she couldn't read the label. She drank quickly, feeling her

9

throat burn, feeling the warm strong heart of the alcohol build inside her and ease her.

'Are you afraid?' he asked.

'Go to hell.'

He laughed. 'I'm sorry about this,' he said, not sounding it. 'You're my good luck. They almost had me.'

'You're my bad luck.'

'I sure am. I always was, for women.'

The world slipped and steadied. A man. A male. A rogue male on the run: dangerous, unconcerned for her feelings, using her. All the veneer of civilisation gone. The situation was primaeval.

'Why are the police after you?'

He considered. 'I stole something, but I don't think that's why. I'm a smuggler. That's probably it.'

'What do you smuggle? Drugs?'

'No. Do you want to eat?'

'No. Let me go.'

'I don't think I will.'

'I don't believe this is happening to me,' she said flatly. The whisky curled inside her, a false friend.

'You'd better.'

He was wearing a bush shirt and trousers tucked into boots. There were big sweat stains under his armpits. She couldn't see them now – he was between her and the light – but she had seen them earlier.

'I'm just going outside to take a leak,' he said, picking up his knapsack. 'You stay put, lady.'

She sat by herself. She was having time to feel afraid now, but the whisky made her feel angry. She couldn't believe he would shoot her.

This was one to tell the girls, she thought. Only, it's not like the movies. I feel grubby and low and I don't know what to do. I don't feel sassy and clever, not one bit.

He came back in and ate by the cave door. Then he checked his watch, settled his knapsack for a pillow and went to sleep.

After a terrible length of time, maybe fifteen minutes or so, Kate began to inch towards the cave mouth. He didn't move. She left her bag where it was. The raffia creaked. It was a pity her camera was in it, but you can buy another camera. There's only one life.

In his thirties, she thought, moving with deadly silence inch by terrible inch. Neat body. Looks strong. The riffraff of Europe, I suppose. A criminal drifter; a thug; a woman-hurter.

He was composed in sleep, his mouth shut, his chest gently rising with each breath. She was very close now. The gun was in his right hand. He lay on his left side. Should she climb over him or take the gun?

He would wake. She would run. He probably wouldn't shoot her but he would catch her easily, bring her down crashing to the harsh ground with the breath sobbing in her throat and the fear out in the open.

She didn't want him to know she was afraid.

She reached out, took the gun and he woke instantly. He went for her wrist and she pulled back, her finger curling on to the trigger. They fought briefly and she shot him.

The sound in the cave was shocking and he jerked sharply in her hands. Then he had the gun back and he hit her so that she fell away from him, back into the cave. He sat up and unbuttoned his shirt. His left upper arm sleeve was black.

He got the shirt off and Kate saw blood all down his arm. He fished in the knapsack and brought out a little box. He fumbled it open with one hand, the other holding the gun pointing at Kate. He now tried to open a little bottle, clamping it between his knees. As the top came off, Kate smelled the sharp sweet whiff of disinfectant. He got a cloth out and tipped the disinfectant on to it.

'I'll do that,' said Kate. Her voice sounded very strange to her ears. She took no notice of the gun and came forward on her knees in front of him. She took the disinfected cloth and began to wipe his arm.

11

He had a ragged groove cut across the muscle. It bled profusely. Kate took a second cloth soaked in disinfectant and began to bind the wound. She felt him gasp slightly.

She couldn't look at him. She felt sweat gather between her breasts and at her hairline. When she was done, tying it cruelly tight to stem the blood, she mopped up the blood from the rest of his arm. Then she sat back on her heels.

She brought her face up slowly until she met his eyes. They were close to the cave entrance, but he had the light behind him still, though it came in slantwise from the angle of the cave mouth. Her chest was rising and falling and there were sparks in her mind, stopping her from thinking coherently.

She wanted very desperately to do it. Very desperately indeed. No one would ever know. She would be believed, if she survived this, not him. She could lie about it.

She brought up a hand and laid it trembling on his naked chest. It was warm and hard and she could feel the texture of his skin under her palm.

His hair was dirty and dust was creased into his skin. His chin was rough with stubble. Kate bent her head and kissed his chest. She could taste salt on his skin and she kissed it again. She let her lips stay against his skin and she felt his heart pound.

She leant forward slightly and put her lips to his arm. She didn't kiss the wound, or even by it. She licked the blood, a tiny trickle fresh from under the bandage. She felt his head turn as he looked down at her leaning in to him.

Now she twisted her head and kissed his neck. He moved again, lifting his head slightly. She kissed him under his chin, feeling her hair fall heavy from where it was bound back and brush his belly. She could hear him breathing quite harshly.

She came up on her knees slightly and faced him, very close. She touched his lips. They were dry and slightly parted. She leant in quite slowly and deliberately. She wanted to remember every second of this terrible unforgivable thing she did.

She pressed her mouth against his. She felt the dryness of his lips and the roughness of the unshaven skin around his mouth. She opened his mouth with hers and tasted him: cool and whisky-flavoured. She kissed him and felt him stir and respond.

She began to tremble. Her palms were flat to his chest now. She twisted her face in an agony of desire and kissed his mouth. She felt his slack body stiffen and his arm came up behind her, pressing her closer. He kissed her properly.

Should thieves and brigands be so good at this? Could a man who could cold-bloodedly cut her with a knife kiss like this, like one who knew?

Kate pulled back. She felt drunk and almost faint, desperation and sense warring violently in her. She undid the buttons on her shirt and took it off. Now her breasts were naked between them. She untied her skirt.

His lips were on her breasts, kissing them, kissing her nipples, licking her skin. He knew how to make love, how to pleasure a woman. One hand was warm against her; the other held the gun. He moved forward over her and she fell back, her skirt falling away. The floor of the cave was cold and gritty under her skin.

That was it, finally. It was the floor of the cave that tipped her over the brink. She was wallowing in it. She had degraded herself totally. She was beyond excuse. She wanted to be screwed by this man so badly she would have screamed if something had stopped them now. Let her lay on the floor in filth. She was filth.

She wriggled and reached till she got her pants off. She let herself go with desire, rubbing her body against his, aware of his lesser arousal and the fact that he had some control still. She didn't. She fumbled between their bodies for his trouser belt. He rolled on to his back, one arm obviously stiff with pain and one hand holding the damned gun, whilst she tore at his trousers to get them off, struggling absurdly with his boots.

She wanted him. She would have him. There was a lover in the bastard and she had found him out and would use him.

She climbed on top of him, exulting that he was erect, his cock pale and heavy in his nest of dark hair. She sat over him and grinned into his face. Her breasts hung forward and she laughed and pushed a nipple whorishly into his mouth.

It wasn't like this with Paul.

Dammit, it wasn't like this with anyone. This was dreams, not reality.

She shut her eyes and moaned, rubbing her inflamed vulva on his thigh. Her hand came into his groin and she felt the thing she wanted.

She backed sharply down his body and bent over his cock. She kissed it.

'Jesus.'

It was his first word since she had shot him.

If she had burned before, she was exploding now. She took the whole thing into her mouth and sucked hard. His body jumped.

There were tears in her eyes. Why wasn't lust always this easy? She moved up his body and lifted herself over his mouth-wet cock. Again, she made a little animal moan in her throat. Her blood was singing sharp with the violence of it, the violence barely under control. She was mad with lust.

She reached under her and held his sex. She lowered her body till she felt the tip of it press against her flesh. She let go of it then – it was hard enough – and put her hands to herself. She held her own sex open and pushed down on his cock.

She shouted as he went into her. She felt him thrust up and she got her hands out of the way.

They were straight into it. She couldn't wait. His size was fabulous in her and she was in orgasm almost from the first thrust. She didn't care about anything any more. She was grunting and calling out all the time he thrust into her, lifting herself and lowering herself in sharp jabs to add to the slap of their bodies as they crashed together. She wanted him hard as he came and her own excitement was so beyond anything that she had no time nor desire for finesse and no need to impress him with her sexual technique.

He rolled her over his good arm and brought himself on top of her. His weight crushing her body was even better. She pulled her knees hard up and gripped herself by the legs so she was reared up to accept him as deeply as he could come in her. She bucked upwards hard to keep the thrusting at maximum. Her breasts hurt deliciously, caught between their straining bodies.

She felt him come but it was okay, she was there at the flood herself. She was laughing, she felt so great. There hadn't been an orgasm like this for her for years. Ever.

He pulled out of her after a moment, to one side. He had held the gun the whole time, against her head latterly, although his finger wasn't on the trigger. It wasn't a threat, it was just that he had tried to hold her conventionally but he wouldn't let go of his weapon.

'I feel like a whore.'

Kate came out of the hot soup of her feelings. 'What?'

'You're the first woman who's ever made me feel used, you know that?'

Kate was silent. She hadn't been considering his feelings in the matter.

'Did you do it to get the gun back? Get me off my guard, and all that?'

Kate looked at the cave roof and grinned. She felt terrific and she didn't give a damn for his feelings. 'I did it for the sex. Of course I used you. And if we get caught together and they find out we've had sex, I'll say you raped me.'

'You bloody cow.'

'I was driving along this road once. It was empty and I could see for about three miles in front of me. It was

15

absolutely empty on a dry clear day. I put my foot down until my car was vibrating. I could feel it through the steering wheel, I was going so damned fast. I saw ahead of me a small side turning; and a long articulated lorry was pulling out of it, very slowly, using the whole road to get himself out and round.' Kate was silent for a moment. The cave was getting dark as the sun fell lower in the sky and lost brilliance.

'This was eleven years ago, you understand. I was driving a car without power brakes. I knew I couldn't stop: the car wouldn't take it, the whole damn thing was shaking as it was. Ahead of me as I hurtled towards it the lorry pulled more and more across the road and I knew I was going to die.'

She let the silence grow. Presently she said: 'When I next remember, I was on the wrong side of the road and my engine was screaming in third gear and I'd got the speed down to about seventy. I gradually reduced to about fifty, which was all my trembling limbs could cope with, and I carried on. The lorry must have seen me eventually, of course, and I must have gone round the nose of it. Or flown over it. I don't remember. I saw the lorry in front of me. Then I was on my own the other side of it, in one piece.'

'Why are you telling me this?'

Kate turned her head in the dirt. 'I could die tomorrow hit by a cow. A plane could unload its sewage and I'd be killed by frozen shit falling out of the sky. Or I could become a traffic statistic after all. You threaten me with your silly gun and you're spiteful with your nasty knife and you scare me and make me tired and spoil my holiday, you trashy little criminal waste of space, but I shot you and I'd do it again. I feel alive, you bastard. I wanted sex and I took it and I don't care one damn that you feel used. You were used and it was good. Now I want to go home.'

He made her get on the blanket and he picked the gravel out from where it had stuck in her body. He put the gun away and he made love to her properly, caressing her limbs and kissing her lips and her breasts till again she thought: it shouldn't be like this. Trash shouldn't make a good lover. But he is a good lover, whatever the books say. Is this what's wrong with me? Good men, decent men, bore me. I need danger to make my sex taste good.

When he kissed down on to her stomach she protested lazily, 'I'm not clean.'

He didn't answer, going on down to the musk beween her legs, kissing inside her thighs so that she opened her legs wide and let him in, let him anywhere he pleased. She felt his tongue against her sexflesh, his chin coarse against her sweet swollen labia and suddenly she thought, has he killed anyone? How much of a bastard is he? Why do I let him do this when I know crime isn't romantic, it's sordid and greedy and destructive?

Her thoughts wouldn't stop. I don't believe he will kill me, she thought. I want to treasure this extraordinary thing that has happened to me so that when I go home and cope with Paul and boredom and work, I'll have something to remember. A beautiful savage man fucked me on a mountain. I took him like I was a bitch in heat. God, I *was* a bitch in heat, and then he took me like a lover and he knew all about it. He knew all about sex and we didn't have to pretend, we didn't even know each other's name, it was just the sex, all on its own, that we did. No loving, no words, no pretence, no lies, no lies, no lies. We didn't try to impress each other, how could we? He knew I was an abandoned woman caring only for getting him up between my thighs, turned on by his petty violence. I knew he was a thug, capable of small cruelties. And we both stank of sweat.

A moan bubbled out of her mouth again. He was caressing her open sex with his mouth and tongue. It sent a sweet sexfire through the tendons of her thighs so that they trembled, feeling unstrung and weak. 'I'm going to beg, soon,' she said, writhing in his hands,

17

voluptuous in her degradation, in her infamy, in her atrocious not-to-be-forgiven behaviour.

As he entered her for the second time, her heart leaping and bounding in her chest at the exquisite pleasure of the thing, he said: 'You wouldn't accuse me of rape, would you?'

'Damn right I would,' she said. She felt his cock slide like a torpedo into her soaked and spongy hole. He was over her now, on his elbows, his face just above hers in the dark. She brought up her arms and put them round his neck, nuzzling up to find his mouth and kiss it. 'There's no moral high ground between us, is there?' she said. 'Is there?'

Chapter Two

Sadie said: 'My God, all this is true.'
   'Yes, it's true.'
'You never told the police?'
'I never did. I told you, he ditched me in Paris.'
'How did you get to Paris?'

Afterwards they went outside into the brilliant night. The air ached with freshness, herbal-pure and heavenly. The sun had only just dropped below the horizon, so that behind them was a dark, Van Gogh, star-bursting blue, and at their front was a pale numinous intensity of thrilling light, empty for ever, infinite.

'There's water over here,' he said. 'We can wash, if you want.'

She stood in the cold little spring. The rocks around still held their secret warmth stored from a day's harsh sun. He knelt by her and washed her body slimy with sex and gritty with dust. He washed her breasts and her throat and he washed up between her legs, cupping the cold water and pressing his hollowed palm to her shivering sex. She stood like a queen, like a strumpet, being served by her lover, adoring his hands between the cheeks of her arse, between her breasts, at the secret underplaces of her body.

She washed him, then. She could feel that her service didn't thrill him, as his had thrilled her. Instead, he was amused.

She kissed his cold clean limp sex and stood up by him. The dark glowed round them. He was pale and edge-of-sight, a glimmer in the night like the strewn sun-bleached rocks.

'Damn it, my arm hurts,' he said softly, and laughed. 'I wish I'd broken it.'

'Why?'

'Then I couldn't have done what I did with you.'

'You're sorry already?'

'No. I don't think I'll ever be sorry. But I'll be different. I am different.'

'You're no virgin. What's the big deal?'

'The big deal? You think I'm always like this?'

'Tell me, sexy lady.'

'I've never pounced before.'

'It was good pouncing, especially if it was for the first time. I have to say, I've never been pounced on so violently before.'

'Women generally pounce on you?'

'They don't generally shoot me first.'

'I'm your captive, remember.' Her voice was bitter suddenly.

He drew her icy body close to his, and they stood in the water, cold flesh to cold flesh. 'Sweetheart, you're free to go,' he mumbled into her skin. 'I didn't hurt you so bad. I had to stop those policemen.'

She started to cry, not all soft and tender with release, but harshly, in pain, jagged sobs that shook her.

'Don't be like this,' he said.

'I want to hurt you.'

'You have.'

'How can I go back, after this?'

'Go back to what?'

'My life.'

'What are you talking about? You sound like a village maiden who's been shamed by a passing stranger. Tess of the d'Urbervilles confessing to Angel Clare she's already been had. Christ, the most tedious man in fiction.'

She didn't understand him. 'I don't like the knowledge. I didn't know I was like this.'

His voice hardened. 'Like what?'

'Fucking with a stranger, one who's hurt me.'

He stepped out of the water. 'If you've never fucked a man who's hurt you,' he said casually, 'you haven't led much of a life.'

She didn't say anything. She didn't even know if she meant what she'd been saying to him, if she truly felt what she'd been feeling. She was giving way to emotion like she'd given way to sex. It was voluptuous, glorious, to speak as she felt, even if the feeling wouldn't last. He didn't matter. They'd be apart soon. He couldn't understand what was happening to her. To him she would only ever be a good fuck on a hillside, one out of the blue.

He was speaking. 'It's your life. Change it, sweetheart, if you don't like it. Don't blame me, though.'

Back in the cave he took her slowly, still cold and distant. Afterwards she dressed and went outside alone for a moment.

She saw the distant twinkle and for some time she thought she was seeing the shore with the lights of a tourist village bobbing and dancing in the humid air. After several minutes she started to think. Then she went back inside.

It was pitch black in the cave. She dropped to her hands and crabbed across the floor till she came to his warm body. He had taken clean clothes from his pack and was dressed again. The night was cool up here.

'Did you do anything terrible?' she said soberly.

'Like what?'

'Kill anyone. Maim someone.'

'You get a sexual buzz off this?'

'No.'

'I'm not violent till I'm forced to be.'

21

'Self-defence?'

'That's how I see it.'

'I think the police are coming. There's a string of lights coming this way. Maybe they're looking for you.'

He was out of the cave door in seconds. Seconds later he was back in, rolling up his blanket and stuffing the stores from the cave into his knapsack. He flicked on a torch and shone it round the cave till he was sure it was empty. Kate picked up her raffia bag.

He checked the lacing on his boots. 'Are you going down to meet them?' he asked.

'Where are you going?'

'Lady, I might fail the next little moral inquisition. I don't think I'll tell you.'

'You promise me you've never done anything really bad? You're just a thief?'

'I don't need this. You keep your hang-ups to yourself.'

'Because I'll help you if it's true. If you've never really hurt anyone.'

'Help me? How?'

'I'm renting a place. Come back with me. They don't know who I am. They won't be watching it. I'm just one English female tourist.'

'I'll take my chances alone,' he said. 'Goodbye, darling, it was a fantastic fuck. Do some other man a similar favour sometime, huh?'

She kept her voice steady. 'I've got over the how-dare-you-change-my-life stuff. I guess we're even. I'll tell them you've been gone some hours. I've got a self-catering apartment in a block on the Velissaríou in Corfu Town. Number twenty-nine Mitrópoli Building.'

He blew her a kiss and was gone into the wine-dark fragrance of the night. She thought that would be the last she saw of her savage stranger, her thief, high on Mount Pantokrátor.

She acted dumb and frightened with the police and they were so grateful she wasn't going to complain or

22

make a scandal that they petted her and let her go back to her apartment. She lay in what was left of the night in her own cool bed and smiled to herself. She had been juvenile and a shade clingy at the end, but on the whole she had behaved well. She regretted the tears and letting him see how arid her real life had suddenly seemed against the technicolor experience of becoming, albeit briefly, a hostage, but otherwise she had kept her end up. As for the sex, it had been sharply brilliant. Whether it was her own ferocity that had made him so superb a lover, or his natural talent, she had no idea. Probably the former. But it was nice to think that somewhere in the world there was a man who could make her bones melt and her sex foam. As for Paul, she would have to consider seriously whether the louse was worth keeping. He had eaten into her vitals like that vulture in Greek mythology with poor old Prometheus (she wasn't entirely ignorant even if she didn't know why Angel Clare was the most tedious man in fiction) but maybe his time had come. Loving him was something she couldn't help, like having a heroin addiction. It was time she went cold turkey.

He came with the new day. She hadn't expected him and was almost put out. Part of her said sharply that she was lucky to have got off so lightly. All that twaddle about not hurting people; she must have been crackers. He was a bad lot and sexy with it. He was probably a con man out of his depth and being charming was part of his equipment. That is, he wasn't exactly charming, but he had a certain charisma. And a fantastic body.

He leant against her doorframe, his face lined and sunken with tiredness. 'My transport arrangements have broken down, sexy lady. Do you still feel like helping me?'

She was wearing a kimono, having risen late, showered and sat long over her breakfast. She hadn't felt like going out and had been planning to lie on her balcony and read and listen to music.

23

Her body shivered. It was a kind of sexy music all of its own. Do it, her body murmured. Do it. Take what he offers. He'll sleep with you if you help him, and that's what you want. You want his balls. You want to see if the magic is there, even when you aren't afraid. What's one crime more or less in a rotten world? This might be the only man ever to turn your pussy into a powerhouse. Take him. Take what he offers and damn the rest of it.

'You've really got it bad,' he said oddly.

She must be letting her thoughts show. She looked down, stepping back and letting him in. 'How's the arm?' she asked.

'How's yours?'

'Okay, you bastard.'

'That's better.'

He showered, shaved and ate. He got to look munchier and munchier and Kate had to remind herself that he was a real, unpredictable man and not some male plaything available for her delectation.

'Being clean suits you,' she said.

'Do you want to go to bed now?'

'What help do you want?' she asked in a level voice, controlling herself. That's what you got for letting a man know you liked it. Right, she would learn her lesson. Was there no damn man in all the world you could be honest with about sex? Probably not. It was a stupid notion.

'If I left the island with you, they wouldn't spot me. They're looking for a guy on his own and they don't have a good description.'

'I'm on a package flight out of here tomorrow.'

'Skip it. Come with me on a ferry to Italy. We can take a train from there.'

'A train where?'

'Back to England.'

'You're going to England?'

'Initially. I have to get back to the States, actually.'

24

'You're smuggling. If you get picked up, I go to jail. No thanks, robber baron. I'll catch my flight.'

He hefted his knapsack. She could see it was almost empty. 'Nothing to smuggle anymore. I posted it; quite the safest way to get stuff across borders. I just have to go and collect it at the other end now. If I get picked up en route, just say you met me casually travelling and know nothing about me except what I've told you. Once I'm out of Greece I'm okay anyway. I've no argument with the Italians or the French.'

'You make it sound easy. They'll check the ferry.'

'They won't check it very hard. They'll assume I've hired someone to take me off privately. So I have, only he's in hospital having his appendix out.'

He watched her thinking about it, about him. 'There's a ferry this afternoon,' he added.

'The gun,' she said.

'I gave it back to its owner. Too dangerous, I thought. Women shoot me, even with less excuse than you.'

She couldn't tally this charming scapegrace with the genuinely frightening man of the previous day. She frowned as temptation teetered under the cold instruction of common sense. She was a secure professional woman, not young, but independent and resourceful. This man threatened her. He tempted her to be foolish.

'May I sleep while you think about it?' he asked politely.

'Through there.'

'Thank you.'

He left his knapsack and jacket, taking himself quietly into the other room like a cat. 'What's your name?' Kate suddenly shouted.

His head appeared round the bedroom door. He held a slim blue book in his hand. 'My passport, ma'am,' he said, and grinned.

They left on the evening boat, Kate shivering with excitement and trying to mask it. She hadn't touched him the entire time, determined he shouldn't think she

25

did this crazy thing for sex. She couldn't even admit to herself that it might be her major preoccupation. They ate together before they left and went to the boat together. He was an amusing companion, but when he took her arm she jumped nervously and pulled away.

'What's the matter?' he asked quietly. When she didn't answer, he went on: 'The idea I had in mind was that we looked like we were lovers travelling together. I thought I made that clear. Is that not how you want us to travel? It's the best disguise for me, you see, travelling with an authentic tourist. Have you changed your mind?'

'You're going to make love to me as a disguise, to conceal the fact that you're a criminal?'

'Yes. But I'll try to do it nicely.'

She let him take her arm. She must remember to conceal how much she wanted him, when they finally lay together. He must think she was using him as she had before, as he was using her. Then it would be all right. If only she weren't so hungry. If only she weren't so ravaged by her desire for his body. Her insides were being gnawed by lust.

They made love in Brindisi and it was certainly all right. They booked in a small hotel for the night and alone in the room he came over to her and put a hand on her shoulder. She turned round and he pulled her against him, his mouth seeking hers with passion and force. He didn't feel like he was acting. His bad arm he kept low; it obviously hurt to lift it, so he used it to hold her waist. His good hand was at the back of her neck, under her hair, and his body was all fluid motion pressing into hers. She heard his breath catch and felt the change in his body as he pressed against her. Now his hand was under her clothes and her head was tilted back as his lips bruised hers. He kissed her neck, the exposed vee of her breasts, and it seemed to her he trembled with desire so that she needn't be afraid of showing her own emotion. It would be churlish to be off-hand with so fine a lover. They fell on to the bed, he pulling her clothes apart, telling her she was beautiful, kissing her flesh with little sucking kisses, sliding a hand between her thighs and touching her so the flame of her desire leapt and she longed to be filled.

She had longed to have him in her, penetrating her, all the time they had been together, only now she didn't have to hide it because he was swollen big with his own need and he had his clothes off as well as hers.

He wouldn't come out of her afterwards. He lay big and easy in her wet soft place and she felt her belly melting and peaceful with the release of her need. The magic was there, it certainly was. It was a damned shame he was a villain and could be no part of her life beyond the next couple of days. She had a capacity to enjoy sex which was why she felt horny all the time. She didn't get satisfaction from Paul, from her lovers before Paul, like she did with this man.

He played with her breasts. 'You're beautiful,' he said. 'What perfect boobs.' He kissed them and played with her nipples, sucking them and rolling them in his fingers. He kissed her throat and ran a hand down the curve of her spine till it rested, palm open, across the curve of one buttock. He went quiet then and she saw he was asleep.

Men are so vulnerable in sleep, she thought. We all are, but men are stronger than women most of the time. When they are awake, that is. Asleep, they are vulnerable. Women sometimes kill men when they are asleep.

Kate looked at her lover and thought he was good. A broad clear brow. Tanned skin with crinkles at the corners of his eyes. A wide mobile mouth with sensitive lips. Good teeth. Good eyes, when they were open: hazel with clear whites. Flat neat ears. A graceful neck without bullish orange-peel flesh and loose fat. Thick straight hair a warm streaky brown. A wide chest with well-developed muscles. A neat waist and hips, fat free. Strong legs, nicely shaped.

The total was not anything that hit you in the eye. He

was an ordinary man at first glace; it was in the detail he scored points. There was nothing wrong with him physically, so that though many men were better looking, few were as unflawed. Nothing special to look at, but not a bad point there. It was a pity about the character.

It was the sense of danger that kept her quivering. He definitely had an air about him. You could tell he was rogue if you were close enough and they didn't come closer than Kate.

They travelled north as far as Milan and picked up the Orient Express. They went through Switzerland and into France. He was charming, amusing, simply beautiful in bed and quite distant. In Paris they had to change from the Gare de Lyons to the Gare du Nord. He went with her until they were about to board the train to Calais. 'I'll just get a paper,' he said and he disappeared.

When the train pulled out Kate didn't worry. She was almost relieved. He would have been an embarrassment back home in her tidy life. He wasn't a Home Counties man. If he had moved in with her she would have found him hard to dislodge. He was a rogue, a delicious naughty enterprise. England would have diminished him, made him vulgar and weak. He would have become petty and small. It was better that it was all over. Now she could enjoy the wickedness of the memory, especially the sex, uncluttered by the guilt of his presence. It was okay to break the rules on holiday. It was not okay back home in stuffy England. There harbouring a violent thief would merely be sordid. She was glad he was gone.

She checked her answerphone. Paul had left a message on it saying that he loved her and could they do something on her upcoming birthday. He would try to be free. There were few other messages, a couple from girlfriends, that was all. Her good friends knew she had been away. Kate drank wine and tried not to think about sex with her thief. There would be other men now. She needed excitement in her sexual life. She needed danger. She would liberate herself from Paul and fill her bed with sexy numbers who wanted pussy and didn't give a damn for companionship. She was tired of companionship and love and all that crap. A little undiluted bonking would do her soul good. Even thinking about it made her soul expand, like her body had expanded and relaxed under the Mediterranean sun. She was up for promotion. If she got it, and she damn well ought to get it if there was any fairness in the world, she would be busy for a while and that would be a good thing. It would mean she would travel a bit for work and that would be a good thing too.

The following week she turned thirty and failed to get the promotion and threw up her job in the process.

Damn damn damn. There had to be more to life than insurance. What would she do? Who with? And why? Perhaps John, her erstwhile boss, was right. She was acting like a hysteric. She couldn't be menopausal at thirty, but suddenly her life was up for grabs and everything that had been okay wasn't any longer. It couldn't be anything to do with a bad man in Greece, a bed-partner on a train across Europe for a matter of thirty-six hours or so. It was romantic to be dumped in Paris rather than, say, Wantage, but it didn't change your life.

What could a thirty-year-old ex-insurance executive do, she wondered. Female ex-insurance executive. With itchy pants and itchy feet.

She phoned Paul up at his work.

'Darling,' he said. He had a gorgeous voice. 'I'm sorry about your birthday. Francine had a migraine and she hates me going out if she has a migraine. Could you be free Thursday? I could come over.'

'Paul.' Kate cut across him ruthlessly. 'I'm only going to have real men now, men who fuck me with abandon and expertise and send me up the wall with passion. Men who take me out and aren't afraid to be seen with me. Men who don't check their watch in bed with me. Men who like oral sex. Men who don't snore and who don't have a partial denture.'

'Are you drunk, Kate?'

'No.'

'Is it, ah, the wrong time of the month?'

'Go to hell, Paul. And don't phone. It's sex I need, not hormone replacement therapy.'

She felt terrible after this, but it still made her snort with laughter. Maybe she had put in too many years being old. It was time to be young a little, before it was too late. If she had to go down the tubes here, let it be in style. If there had been any more bridges to burn in her life, she would have been rushing round with the firelighters making her arsonical round complete. But they were all gone, except she had her house still and money in the bank. For the time being. That wouldn't last. She would come to her senses and start looking for another job in a week or two. Meanwhile, she must cast round for some way of filling her time, filling the vacancy in it that nagged at her and stopped her sleeping properly.

Two days later, she nearly found a permanent solution. She stepped off the kerb near where she lived, intent on going down to the corner grocery because she had a sudden desire for asparagus, even the tinned variety, and a red car appeared out of nowhere.

It was like the lorry in that far-off almost accident. Suddenly Kate knew she would die. Time staggered. She stopped mid-stride in the middle of the road and cranked her head round at the hurtling mammoth about to crush her. All the world was flying metal. It reached like the angel of death to wrap her round and all she could do was to open her mouth a micrometre at a time ready to scream. No scream can hold off death, and it was three-quarters of a tonne of death that was accelerating towards her. There would be hopheads at the wheel, but what did that matter? My final thoughts, thought Kate in the split second between noticing the roaring monster and realising she couldn't escape it. My final thoughts are – oh!

She was jabbed so hard in the back she went flying. The car veered miraculously away and she lay in the road with her saviour.

'I couldn't move,' she whispered. 'When I saw it, I couldn't move.'

'You were running. You would have escaped it anyway.' He sat up and dusted his jacket. 'Are you hurt? I'm sorry about the melodrama. I thought it would hit you.'

'Oh God,' said Kate, and threw up.

There were witnesses, but Kate could see they were relieved when she said she wouldn't report it. No one had the car number and the police couldn't keep up with hit-and-runs, let alone miss-and-runs. She tottered back to her house with the helpful stranger holding her arm.

He hesitated on her doorstep. 'Perhaps I shouldn't come in,' he said. 'You'll be all right now. Is your husband home?'

His voice lilted slightly, the intonation faintly foreign. Charmingly foreign.

'You saved my life,' Kate said. 'Come in and have a drink. I'll brush the road dust off you, too. That's a good suit, too good to rub in the dirt.'

It was a good suit. Now she looked at her rescuer, she saw he was a very sharp number indeed. Absurdly, her spirits lifted. How nice to be rescued by a guy who didn't look like a loser. This man was out of the movies. His suit was exquisite in its tailoring, and his heavy cream shirt looked like it came from the same superior menswear stockist. And the silk tie. Gold cufflinks, too. This man knew about good living in a designer-crazed age. He had black hair he was smoothing back (my, how the cufflinks winked) and dark eyes, but his skin was pale honey.

She began to tingle. 'My name's Kate Matheson,' she said. 'I'm so very grateful to you.'

'Raoul Martineau.' French then, she thought, as they shook hands with absurd formality. His hand was dry and warm and firm.

A wave of shakiness swept across her. Damned cars. Damned roads. She felt sick again and once was too often. She must go up and clean her teeth.

An hour later he said, 'I must go.'

It had been a quick hour. He wasn't just easy on the eye, he had conversation. This was nice. So often the pretty ones were dead between the ears or were so vain it came to the same thing. This one was too smart to be called pretty. His smooth good looks were bone deep and as natural to the man as his classy threads. He worked in London for a specialist geological group, of all things. They were mineralogists, survey specialists, based here but working all over the world. They did aerial surveys. Apparently, you could deduce what lay under the ground from certain surface features, if you knew your stuff. Raoul worked in the office, he wasn't a field man, but he knew all about interpreting magnetic anomaly maps of the areas their field operatives overflew.

Kate thought him fascinating.

They reached her door and she was saying goodbye and thank you again when she felt the stillness in him.

'I'm so glad you aren't dead,' he murmured.

'So am I.' Kate looked into his eyes. Jesus, she thought. White flame went through her. Then she was hot, burning hot, her heart hammering. His lips touched hers. The moment was ecstatic. It was all to come. She wanted it and he was going to give it to her.

It was like a taut elastic band snapping. Life and death were bed-partners, after all. You were born in bed, you made babies in bed and, if you were lucky, you died there.

She wanted him right now, in her heat, the brush with death still sharp in her.

'I was frightened,' she said, pulling back from Raoul's

face. She could feel her eyes widen, remembered terror enlarging her pupils.

'I know,' he said, and his hand slid under her blouse and closed over her breast.

'Take me to bed,' she pleaded. She writhed slightly; her breast felt so gorgeous.

He stood back from her and she saw his face was blazing. 'No,' he said. 'I'll take you here.'

He put his hands on her thighs and wrenched her skirt up. He grabbed her panties and tore them off her. He opened his own trousers and then he hooked his hands under her thighs and lifted her clean off the ground, pushing her back against the wall. His lips were on her throat as he drove urgently into her. She crossed her ankles behind his back and gasped as he pumped his hips hard. It felt like electric shocks inside her. The man's muscle radiated heat. She gasped and moaned, writhing on his impaling sex, and when the bursting weakness came in her she laughed exultantly.

He lowered her and stood leaning against her, panting. Kate pulled his head so it was bowed, resting on her shoulder. She bit at his hair. 'That was so good for me,' she said fiercely.

He looked at her. Faint amusement tugged at the corners of his mouth. When he spoke, his accent was more strongly marked. 'I am glad I was able to rescue someone like you,' he murmured. 'Think how dull you might have been.'

She leaned back against the wall with her eyes shut, her teeth bared in a grin as she hauled air into her lungs. She could feel her blood flowing vigorously round her body. Her toes were curling with pleasure. She laughed out loud. 'It's an affirmation of life.'

'More than that, surely.' He had one hand flat against the wall and he leant over her, looking down into her face.

'You fuck beautifully, Raoul.' She felt delirious. She could say anything.

He moved her collar and dropped a kiss on the naked skin of her shoulder. 'Once is not enough, pretty lady.'

They went upstairs. He lay on her with his eyes open looking down into her face. His was a blank, yet if his features were frozen, he was fire down below. His fingers probed her before he entered her. They had their clothes off this time.

It was a very foreign coupling, quite frightening in its way. He went about his business with a mechanical perfection that both stirred and repelled her. Kate found him fascinating. There was more than a touch of cruelty in him, yet his passion was real, knife-edged and alive, and it made her flutter inside.

His fingers were hard in her and she saw a slight twitch in one cheek as he pushed deeply and then opened his fingers wide in her elastic heat. He touched something, did something she didn't understand, and she felt galvanised, her flesh jumping as a fire of lust flamed through her. She smelt fresh sweat as he probed, and she jerked again, helpless at his clever and curious knowledge of her body. She saw his thin lips curve slightly with pleasure as she jolted at his behest. She tried to reach down and hold his sex but he drew his groin away from her and smiled suddenly. 'Later,' he murmured. 'Not yet.'

He entered her then. He was very hard, as if he had not made love only recently. He stabbed her and then, quite blank, he drew back and pumped with rapid movements at the entrance of her sex with the head of his, so that he pushed the fattest part of his sex through the narrowest part of hers. It was extraordinarily arousing. Kate found her fingers curling in the firm muscular flesh of his back. This controlled manipulation of their coupling made her want to sink her nails into his skin.

Suddenly he was shafting her deeply again. He must have tenderised that special spot in her because fiery darts of lust were burning her inside and she could feel she was losing control. He wasn't. His face was a mask while his balls were on fire. Kate began to gasp. Her nails sank into him despite three years' training with another woman's man, one she daren't mark however excessive her passion might be. Raoul was dragging her up on his tide. She saw the nerve jump suddenly in his cheek again and then his face flushed and she felt herself wet and full. Her pussy rippled and her belly flooded with peace. She bore down on his shuddering cock so that he lost nothing of his climax.

He went slack as her movement stopped. He bent down and nibbled her ear. Then he lay beside her and smiled, the grimness leaving him.

'Are you married?' Kate asked crudely.

He laughed. 'I cannot stay faithful. I adore women too much to limit myself to one. Mind you,' he added lazily, 'some tempt me more than others to that unfortunate state.'

Kate nodded in satisfaction. She felt like a cat with cream on her whiskers. 'Do you want anything?' she asked. 'Tea? A glass of wine? Tell me what you like after sex, Raoul. I'd like to know.'

'I want to punish you,' he whispered.

'How's that again?'

'I think you have marked my back.'

'Maybe I could make up for it, if you told me how.'

'I visit you again, or you visit me in my apartment, and you do whatever I say.'

'Is that a punishment?'

'Maybe, my little English lady. I think I am more wicked than you. Maybe you won't like me on closer acquaintance.'

'Maybe I will.' Kate felt cold inside, cold and excited.

'Then I take your phone number and I ring you tomorrow and we fix something, *hein*?'

'That's fine by me.'

He left her then, visiting her bathroom and reappearing as immaculately groomed as he must have been before he threw himself in the road to save her life. Kate lay in her bed, the sheet half pulled across her, one breast lying ripe and exposed. Raoul shot his cuffs and shook his pockets until they were comfortable, smoothing his jacket and running a hand over his hair in the gesture she had already seen that should have been effeminate but on such an icy man was not.

'I phone you tomorrow,' he said. He was lighting a cigarette. His movements were neat, economical, cat-like. His grace was entirely masculine, however.

Kate nodded.

'Au'voir, chérie.'

'Au'voir. Et merci.'

'A demain.'

After he was gone, Kate wondered what he had been doing in west London, as far out in the suburbs as this. Strange that he hadn't said.

She lay back in her bed, feeling the pleasure in her body, the sweetness of her used sex cool and wet from a man. Not a domestic man, not a domestic man at all. Perhaps even a dangerous one. Kinky. Would he be into pain? She hoped not. She didn't think she was, herself.

What was she, though? On that never-to-be-forgotten holiday she had practically raped a man who had nakedly threatened her life. So? Did it matter? She had responded to a one-off situation oddly. Hadn't he become tame, after her sexual frenzy? Hadn't he become sweet under her hand and gentle with her?

Kate laughed. Was that the way? Would she enter a phase now where she brought men to heel by the ferocity of her loving? It was a hell of a way to separate the men from the boys.

What of Raoul? He was a tiger. Kate didn't think she could tame him; no, not at all. Curiously, the thought brought both relief and excitement.

Wasn't there some proverb about riding the tiger? If there was, she couldn't remember it. She was falling asleep. Riding the tiger. No, the memory wouldn't come.

Never mind.

Chapter Three

*T*hey didn't go to his apartment, and on the whole Kate was glad. She felt instinctively that she should tell someone where she was. There was definitely something about Raoul. The suave exterior of the man was perfect but as to what went on behind it – Kate felt he was a man of subtle and devious tastes, a man who understood his own nature and had few inhibitions about satisfying it. He was a private man, supercilious even, but unpredictable.

A woman walks with care in the sexual jungle and Raoul was one to avoid, if safety were the main criterion. But Kate, just out of her twenties, felt she had been dull too long, safe too long, and her very soul thirsted for stronger pleasures.

They ate together and he took her to a party.

'It will amuse you,' he murmured, and the look in his eyes was at once sly and amused. Kate felt excitement. The man made her spine shiver. She felt hot between her thighs. It was nice.

It was a private club, one of those large buildings in London with a classical façade in dirty stone. They had a drink in a bar, a room so plushly discreet Kate wondered if she was in a whorehouse.

'Are you interested in people?' Raoul asked.

'I'm no social worker.'

'I mean, do you find their vagaries delicious, amusing? Do the byways of human behaviour appeal to you? Do you observe?'

'No,' Kate said. 'I find people difficult. If they're good, they're boring. Sometimes if they're bad they're boring too. Maybe it's me.'

'Do you wish to observe? In my company.'

'Yes.'

'Come with me now, then.'

They went next door to a dim fragrant room where music was playing softly. People moved in it like actors in an art film, passing slowly through the shadows lapped with warmth.

Kate's eyes adjusted. She saw that some of the people in the large room, which opened into another like a museum gallery, wore children's masks. There was a lion, a chimpanzee, an elephant. Some wore half masks that began above the nose leaving the lower face bare. These were of card but astonishingly effective. She saw a Regency buck, an American Indian, a monk.

There were men and women in the murmurous dark, some sitting, some on the move.

Kate and Raoul passed through. She saw people like themselves, couples or singles in conventional clothes, watching.

The masked ones were dark clothed. Kate saw pale patches and felt her skin crawl. Their faces were shrouded and hidden but their genitals were exposed, men and women. Here, in this inner room, they came together. She saw a woman standing by a man stroking his sex which stood pale and stiff before him. She saw two men, one paunchy and heavy, one slim and lithe, each stroking the other's sex, facing each other, masturbating each other, lost in their private world whilst outsiders looked on.

A woman bent over the arm of a couch. A man took her, grunting as he finished his business in her. She stayed where she was and after a moment or two another man came up to her. Kate trembled. She saw him lift his sex and slip it in. The woman moaned and stirred and the man pumped at her.

She looked up at Raoul. She could see his eyes gleam in the uncertain light. He bent towards her and his lips touched her ear. 'Do you like it, pretty?' he murmured. 'Does it amuse you?'

What was the truth? That she enjoyed seeing what she saw? That she was thrilled at the breaking of the code? That she felt weak with excitement and desire?

'It's an experience,' she said huskily. Shouldn't she be repelled?

'Novelty is always nice.'

They continued to walk among the quiet copulations. Kate realised there were more people around, more spectators. The lights seemed a little brighter. The sex was noisier, more frantic. The alcohol consumed by the spectators was adding a glitter to the room, a kind of frantic sheen of excitement.

She felt drunk, though she had hardly sipped her drink.

She saw the first couple go down, not the masked zombies but people like herself and Raoul. The woman cracked first, pulling at her man who must have been in his late fifties. They fumbled and groped into each other's clothes with people laughing and pointing around them.

The woman was grotesque. Her make-up was smudged and her legs came up awkwardly, gracelessly. The man puffed as he knelt between them, grunting as he dropped his trousers and his large wobbling bottom came into view. His sex was vast and purplish. He shoved, holding it to get it into the hairy maw of the woman. People clapped and laughed, watching them. Then he was over her, his face so red Kate thought his heart would give out. He shoved hastily and then he stopped. He knelt up, pulling out, his big cock softening and gleaming. Incredibly, he looked smug. He must have come in under a dozen thrusts. Kate turned away, sickened at last. The woman still lay on her back with her legs drawn up, allowing people to stare into her exposed sex.

'What is it?' Raoul said. Kate had forgotten him.

'That was terrible.'

'To see them do it in public?'

Kate laughed suddenly. 'To see them do it so badly.'

Raoul's grip tightened on her arm. 'I will make love to you. It will not be as they were.'

'Not here.'

'No, not here. We will have our sport in private, *hein*?'

He lived, predictably enough, in Docklands. At the top of the stairs inside his little apartment was a huge window and through it Kate saw the fat black jewelled ribbon of water that was the Thames. He had no bedroom, only an open balustraded balcony with his mattress and bed linen on it.

You could see the river from the bed. Almost an entire wall of the apartment was glass. Raoul was slow and careful, lingering over her body, biting her gently, tugging her flesh until it was aroused.

All the walls were painted soft cream. There were almost no decorations: a blue-painted vase with flowers in it; a Matisse on the wall; a porcelain horse in an alcove, so strange it must be Chinese. There was almost nothing, but what there was was superb. The rug on the bare floor was softly rich, providing almost the only colour in the room.

He had strange likings, licking and kissing in her armpits like a cat nuzzling. She had little chance to do anything herself. He had some private agenda, and for all he took his time, he was purposeful and determined.

He had a hand under her chin now, thrusting her head up and back so that he could kiss the pulse in the exposed throat below him. Kate felt his strength, the ease with which he exerted his muscular power. She loved it, running her hands over his smooth skin and

40

feeling the hardness of his firm body, but it frightened her too. He could snap her neck with one flick, if he desired. She was vulnerable in every sense. Yet he remained controlled, arousing her, pleasing her, thrilling her body till it seemed to her that her sex gaped, so strong was her yearning to be filled.

He lifted and opened her legs. I am in the hands of a true voluptuary, she thought. This man is dedicated to satisfying himself. He is consumed by the desire for sex. The strangeness of the experience uplifted her. It was like but unlike anything she had known before. This new country she explored, what did she think of it? Did it matter what she thought? Was it not enough that it existed, that it excited her and aroused feelings she had not known she could feel. She stood on a new-found-land and Raoul was there to lead her gently through its strange enticing coverts.

He entered her slowly. His penis in her sex was a vast invasion of her mind. She felt the texture of her personality yield as he pressed into her. His icy precision enfolded her, freezing her so that the passion between them was a sculpture in ice, glittering shards and probes that splintered into hard patterns of crystal desire, coruscations of sensation that whirled kaleidoscopically so that the movements within her hurt in their ferocious intensity and the pain was an exquisite consumation of pleasure.

He fucked her with his teeth bared. He twisted himself, he thrust hard, he thrust soft, he bit her neck, he squeezed her breast and all came together, each separate sensation like some precise placing of parts, till an architecture of lust was constructed from her frailties and his strength.

It took her some time to come back to herself. Her body was a new place to her. She looked at the beast beside her and saw how he had taken her fibre and used it for himself.

Did it matter? He was brilliant but chilling. She disliked losing herself to him; she disliked his absolute

41

mastery over her sensations, his orchestration of her experience, but she could learn from him. She was in the hands of a man unique to her experience. Could she not play with the devil and let him be, when she had had enough?

'What do you think about, *chérie*?'

'You are a devil. You ravish me. Are you like this with all your lovers?'

He put his tongue on her nipple, flat and warm, and rubbed it there.

'I like to do well what I do,' he said. His eyes watched her.

'I can see how you're not married.' She laughed.

'If she was always a virgin, it would be good. I would go out and find exquisite women, sensual experts. I would employ them to satisfy my varied, my varying desires. Always I would come home to innocence. To ignorance. I would teach her carnal joy. I would make her lose herself in my lust. I would control her. But I would want for her to be a virgin the next time, tight on my sex, dry till I loosened her. I would rupture her flesh and make her entrance mine.'

Kate shivered. 'I'm not the woman for you. I'm too, too ordinary.'

'But that is my pleasure.' His voice was so low and soft he almost purred. 'You do not know what you are. I will teach you. I know what you are capable of, how much pleasure you can have. I see your nature. I know the men you have been with have not been enough for you. You remain unsatisfied. I will teach you, pretty. I will teach you to take what you want as I have taken what I want from you. Then we will part and you will go off and be able to satisfy yourself with a man, as I can satisfy myself with a woman. For the rest of your life.' He touched her neck again with his lips, her naked shoulder.

'Why?'

'Why?' He laughed. 'I am the dark prince and you are my sleeping beauty. There have been others before you and there will be others after you. It amuses me, pretty. Especially you English. To wake you is divine.'

His certainty offended her. 'We're so dull, then?' she enquired sarcastically.

'You are like dirty oil paintings, jewelled colours lost under the patina of daily life. Do not resist me, sweet Kate. You are waking already.' He laughed again, teasing her. 'You must not resist me when I offer you so much.'

Kate, dazed, back in her own house, knew that it was true. Raoul held for her the keys to the sexual kingdom. She was bored with the received wisdom on the subject. None of it seemed to fit with her own feelings and she had, unthinkingly, accepted that she was wrong and what the world said was right. The truth was she wanted to make a carnal exploration and couldn't see why it should cause feelings of guilt. Food and sex were the two great sensual pleasures of life. No one attacked the gourmet as corrupt. Television was dedicated to cookery, endless cookery, and when it wasn't going on about cooking, it was advertising food. Constantly. Yet sex was undoubtedly the superior pleasure and it was subverted, cloaked, presented slantwise as romance. Any serious exploration of the subject became risible just because the seriousness was so inappropriate. Sex was joyful. Sex was fun. Morality crowded and twisted and perverted honest enjoyment of a harmless human activity till people became guilt-ridden, repressed, furtive or alienated.

Paul had offered her love and given her bad sex. Maybe it was time she forgot about love and tenderness and equality, and went straight for what her body craved. She was a passionate woman. She lusted for men. She got hot between her thighs. It had never exactly made her ashamed, but in some mysterious way she had felt odd and at fault.

Sex should be dangerous. It was a dark fire. It should be an adventure. Society trained its members for the dullness and routine of monogamy, that most unnatural state. Kate had only escaped it herself through a chance set of circumstances. She had been engaged when she was twenty-one, deeply in love so she had thought, and on the brink of marriage. Colin had died in a road accident, and within three months she was in bed with another man, enjoying it.

She learned her lesson and learned it well. Had she and Colin married, she would have desired other men. Not immediately, perhaps, and no doubt she would have concealed her emotions from herself for as long as was possible. But she would have tired of him. Her feelings were not as all-important and profound as she had believed them to be. They were temporary and exciting and shallow.

Marriage was convenient socially and economically and fiscally. It was very useful if you wanted to raise a family and if the State wanted to tax you. For all other purposes and notable among them was sex, it was useless. Indeed, it was counterproductive.

They were conned. All of them, men and women. They were set an ideal, that of monogamous sex, and told it was decent, it was good, it was worth aspiring to. Most of them fell by the wayside, of course, and felt guilty according to their natures. But it was no ideal; it was emotionally degrading to aspire to sex with only one person. Through being corralled and straitjacketed, a huge human happiness was systematically destroyed.

Lust bubbled in fat slow plops like a mud geyser in hot springs, exploding at cyclic intervals in a burst of energy that was terrifying and dramatic. Try to hold it down and you would be burned.

Yes, she would voyage with the terrifying Raoul and learn of the sexual side of her nature. He was a man who did not trouble with the limits society conventionally set. He was an intelligent man. If it got too much, she could get out.

She didn't think it would.

* * *

She woke in the night from the flames of her dreams. Something had alarmed her and she lay in the dark with her heart thumping uncomfortably. Her mind was in a wet hot turmoil, reeling from thick thoughts that slipped and slid as she moved further into wakefulness. What was wrong, that she felt so anxious, so disturbed? Was it her dreams, or had she heard something?

She tried to slide back down the deep slope into the softness of her all-enveloping sleep, but gradually her thoughts hardened and sharpened and so, reluctantly, she heaved herself from her bed and pattered downstairs. Better to break the pattern completely and start again. She would make herself a hot drink.

She didn't put on the main kitchen lights, reluctant to offend the darkness of the night. The streetlamps outside were dull and tired but all the houses were black and silent. She dropped her blind and put on a small sidelight.

The house was very quiet. It made tiny settling noises, for all the world like a sleeper twitching slightly and mumbling in sleep. When the noise came it was distinct and wrong. It had no part in the silent dullness of the night with its background mumble of distant traffic like a far-off sea. The sound came, familiar but unidentifiable for the moment, and then it was gone.

Had it really happened or was it the echo of a disturbed mind?

Kate padded through to her living room, and from there to her sitting room. She came back into the hall and stood there for a moment. The sound was familiar and yet she couldn't place it. Something about it was wrong. Was it a noise that belonged to work that should not be here at home? Was it a noise of the day that shouldn't happen at night?

She saw then the slim package on the mat. She had heard her letterbox flap being used. Someone had delivered post to her by hand at four-thirty in the morning. That was what was wrong.

She picked up the package, a folded-over A4 size. It

was a padded envelope addressed in typescript to her. It felt full of banknotes, as if a wad of a thousand pounds or so were stuffed inside. Grinning to herself at the absurd fancy, Kate took it through to her kitchen where she used a knife to slit the tape that held the thing together.

She sat frozen, minutes later. The opened parcel was in her dustbin, outside. If her dustbin had not been inside her locked back yard, she would not have gone out to it. Out there in the night stalked things she never wanted to meet.

She struggled to be rational. Perhaps the parcel-maker had walked blindly through the night till he saw a light on and then chosen that door to receive his disgusting packet. How he could have seen the dim kitchen light from a window with the blind down at the back of the house when he was at the front, Kate didn't know. The malevolence of the stupid and unpleasant act need not be directed personally against herself, however. She must hang on to that thought. A person who could deliberately parcel up excrement and post it into someone's house maybe didn't need a specific target. Everyone would be upset. Anyone would be frightened and disgusted. To be so upset was to play into the hands of the perpetrator. She was suffering from an emotional low because she was in the suicide hours. Everyone was low at this time; it was a physio-logical fact, something to do with metabolism.

Kate drank her tea and went back to bed.

The next morning she discovered that during the night someone had cut off all the flowerheads in her front garden. It was a common act of vandalism, and Kate didn't even like gardening, merely going through the motions to make her property look nice, but she felt aggrieved.

She was jumpy for the rest of the day. She ascribed it to a broken night, though the odd one never usually bothered her, and to the fact that she had little to do.

The truth was, she was a worker. It didn't suit her to lie about all day and she felt bored and over-imaginative. What must it be like, she thought, being trapped with young children? She, at least, would be going back to work soon.

She cleaned the house, a supremely boring job that gave her no satisfaction, and did what she could in the garden. She chatted to her neighbour on one side, an elderly lady who sympathised with her over the flowers, but on the other side they were away. She was restless and discontented when she went to bed that night. She would begin job-hunting the next day. She couldn't stand this vacancy in her life. All her friends were working and she didn't even have a dog to take for a walk.

The phone was ringing. It had taken her a long time to get to sleep and now she struggled up through the muffling layers of drowsiness as her hand reached out and groped for the receiver. She knocked over her alarm clock and woke up a little more. Then she had the receiver.

'You're awake?'

'Mmm.'

'Get out, quick. Next door's on fire. The brigade are coming.'

The connection was broken. Kate hung on to the receiver for a moment, aware of the comfort of her bed, of her desire for sleep. She dragged herself upright and rubbed her face and hair. Then she hauled herself out of bed and struggled into her dressing gown.

Think. A fire. What was so valuable she must take it with her? She picked up her handbag – she always took it upstairs at night – and that meant she had her purse and chequebook, her credit cards and driving licence. She was a true child of bureaucracy and knew that documentation mattered more than insured possessions.

She looked out of the window across her garden. The

47

bland back-walls of the houses behind hers gave nothing away. All was quiet and dark.

Was it old Mrs Milverly's, poor soul, or the Pratchetts' house currently empty on the other side? Kate was halfway down the stairs before she stopped.

It hadn't been Mrs Milverly on the phone. It had been a man's voice. John and Celia Pratchett weren't home, though. They weren't due back for another week.

Who knew her name? Who had phoned her?

She ran her mind along the street in both directions. She didn't know many of them; it was a private, quiet neighbourhood, not street-party country at all.

She reached her front door. There was no smell of burning, and safety was three feet away. There was no noise of fire engines.

Kate stood in her long towelling dressing-gown, clutching her handbag, and wondered about the man on the phone. She didn't feel like stepping out there. She didn't feel like leaving the protection of her own house. She sat on the floor and, despite the warmth of the house, she shivered. Ten minutes went by. She heard a car start and rev up outside. It pulled away. Maybe she should have watched it and taken the number, but she didn't think she would have seen the number-plate well enough and she didn't want to show herself at the window. She went to the phone and looked up the number of her local police station. A weary sounding desk sergeant answered her and confirmed that there had been no fire call-out in this area in the last hour. Kate explained why she was asking and he wrote it down. Then she went back to bed.

'Kate.'
'Speaking.'
'It is Raoul.'
'Hello.'
'I must tell you. I have to go abroad, my pretty. I will be away some time.'

Kate felt the emptiness swell within her. It wasn't

48

that she gave a damn about him, but he had added spice to her life, and she felt very low.

'You will amuse yourself without me, *hein*?'

'Of course. Are you going somewhere interesting?'

'With some friends. I fulfil an old promise. I have a place in France, a little primitive but with an air. We go for a week or two.'

'That sounds very nice. It's a lovely time of year.' Kate was aware that what she said was banal but she could not say what she wanted to say: that she was afraid.

'It is a holiday, I admit. I shall miss you, my English Miss.'

'Good. I shall miss you.'

'Tell me pretty. Is it right you do not work at this moment?'

Kate felt her heart jangle inside her. 'That's right. They didn't give me the promotion I wanted and I told them to stuff it.'

Raoul chuckled. 'You could come with me, if you wished.'

'That might be nice,' Kate said cautiously, trying to mask the longing she felt. It was not Raoul's person that she longed for, but the excitement he generated. 'But your friends, what about them?'

'They are like me, I think.'

There was a silence. Kate silently cursed the phone. She wanted to read Raoul's expression as he made this extraordinary statement.

'Men?' she hazarded.

'Oh yes, all men.'

'Will they want a woman with them?'

'That depends on the woman.'

'I don't think I understand you.'

'I think you do. If you allow yourself to. They are four of my very old friends. We like to meet up every couple of years and find out what we are doing. No wives. But you are not a wife, *chérie*. You are an explorer.'

49

'I'm not a domestic, either.'

'We have one for that. A girl from the village. My place is in the Pyrenees, you understand. It is very old, very draughty, and very inconvenient. You are English, so I expect you will like it.'

Kate laughed. 'It's one hell of an invitation. If you're sure the others wouldn't resent my presence.'

'If they do, you are not the woman I take you to be.'

It was Sadie, curiously, who struck the note of caution.

'You've known this guy less than a week and you're going to his place in the Pyrenees? Isn't that a little foolhardy, Kate?'

'He isn't nobody from nowhere. He has a job here. He owns a house in France. I hardly see him as a mass-murderer.' Kate giggled. 'A shade vulgar for Raoul, that would be. He is a man with delicacy, with finesse. No, I think I'm safe from his night-time roamings with a meat cleaver.'

'I'd like to meet him.'

'He's delicious on the eye. A real smoothie.'

Sadie looked at her friend. 'I detect a note of, hm, no, an absence of cuddliness in the way you speak about this guy. Have you fallen for the gold cuff links?'

'He isn't cuddly,' said Kate, suddenly sober. 'He's the most sexual man I've ever met.'

'Sexier than the one in Corfu?'

Kate looked puzzled. 'That was me. That was some kind of aberration. He scared the pants off me – no, not literally. I mean, I've never been seriously frightened of a man before. It wasn't any sort of sexual fear, I'm not that creepy. There wasn't anything sexual between us till I made it. I don't know what happened. Maybe I just got so overwhelmed with feelings I knew nothing about, not having been held hostage before, that I translated them as sexual. Maybe I instinctively knew that if I screwed him, he wouldn't be a physical threat any more.'

'Like chimps presenting their arses in appeasement,'
Sadie said helpfully.

'You have this way of putting things.' Kate's voice
was dry. She remembered standing in the water high
above the world in the star-washed night air, his hands
cold about her body, cleaning her. 'He was a real man,'
she added uncertainly. Her recent experiences had her
off-base. She felt truly weird. Sadie had been very
sympathetic, but it had been the standard men-are-
threatening-bastards feminist response: Kate was a per-
sonable woman living alone, making her own way
through the world; she would be a prime target for any
passing macho weirdo; it all went to prove men felt
threatened when women managed alone.

Kate could work this sort of thing out for herself, but
this was an occasion when it didn't seem to satisfy.
What she wanted was to have someone dismiss the two
threats against her as coincidence, not to see them as
fitting into the ideological framework of the sex war.
She was a bit sick of the sex war, if it came to that.

'A real man? Kate, listen to yourself!'

'No, you listen. Men are like peacocks now. They can
make theselves smooth like Raoul. That is one hell of a
smooth man, Sadie. But Raoul's powerful, too, like a
big snake. Beautiful and powerful and, and alien.'

'Alien?'

'Utterly unlike me. Utterly male. Predatory. Tough.
Strong. So was thingummy in Corfu, though he was
different. He was all sweated up and about to be shot
by the police. I mean, I shot him. I literally put a bullet
through his flesh.'

Sadie shivered. 'Then he had you. Yes, I see.'

'No. I had him. He cooperated, but I practically raped
him.'

'Is it seeing real emotion that's turning you on?'

Kate looked at her friend. 'Maybe it's feeling real
emotion that's doing it. I feel alive. Nervous, yes.
Exhilarated, yes. Excited, yes. But suddenly men are
men, not failed women. They're different. They're chal-

lenging. They're real. No one's trying to typecast me, turn me into a servant, a *hausfrau*. One used me to shield him from the police. One wants to play elegant sex games with me. These men are not in the same league as the sort who buy you children's takeaway food and then puff on top of you while they tell you the boss gives them a hard time.'

'I ought to tell you not to go,' Sadie said, 'but the truth is, I'm jealous. I wish I was going.'

'And when I come back, I'll jobhunt,' Kate said firmly. 'That'll bring me back to earth.'

They travelled separately. Raoul had some ancient relatives to visit as he passed through France; duty calls, he explained, that would be oh-so-boring. Moreover, he said, if he turned up with someone as young and attractive as Kate, his aged aunts and cousins would assume he was settling down at last. He would be involved in endless explanations and it would all be very unpleasant and tedious. It was better to travel alone. So Kate flew Dan-Air to Perpignan, where she swapped to a train.

Here she began to doubt that her tourist fervour had guided her well. She had chosen this route, which left her with a long train journey west to Tarbes, hoping to see a little of the country. She became hot, tired and sticky and by the time she arrived in Tarbes it was late in the day and she wanted nothing but a long cool shower and her bed. Since Tarbes appeared to be a town of surpassing dullness – unless you happened to be an arms manufacture enthusiast, which Kate did not – this did not matter.

The next day she took a train to Lourdes. Here her cynicism fell away. To the south the mountains climbed up into the sky. The *Cité Religieuse* foamed with people and Kate was overwhelmed by the foreignness, delighted, stimulated and not a little lonely. It would have been fun to share this bizarre experience with someone she could talk to. She felt remote from the thrusting humanity around her all intent on benefitting from a kind of saintly health service, yet she was pleased to see them. She left crowded Lourdes with regret, taking a bus to Luz. Now she was following instructions.

The mountains rose before her: jaggedly beautiful; remotely calm; peacefully there. The bus stopped in the lower part of the village. She stood while her cases were unloaded. High above her, at the top of the village, was a fortified church. It seemed odd and out of place to have crenellations and gun slits in a house of religion. Still, it did reflect a certain realism. Religion caused more wars than it brought peace. Here they had known they would have to fight for what they believed in.

It was hard to believe she was only a bus trip away from Lourdes with its seething thousands of visitors. This place felt empty by comparison. Such people as there were wore approximations of climbing gear and they looked at her chic skirt and jacket with disgust.

She sat at a café drinking campari and soda, full of ice and with a mint sprig in it. In sunshine herself, she watched clouds gather over the peaks, darken and shoot jagged lines of fire. Thunder rumbled in the distance. She had heard of the summer storms in the Pyrenees. She had not expected to see one so soon. The air was humid and oppressive and Kate felt both lethargic and anticipatory, an uncomfortable combination.

'M'selle Mat'eson?'

She jumped slightly, half-asleep. A man was bent over her, hard to see against the dazzling sky. 'Yes?'

'I have come from the Maison du Lac. I have a car. Are you ready to leave?'

Her glass was empty. Kate looked over the village street. She would come here again and potter as a tourist should. She stood up and smiled at her guide. 'You are Raoul's friend,' she said. 'I'm so pleased to meet you.'

He had heavily pock-marked skin, quite clean and healthy, but pitted as if by some old virulent disease in

53

a way that was almost disfiguring. Yet his features were regular and good so that the extraordinary corrugations gave him a craggy charm. It was a face full of character, prematurely old perhaps, but not displeasing.

'My name is Pierre Dupont. It is our pleasure to have you among us.'

They moved together towards the car, a large open Renault. She was pleased at the quality of his English. As Raoul knew, her own French was very poor. Pierre was a heavy man, and his rolling gait, gravelly voice and pitted skin made him almost a caricature of a stage villain. He would make a wonderful movie thug. There was a touch of the Mafia about him. Really, he ought to be called Tonio . . . 'I beg your pardon?' He had been speaking and, lost in her absurd fantasy, she had missed what he said.

The road took them a surprising distance from the village. It dipped down and ran between a thick fir wood so dense it appeared black between the trees. It narrowed and became rutted. Then it began to climb via a series of breathtaking hairpin turns through a tumbled terrain full of little cultivated fields: tiny squares at slanting angles on the stony hillside where ground had been painstakingly cleared to grow a little patch of pumpkins or potatoes or whatever they grew here. Cabbages, probably.

Streams ran between rocks making tiny cascades and waterfalls. Sometimes they ran across the road. She saw a wayside shrine, a litle house shape in weathered wood with the paint peeling off, the Virgin within with one hand raised in blessing, the stiff fingers little pink pegs raised or bent as was prescribed by tradition.

Pierre was quiet, concentrating on his driving, for which Kate was grateful. The air was cooler now as they climbed and quite scented. The land was wilder with fewer fields. Wild flowers grew in tiny natural meadows. Kate saw goats, scrawny and evil-eyed with bells clonking about their necks. Otherwise it was an empty place, apart from the birds. And themselves.

She was hungry. She felt shy now. Raoul wouldn't arrive until the following day, she knew. She would be with the others, or such of them as had arrived. It would irritate them to make laboured conversation in English for her sake. She must make an excuse and go to bed early, leave them to get on with it.

The road dipped again. Now they ran through a narrow gorge with high cliffs on either side clad in wet lank vegetation. They climbed laboriously up this road, seeing no one else, though Pierra broke his silence to say that each year, while the snow lasted, the place was full of skiers. Kate found this hard to believe. Suddenly they reached the top of the cleft they had been climbing. Kate gasped and Pierre smiled and pulled up.

Ahead of them was a towering cirque, a rocky amphitheatre snow-touched and soaring up into the sky, cradling within its sheer grey flanks a great bowl in the mountains.

'It's incredible,' Kate said.

'Beyond it is Spain.' Pierre was lighting a cigarette. 'It was used by the *passeurs* in the war, guiding the French to safety in Spain. Previously it was used the other way, to help those who wished to escape from Franco's Spain.'

'You mean it's passable?'

'For the knowledgeable. Of course, climbers come here. There is a glacier at the top. The permanent snows, *hein*?'

'Yes.'

The car swung down a dizzy track. The utter emptiness and desolation began to oppress Kate. She was an urban soul by inclination, and the shattering countryside overwhelmed her.

Below the towering wall of rock they began to weave between a broken country full of small jagged cliffs and hanging greenery. They crossed little bridges where water foamed and quite suddenly, rounding a corner, the view opened up and Kate saw ahead of her and below a silent dark lake of still waters caught in the bowl of rock. The whole vista hung like some picture of a Gothic past. Islands dotted the lake with single pine trees and clusters of scrub. Green sunlit meadows ran down to its borders and the track was a white thread of civilisation, contrasting pleasantly with the remote savagery of nature.

The lake was oval, bright in the sunlight on the side nearest themselves but dark where the rock cirque shadowed it. Towards one end but well out into it, an island larger than the rest had a bleak grey building upon it. It looked like a small tower with an outlying sprawl of lower buildings.

'The Maison du Lac,' Pierre said quietly.

Kate was speechless.

Pierre put the car into gear and she began the final stage of her journey.

Chapter Four

She was glad she had bothered to bring good clothes. They dined on the terrace overlooking the still, slate-blue waters of the lake. She wore a clinging silk jersey dress that outlined her figure, emphasizing her narrow waist, her rich breasts.

The air was fresh and warm. The sun was caught here all day, but the waters remained cool and they made it a pleasant thing.

The house was more extraordinary and less terrifying from close up. Certainly it was grey and had a fine bleak tower, crenellated as had been the fortified church in Luz. But the long extensions at a more reasonable level had gracious mullioned windows. Huge tubs stood on the terrace, gay with geraniums. Their bright vermilion offset the atmosphere, adding a note of gaiety.

Three men were there, and Anna the maid. Her company comprised Pierre with his ugly skin but pleasant manner, Lucien who looked like a fallen angel with flopping brown hair, a golden skin and piercing blue eyes, and Jean-Marc, a withdrawn man who watched.

The meal was superb, a lobster bisque followed by steak and salad. All the men wore evening clothes and as the wine mellowed her, Kate saw she was in for some gracious living. The formal blacks, the shattering backdrop of the cirque, the fragrant air, the still lake, all combined with the fine wines, the candlelit meal to give an ambience that warmed her spirit. She felt rich and lazy: pampered. Lucien chattered in French and English during the meal and after it he and Jean-Marc played chess. Pierre put on some Mendelssohn and appeared to go into a cultural abstraction. Kate wandered outside for some time and then came in and said she was going to bed.

Her room was sumptuous, panelled and brocaded like something from a former century. She quickly fell asleep.

Deep in the night she woke to hear female giggles. Was this the leaden Anna? She thought she detected Lucien's quicksilver tones. Then she heard a woman's voice again, low and murmurous.

The walls must be solid. How could she hear? Kate climbed out of her vast bed and padded across the room to her windows.

They were on the terrace. Lights set along the parapet overhung the water, for here the masonry came straight up from the lake bottom. The terrace was furnished at one end with chairs and tables more suitable for lounging than eating. Really, Raoul must be indecently rich to support all this.

Figures flitted by, and in the dim light Kate saw how pale they were as they ran past. Again she heard female laughter and a male voice, teasing.

Incredibly, they were at naked play. Kate could almost see Anna's heavy beasts flop as she ducked and weaved about the chairs, dodging Lucien. If he was not naked, his garment must be so small it counted for nothing.

Kate stared. Their behaviour was so public. True, no strangers could see them, but to conduct their noisy amours so that anyone in the little chateau could watch seemed to border on perversion.

Despite herself, Kate could not resist watching. She saw Lucien catch the willing Anna and press his naked body to hers as he kissed her. They were at the balustrade now and the lights that lit it, lit them. Kate saw the crevice between his buttocks as he pressed against Anna, his hands at her breasts. Her hands came down his back and found his buttocks. She clutched them and Kate saw by his manipulation of his body that he was preparing to enter her, bent back as she was over the stone, the water behind her. He was going to enter her in full view of anyone who cared to watch.

Now his hips were jerking. Anna was making small noises that were caught and echoed upwards on the still air. Her body shuddered as his thrust into it.

After some minutes, he stopped. He pulled back and sank slowly to his knees. Kate saw him nuzzle and kiss at Anna's stomach. Kate's insides knotted. She was hot between her thighs. The man could make love. She almost envied Anna, not for Lucien but because she was with her lover, being adored. Kate was alone.

Suddenly, a moon lifted above the wall of the cirque on the south side of the lake. Silver light spilled ghost-cool over the water. Anna cried out and turned to face it, ignoring the man kneeling in front of her.

She lifted her hands to the moon. Lucien stood and ran his hands over her straining breasts. Then he stood back and slapped her rump.

He went to sit down. Anna turned and padded quietly into the house. Minutes later she was back with a tray, still quite naked, and Lucien took what was on the tray. Anna turned away and vanished back into the house. Lucien drank and smoked for some time. Then he too rose and re-entered the house.

Kate went back to bed. She was less shocked than amused. There was something very robust about the naked lakeside friskings in this fabulous mountain scenery. Sex was as ancient as the louring rock and considerably more interesting unless you were a geologist, which, funnily enough, Raoul was. Of a kind. Kate could not exactly remember what Raoul had said about his friends but she admitted to herself that she was surprised by them. What held together the benevolent Mafioso, Pierre, the young imp, Lucien, the taciturn Jean-Marc and the smooth and snaky Raoul? Not schoolfriends, surely, for their ages ranged from Lucien in his twenties to Pierre in his forties. There was an unknown, too, the fifth man coming on the morrow with Roul. What would he be like?

As for Anna, if she enjoyed romping with her employer's attractive guests (and Lucien was really very attractive, there was no doubt), then all power to her. Life could not hold many excitements for a Pyrenean peasant girl in domestic service, and since one had to assume she romped from choice and not necessity in this egalitarian age, one could only view her behaviour with indulgence.

She woke once more to a grey dawn. Again she slipped from her bed and went over to her open window. A wind soughed across the water, breaking its cold grey surface into a thousand steely ripples. Trees bent and swayed as the wind bounced round and round the bowl. Kate saw that the sky was not overcast but clear. It had the dullness of the predawn, but stars still shone dimly. Putting on her dressing gown, Kate let herself out of her room.

She hurried on silent slippered feet along the quiet corridors. She reached the main staircase and ran lightly down its broad wooden treads, keeping to the carpet in the centre to avoid creaking and unnecessary noise. She did not expect the main door to be locked here on this island only reachable by boat, and it was not. She stepped out into the cold blowing dawn and heard the shrill angry peep of some water bird skimming the broken surface of the lake.

She walked across the terrace that fronted the entire house and stopped at the parapet. Below her the water slapped and fretted against the stone blocks that supported the terrace. The wind took her hair and span it up and around her face. Her dressing gown blew open and she tied it more securely because it was cold, if exhilarating, where she stood.

She inhaled great lungfuls of clean moist air. She missed the smell of salt she associated with water, but there were resinous undertones and the scent of wild herbs from the country around the lake. She shook the hair from her eye and held the parapet, feeling the stone comforting and rough under her hands. Raoul was coming today. Her body thrilled. It he had been extraordinary in London, her familiar ground, how would he be here where he was a petty lordling in a noble savage land? His body had authority over hers already. What more might it have here?

'M'selle.'

She jumped, startled. Lucien was there, fully dressed.

'I was looking at the dawn,' she said, her heart still thumping from the surprise.

'*J'aime l'aube aussi.*' He stirred and looked over the disturbed waters, his eyes dulled to a matching grey in this light. 'See,' he added quietly, 'I go into the mountains at this time alone.'

She saw indeed that he wore knee-length hiking trousers with long woollen socks and stout shoes. He had on a combat jacket. A light rucksack was slung on one shoulder.

'Are you going climbing?'

'A little. Half climbing, half walking. I do not know the word.'

'Scrambling.'

'So. Scrambling.' He smiled.

Late at night he tumbled Anna. Now in the early dawn he went mountaineering. He had a remarkable fund of physical strength, Kate thought.

She shivered suddenly.

'You are cold?'

'A little. This is strange after London.'

To the east the mountains turned black as the sky

61

luminesced behind them. 'There is no need ever to be cold here,' Lucien said. 'We are like those musketeers, yes? All for one, and . . .'

He stopped. He raised a hand and touched Kate's cheek with the back of it. Then he moved it round and very delicately ran the tip of his finger over Kate's slightly parted lips. She saw his eyes change colour and a kind of settled deadness held his body taut. Very slightly, his nostrils flared.

'Raoul comes today,' Kate said.

Lucien did not move for several seconds. Suddenly his face eased and his ready smile came back. 'He is my lover,' he said. 'And yours, I think. We must be friends, yes?'

He didn't wait for a reply, turning on his heel and going down to the boathouse. Kate stood turned to stone, absolutely shocked at what he had said.

After a while, she turned stiffly to go back into the house. To the east, the sky was now a brilliant yellow and the peaks to the west were high enough to catch the rising sun. They flushed the most delicate rose.

She was opening the door to her room before she realised it was probably a joke.

She sunbathed and read on her own the next day. The amenities of the Maison du Lac were superb. She had breakfast in bed brought to her by Anna, full of a sloe-eyed slumbrous calm. Jean-Marc and Pierre played *boules* on the green behind the house after breakfast, having courteously invited her to join in. Then Pierre went out on the lake to fish in one of the boats while Jean-Marc vanshed indoors to deal with some mysterious paperwork.

They met at lunch – omelettes and salad – and sat together on the terrace afterwards lazily discussing the region and what it offered. It appeared they were all keen walkers and amateur climbers. Kate wanted to talk about their friendship with Raoul, but it seemed presumptuous somehow.

Both remaining men went off the island that afternoon. Raoul would not arrive until evening. Kate decided to explore.

The island was like a large triangular wedge of cheese lying on its side. The boathouse and harbour were down at the shallow end. The other end reared surprisingly high above the placid lake waters and, peering over the cliffs, Kate could see down to where great pale rocks loomed under the dark water like strange seabeasts. Water monsters. It took her quite a while to walk round the island and some parts were so tangled and brambly she could not penetrate them without risking her clothes.

She did not feel alone. Things lived amongst the bushes and shrubs and trees; quite large things at that. She would ask Raoul. She knew the brown bear survived in the Pyrenees, but though it was well-known that bears could swim, she doubted one was here. Maybe the birds were exceptionally noisy, crashing through the undergrowth. The men would know.

Close to the house were trim lawns and fruit trees. All else was wild with broken rocks and sudden tiny valleys. Tiny emerald lizards skipped away as she came by, birds shrieked indignantly and Kate felt herself to be the intruder she was.

It was with a sense of relief that she entered the house.

She went first to the kitchens. It occurred to her it would be polite to ask Anna, as Raoul's representative in his absence, for permission to wander the house, which was very large. She could not find her, however. The modern kitchens were impressively clean and quite cavernous in a ceramic way. Every modern help a cook might want was supplied. When Kate opened the fridge door, she found it was more in the nature of a vast walk-in cupboard, each shelf neatly labelled and stacked. There was a similarly large freezer and an even larger cold store where fruit and fresh vegetables lay piled. It was hardly easy to reach a shop, thought Kate, and whoever had provisioned the house must surely have had professional experience. It required considerable logistical skill to cater on this level this far from fresh sources of food.

Kate felt reluctant to explore the lower regions too thoroughly in case Anna had her private room here. It would be terrible to barge in on her. She came up into the sunlit silence of the upper levels instead, roaming the long corridors and taking a peep now and again at the solemn march of bedrooms.

Up again, into smaller rooms of almost attic proportions. Anna couldn't manage this whole vast place alone. There must be more help from somewhere. Then, surprisingly, she found a gallery devoted to archery with straw butts set up at one end and bows and arrows stacked at the other. That might be fun to try.

Ornaments. Statues. Pictures. Soft furnishings. Heavy furnishings. Nothing was very new, but it was all good and in good order. One would have to be a millionaire to keep up a place like this.

A door at the end of a corridor was shut. Kate tried it and found it locked. Then she saw that beside the door there was an alcove. A large and heavy key rested on a shelf within it. When Kate tried it, it was stiff but it worked.

The door swung open to a large dusty room, bleak to the point of austerity. The stone walls were unpanelled and unplastered. Slit windows opened to the outside, unglazed. She was in the tower.

In some respects it was like a mill: one room upon another with open wooden steps little better than a ladder leading from one level to the next. Here dirt had the upper hand. Feeling like someone out of a Brontë novel, Kate moved in to explore.

Upstairs were dust, slanting sunlight and the fat drone of gorged flies. A faint smell grew to become repulsive and eventually Kate found out why. Something furry had died up there and its rotting remains lay on the floorboards of the uppermost room. Kate hurriedly retreated. She had no desire to see something move not of its own volition but from the writhings of what fed on it as carrion. If up was barred to her, she would go down.

It seemed the only direct link with the main house, the inhabited part, was through that upper-storey door. Here below the two buildings were walled off from each other in no uncertain way. Moreover, a dankness was creeping in.

Kate was made forcefully aware of her own lack of credibility as a heroine. She could not go up for fear of rotting dead things. She was reluctant to come down because of the damp. It was getting dark, too. She climbed down one more level. The boards seemed to give soggily under her feet and the wooden handrail was unplesantly spongy in her hands. Perhaps it was common sense and not cowardice that made her reluctant to do this.

Now she was down. It must be about ground level if not below. The floor was paved rather than boarded as the other floors had been. It was windowless, but light spilled down from where she had entered.

The crepuscular edges of the room seemed tenanted. Kate moved cautiously forward, her eyes adjusting to the gloom.

Fixed to walls were artefacts from a macabre past. She might have been on a Hammer film set. Great ringbolts were set into the stone walls and from them dangled manacles and chains. Spikes, neck braces, a rack-like affair – all clamoured of a dim horrific history. Confronted with the sins of the past, Kate was horrified.

What unimaginable tortures had occurred here? Had men screamed as their limbs were torn apart, flesh unzipping from flesh, tendons tearing, blood spurting? Had women wept and fainted? Had people starved slowly in chains, raw sores on wrists and ankles.

'Kate,' said a soft voice.

She cried out. The dungeon was suddenly very dark as someone filled the gap through which she had come.

'Kate,' he said again and then he was descending.

'Raoul,' she said huskily. 'So soon. This awful room . . .'

'Is a joke, *chérie*. My ancestors may have had an exaggerated sense of humour and too much money with which to indulge their delights, but I can assure you this was a playroom, and has never been used for a serious purpose.'

He had her suddenly. She was in his arms, feeling his hard body, feeling his strength and warmth.

His lips locked with hers. She was still in shock from what she had seen and imagined and from his sudden presence. Her emotions seesawed and the press of his mouth both fierce and sudden, the arrogance of his assured attack, had her fumbling like a girl with her first lover. Raoul forced her head back and opened her mouth. She tasted his tongue, felt his teeth. A shout of desire echoed through the confusion of her pain. His loins pressed tightly against hers. She felt the rage of his lust as it warmed and roused her.

She drew her head away, panting. She could hardly see his features, only the gleam of his eyes. 'I'm dirty,' she said. 'I've been exploring.'

'I take you here, in the dirt.'

'Not here!'

'Yes. Turn round. Bend over. Now.'

He forced her trousers down and her pants. She was bent double, facing forward. She felt him drive between her buttocks, push for a moment and then slip down to enter the gape of her sex.

He gripped her hips as he slammed into her. She put out a hand blindly and held herself steady against the wall. She straddled her legs as best she could, feeling the rush of his sex, his swelling size, the slap of his balls warm against her thighs. She rose up on her toes, willing him to go on and on and never stop, but when he did it was good too because she was in orgasm around his sex and her own rippling tremors of sexflesh were indescribably sweet to her.

Her palms could still feel the imprint of the cold gritty stone surface of the wall where she had pressed against it. She pulled up her trousers silently and they made their way up into the light. Raoul kissed her again at the head of the ladder, pulling her blouse open and kissing her breasts. She pulled away and tried to escape up to the next level. Again he tumbled her to the floor where he kissed her belly, opening her trousers against her feeble resistance.

When he released her, she met his eyes. They were coolly amused and calculating. She fled again. This time she made it up the steps and into the next room. The door to the main house stood open. She ran through it into the corridor, holding her clothes together. With Raoul silent and swift behind her she ran along the corridor as far as the staircase. She plunged madly down the stairs and out along the corridor where her own room was. Looking over her shoulder as she ran, laughing, she didn't see what Raoul must have seen.

She cannoned into Jean-Marc.

She gave a small scream and dropped her trousers.

He stepped back, and for the first time she saw his rather tight face relax. It was no knowing smile that he revealed. Instead there was a flash of Satan, of Pan, of the *homme sensuel*.

Three of them. Raoul. Lucien. Now, the inscrutable Jean-Marc.

Crimson-faced, Kate stopped to pull up her trousers. Raoul was at her shoulder.

'Jean,' he murmured.

'Raoul.'

'You have met my lovely English Kate.'

'It has been my pleasure.'

'She is embarrassed now.'

'She need not be.'

Kate looked at Jean-Marc. His eyes were brilliant and cold under hooded lids. Her dishevelled state evidently pleased him. A frisson ran down Kate's spine. Raoul was there: solid, warm – but was he protective? His ties to these his friends were greater than any bond between himself and her. Kate moved from between the men and slipped into her room.

She chose a low-necked short black dress for the evening, the skirt bias cut to swirl about her slender thighs. She wore real amber beads at her throat and her wrist and at her ears, set in gold. She put her hair up into a twist, and allowed a delicate strand or two to frame her face. She used cosmetics to emphasise its piquancy.

Swaying on high heels, the picture of cool elegance, she made her way to join the men.

The meal, of course, was perfect. Unconsciously, like a cat, Kate started to relax. It was all so subtly caressing: the quiet talk of the men; the orchestration of her taste buds; the wine; the music.

It was almost too good to be true. It might almost have been arranged in its social and aesthetic perfection, had there been any point to such an arrangement. There was no stage, no audience to appreciate, so therefore there was no performance. Yet Kate felt the slightest touch of a game in progress and her the outsider. Probably this was no more than the influence of Raoul, with his cool amusement at life. He was the sort of man who effortlessly dominated his company, controlling them with little more than a raised eyebrow. They did not seem to resent this, the heavy and heavily amused Pierre Dupont with his pockmarked skin, the golden youth Lucien, the cold and hawk-like Jean-Marc and the last member of the company, the one who had arrived with Raoul.

He was perhaps the oddest of the bunch. Gauche almost to the point of surliness, he was younger even than Lucien with youth's clumsiness and ability to take offence. What he was doing here Kate had no idea. Pierrre joked with him. Lucien looked supercilious. Jean-Marc watched him occasionally in his cold-blooded way while Roul took pains to include the boy and was gentle with him.

A nephew? A young cousin? Kate didn't know. The tale of old friends was inadequate as an explanation, unless this was the son of an old friend, now dead. Whatever he was doing here, he was Raoul's guest and Kate exerted herself to be pleasant.

The men began to talk French politics among themselves and after a while Kate took her coffee and wandered away. Perhaps Emil was a student. She could hear him asserting himself defiantly, though the conversation was too quick for her to follow. She went along to the far end of the terrace and balanced her cup on the stone balustrade, content to watch the sky thickly brilliant with stars. Half the sky to the south was blotted out by what she knew to be the rearing wall of the vast amphitheatre in which their lake lay. Northwards and westwards she had a more open view. Nothing, however, could quite remove the claustrophobic influence of the surrounding countryside. She was in a bowl. She was cupped by mountains rearng all around. The silent sky blazed above the immense darkness and Kate understood fully for the first time how blackness grows from the earth itself and is a product of it. Each night the light retreats up into the sky, to make a fresh assault in the coming dawn.

Kate shivered. It was creepy here, hearing the faint splash of the water as night creatures moved in it.

She heard noise, yellow light spilled, and Anna came out with liqueurs. Now the men sat smoking and watching the moths bat blindly at the candles on the terrace. Kate took her place among them again, feeling them stir and open to admit her, closing again after she was in.

She tried to make conversation with Emil, but her French and his English were too poor for anything but the most laboured exchange. Lucien stopped behind her chair.

'You will come climbing with me tomorrow, Katya?'

'I think not.' Kate laughed.

'We go in the dawn, up and up together. I will help you.'

'No. I'm content to look at mountains. I've no desire to risk my neck in them.'

'I will keep you safe. It is good to be high.'

'This is high enough for me.' It was quite nice to be teased by the pretty boy. Kate grinned in the dark, remembering his activities with Anna.

She looked across to Raoul. 'What lives on the island?' she asked.

'Lives? Apart from us, you mean?'

'Yes, apart from us. Anything dangerous?'

Someone snorted suddenly as if she had said something unintentionally funny. 'Vampires?' Raoul hazarded. 'I know you English fear vampires very much. We have some bats, I believe . . .'

'Bears,' Kate said firmly. 'Wild boars. I suppose these creatures can swim?'

'I'll protect you,' Lucien said.

'Unfortunately, there are very few bears left here in the Pyrenees,' Raoul said. 'I think what few there are stay well away from mankind.'

'They would if they had any sense,' Jean-Marc said in silky tones. 'Certainly Lucien here would shoot one if he could.'

'Oh no!' Kate could not help but protest.

'Me, I love hunting. *Vive la chasse*.' Lucien chuckled. 'It is in my blood. I cannot help it. You must not mind, Miss Kate. Often the animal I seek eludes me.'

'Not that often. Lucien is too modest,' Raoul said quietly. 'He is superb.'

In her room, Kate bathed and changed at her leisure. This studied elegance belonged to a former age and she was content to behave as though she belonged to it too. A kind of sensuous slowness enveloped her. The luxury of her surroundings, their separation from anything she would call normal life, both geographical and cultural,

70

all conspired to make her feel not exactly a new person, but one with aspects she had never known. She had never seen herself in such a setting and had not known how she might respond. Sliding her clean smooth perfumed body into clinging silk nightwear was all of a piece with this new strange life. It could well bore her if it went on too long. For the moment it was wonderful. The fret and difficulty of life at home were utterly remote, so remote as to be unreal. She had escaped the prison of herself and her everyday behaviour. Here she could be someone else.

She slid into bed. She relaxed back among the pillows and let her mind wander, reliving the events of the day. She expected Raoul to join her, though nothing had been said. She did not intend to fall asleep, but she did.

'Darling.'

Kate woke mistily and felt the man's warmth and pressure on her body. The mattress moved below her as he shifted his weight. She smelt his breath: the faint masculine tang of a cigar; the clinging aroma of fine brandy.

A hand was on her bare shoulder, then lips. She stretched, feeling her warmth and the touch of his jacket. 'Raoul,' she murmured.

His lips were on hers now. She felt the slight graze of his chin. Sexual desire flamed in her and she arched up against him. His hand cupped her breast through the thin silk of her garment and he rubbed gently as her nipple enlarged and lengthened under the knowing caress.

He used his hands too for the long skirt of her nightdress. She felt the silk slip up her thighs as the covers were put back. It pleased her to lie with her eyes closed, yielding to the arousal of her body, slack in his arms. Her powerlessness was delicious. A hand rested on her warm flesh. She strained up into the man above her, rubbing herself against him, kissing his neck, sliding her hands under his jacket to feel his body through the material of his shirt.

He sat up momentarily and slid off his jacket. Then he caught her up, pressing her to his chest, holding her in his arms, kissing her with passion and small murmurous noises. Kate locked her arms about his neck and felt strength flow through her body even as she weakened between the thighs and softened with the welcoming knowledge of what was to come.

He stripped rapidly and came over her on the bed. There were hands again on her thighs, fingers at her sex, touching her clitoris, stirring her sexual lips. She felt lips graze softly on her desire. Her nipples stretched, her breasts swelled and all of her body was suffused with the lust she felt, the lust of wanting and being wanted. She needed to be entered now. Her desire must be satisfied.

Their passion became rougher as each strained into each, their kisses deep and feverish. He held her up from the bed in his urgency, yet at the same time he continued to touch her sexual parts and she opened wide her legs to receive both his caress and his sex. She was shameless in her greed. Such loving, such fire did not come often from a man. She would have him while she could.

He slid one slender strap down her shoulder and kissed it, nuzzling down into her armpit, kissing the breast he was exposing till she was delirious with pleasure. At the same time he penetrated her vagina with his fingers, feeling the warmth and wetness of welcome that waited for him there. She spasmed round his fingers, loving their intrusion but longing for the firm fulness of his erect body to enter her.

There were lips on her exposed belly now. Hands came under her hips and lifted her up from the bed. She fell sideways from the pillows, her head falling back over the edge of the bed as she opened her legs wider and wider to admit the man into her body. Now she was being kissed on her sexual lips. She gasped and writhed. A tongue touched her clitoris. She heard Raoul murmur in ecstasy and knew a white-hot flicker of triumph that she could so move this immensely sexual man.

Now his lips were at her one free breast again. Her own hands were deep in his hair. She felt his body manoeuvring and great trembling threatened to engulf her. She could feel the thrust of his solid member. He was pushing between her thighs. She gasped as the head of his cock touched her vulva. The muscles within it were flexing uncontrollably as they yearned to be compressed and squeezed by the penetrating flesh. Now he was thrusting in and Kate sobbed at the exquisite sensation, as she felt herself filled and her soft hungry flesh crushed by the grossness of the great rod of flesh entering her.

He began to move in her. She wanted to move herself, to reciprocate, to meet his thrusts and respond with primitive passion, but she was rendered helpless by her position. Somehow her hips were lifted up so that she could not drive against him with the muscles of her legs. Her hands held his face to her body where she felt her breasts ache with desire and the longing to be sucked and stretched. She rolled slightly at the joy of his penetrations and felt herself kissed and sucked and bitten in his lust.

Now his mouth was over hers and again she wallowed in the bliss of kissing him and his deeply penetrating tongue. Still he fucked her, hard blows getting harder and deeper as he moved towards the climax of his lust. She was with him, her own orgasm rolling like thunder round the rim of her sex. Explosions of lust consumed her. She hardly knew what she was doing. There were lips, hands, skin at every part of her. She was burning with lust in every inch.

She was almost entirely free of the bed now, lifted up literally as he came to climax in hard shuddering blows in her body. She would have fallen over the edge of the bed had he not held her so tightly, absorbing the shocks through her body created by his own fierce loving. She orgasmed and shook helplessly as her body foamed. Through its roar of her own lust she felt his explode. He was calling out in triumph and Kate felt a wild laughter bubble up in her. This was a crazy consummation, two sophisticated adults, sexually mature, utterly overwhelmed by the primitive forces their own bodies had unleashed between them.

She lay slack on the bed, feeling his lips murmur pleasurably on her skin. She felt faint tremors through her thighs as they slowly relaxed from the beautiful ferocity of the experience she had had. The man was everywhere, all over her, cradling her in his warmth and expertise. He was a conjuror, a magician of sex, and she was his willing assistant.

'Raoul,' she murmured contentedly when she was come back to herself enough for coherent speech.

'Sweet Katya,' he said, the rumble of amusement evident once more. He too had regained control, then. How deliciously he had lost it. And how delicious to know that he would lose it again with her, that this time was theirs yet it was curtailed. There would be no disastrous failure and mess. They would explore love and lust and sex here in the Maison du Lac, out of time, out of the world, and then she would go back and leave all this behind forever so that it would never be tainted, never be messed up in the general inanity of human sexual relations.

The bed moved as he reached to turn on the sidelight. Kate had no memory of turning it off. She must have done it virtually in her sleep, the sleep she didn't mean to have.

She was so glad he was a good-looking man. Its hollows shadowed by the soft creamy light, his face hung over hers, predatory, sensual and with that faint air of hauteur clinging to it. The man was a natural aristocrat.

His lips touched hers gently. 'You liked that,' he whispered.

74

'You are superb, Raoul. You are a lover any woman would be proud of.'

He began to remove her nightgown, sliding the soft material easily up and over her body. She narrowed her eyes in amusement and stretched for him, displaying her slender waist, her clear perfect skin, her full rounded breasts so that he might see and enjoy the animal that she was.

He moved down her slowly and kissed one knee. With the tip of a finger he moved it apart from her other knee so that her wet sex was exposed. He reared up and looked at his handiwork, her bruised engorged vulva laced with his semen.

Kate saw two things. She saw his sex rigid and erect, dry, with the flaming tip of his penis hard and hot and red. It was at once beautiful and quite unsatisfied. She saw too a remote statue-like figure apparently standing in the centre of the room.

Her mind groped for an explanation. It was an oil-painting, brought into strange relief by the low lighting of the room. Had she failed to notice a life-size painting of this beautiful boy, this beautiful naked boy? His body was lithe and muscled, his sexual hair dark and fluffy around a gleaming horizontal penis jutting at her, the testicles hanging like sweet fruits below. His arms were folded across his chest and above his broad young shoulders his head was held slightly to one side, like a dog waiting to see what its master required of it.

Kate forgot her own nakedness and sat up. Raoul was beside her, quite silent.

It was no painting. It was no statue. There was a second naked man in the room with her, one moreover who had just made love.

'Lucien,' Kate said in a choking voice. 'Lucien.'

Chapter Five

*T*he warmth of the room seemed to throb inside her head. Kate felt her heart beating so hard it must be lifting her breasts. Her deceitful body, grossly satisfied, settled and spread in its voluptuous satisfaction.

'Lucien,' Raoul said softly.

Lucien smiled. His cock wavered slightly. Undoubtedly it was wet, sticky from congress.

Kate looked down at Raoul's body, his penis firm and dry, fully erect. He had not entered her, then.

'You knew,' she said fatuously, furiously, to him.

He shrugged.

Lucien moved forward, unfolding his arms. He was quite matter-of-fact about his own nakedness before the two of them. 'Katya,' he said. He sat on the bed and touched Kate's foot.

She pulled away in an angry gesture. She felt the men waiting and knew in a sudden rush that Raoul was bored at her reaction because she was behaving predictably. Conventionally.

She swallowed suddenly. 'You tricked me.'

'An insult,' Raoul said lazily in acknowledgement.

'Would you have let me otherwise?' Lucien asked.

'You might have asked.' She knew she sounded like a spoiled child and was angrier because of it. Abruptly, she lay back with a thump on the bed and shut her eyes.

The silence grew. In the turmoil of her thoughts Kate was aware of herself naked between two naked men. Two beautiful naked men. Two men capable of making love superbly.

It was a chance. An opportunity. She was isolated here. She could do as she pleased. Would it please her to have two men, like this, together?

She began to shiver. Two men. One loving her mouth, her breasts. One adoring her between her legs. Two men. Never tired. Ready to give her what she wanted. Here at the Maison du Lac desire was realised. Fantasy became fact. To think, to dare, was to do.

A hand came suddenly to cup her sexual mound. 'Let this,' Raoul said, 'decide.'

'What do you mean?'

'Lucien has had you. I want you. If this wants me, then so, it is arranged.'

Kate opened her eyes and looked at him. The light was behind him so that his face was shadowed. He had the air of a hawk about to stoop. She was the lure.

She had been tricked but not forced. There was no suggestion of force in the room. Both men waited on her reply.

Lucien moved deliberately and picked up her arm. He kissed the hollow inside the elbow, then he twisted it slightly and kissed the soft under flesh of the upper arm. Gently, slowly, he bowed his bright head and kissed the undercurve of her breast.

The soft warm skin responded. A tremor passed through her. Her sex woke up and she felt a pleasurable ache between her leg and the rearousal of desire. She had been superbly fucked by an expert and another waited to perform the same act. The similar act. Part of its charm was that it was never the same twice. Raoul wanted to enter her body. He had kissed her and caressed her even as Lucien had fucked.

What kind of men were they? What kind of woman was she? Lucien kissed her breast and she sighed.

Desire flowed in a gentle tide through her body. It imparted a lethargy, a heaviness, so that she had no energy to protest what they did, what they wanted to do with her. She wanted to succumb, to linger in the thickets and be ravished by their strong willing bodies.

'I've never been here before,' she said, her own voice the voice of a stranger. She reached out her hands in slow fascination and took hold of each of the two male members by her.

Lucien's was the more elastic, half erect, warm and sticky from her body. He grinned, and she thought what a good thing a young man was. His skin had a faint sheen, satin smooth and muscular, almost hairless. He was a marvellous specimen.

Raoul was painfully hard, the sheath of skin silkily soft in her palm with his muscle rigid and bulging within. An older man, he had less of Lucien's bodily splendour, but his maturity of flesh had its own beauty. There was hair on his chest, not a great deal, but enough to give him a virile grace and promise of strength and sexual endurance.

'I must wash before I take you,' she said suddenly.

Lucien laughed. He swung off the bed and lifted her clear of the mattress. He carried her into the bathroom and stood her under the shower, squeezing himself in beside her. The water poured around them. Kate keeping her hair free but allowing her breasts and buttocks, all her skin to be washed clean.

Lucien brought his hand up between her thighs and washed her there. The spasm of desire that ran through her was not for him.

Kate was shocked. She was making love with two men. That was extraordinary. But that the actions of one should remind her of a third man, not present, and the thought of that man arouse her suddenly and make her long for him, surely that was perverted.

John Sorrell, his passport had said. Probably it was

false. He had put her in fear of her life on a Greek mountain, used her in an archetypal cowardly fashion to protect himself, hurt her deliberately and with malice aforethought, and in response she had torn an orgasm for herself from his body with all the ferocity of which she was capable. This was his fault, then. That sexual response he had created in her had continued through her meeting with Raoul. Her body wanted John Sorrell still, even though it had two other men.

Lucien's lips closed with hers. He was not a tall man, not as tall as Raoul, and she stood dreamily for a moment, the water falling across her, the strong young body pressed into hers, his penis once more erect and between her thighs. She slid her hands down his back, into the arch at its base. Her hands went on to cover the curve and swell of his buttocks. They were very hard and muscular. She let her fingers press into the division between them. She pulled Lucien against her breast, felt his flat belly against hers and felt him begin to move, backwards and forwards, as lust grew in him.

She stepped out of the shower and took one of the huge fluffy towels. Without a backwards look she went through to where Raoul waited.

For some moments she stood, drying herself almost unconsciously as she considered the situation. Rather, she let her emotions play with the situation, keeping the rational processes of the mind firmly at bay. Not that she thought they would let her down. She was honest enough to admit to herself that she wanted to do this thing, that part of the enticement lay in its wickedness, in its flouting of conventional morality. She wanted to do it. It was exciting. The opportunity might not come again. She was not entirely dead to the desire to experiment; not so old, so stuffy that novelty itself held no interest.

Her thoughts whirled. The towel dropped softly to the floor. Raoul lay on the bed, his expression enigmatic, watching her.

Kate stretched, arching her back, feeling her muscles.

She ran her hands down her sides, enjoying the smooth slide of her skin. On pussycat feet she approached the man on the bed.

She began by picking up one of his feet, running her hands into its arch and then on and up on to the ankle. She twisted the foot so that he rolled on to his back. His sex stood up proudly. In a long swooping movement Kate laid herself up the man, rubbing her breast against his legs as she went. She reached out and grasped his sex. Her hair fell across his belly. She drew her knees up behind her and she bent over the body she commanded. She kissed the tip of his penis.

Kate closed her eyes and opened her mouth. Her own sex tingled faintly, feeling twice its normal size and pleasurably sensitive. She felt her hair sweep the man's belly; she felt her breasts being excited by the curling hair on his legs; she felt the swelling turgid column silk-hard within her hands; she tasted his arousal, his desire. His desire for her.

His gland was sucked within her mouth and she ran her tongue caressingly around the sensitive tip. He shuddered faintly in her grasp. She sucked gently, teasingly, knowing he was hard erect and intent on keeping him there without tipping him over till it should please her to have him spill himself inside her. She crooned slightly, kissing his sex, stroking the hard column gently, masturbating him with small firm gestures.

One hand went down and began to cradle his balls. Delicate fingers probed with exquisite gentleness. She longed to see herself bent thus over the man spreadeagled and almost annihilated by his need for her.

She jumped slightly. A hand had slid over her exposed upwardly jutting buttocks. It could not be Raoul's.

She began to nibble down the side of his cock. So. She would pleasure one man whilst she herself was stimulated and pleasured by another. Had that not already happened? Had not Lucien pierced her while

Raoul kissed her and played with her breasts and lips with his hands and mouth? Now she would service Raoul and Lucien would enhance the act by playing sexual games with her body.

Her buttocks were held open and she felt the cool rush of air to her heated parts. Then Lucien's mouth closed over her vulva and he began to kiss and suck her. She almost bit Raoul, such was the frenzy Lucien invoked. It was hard to concentrate, so hard that she was grateful when she was released.

A moment later Lucien's shaft slid into her prepared wetness. His hips jerked and he was taking her hard and fast, as though he knew it wasn't his turn and he shouldn't be there.

For the first time in her life, Kate pulled free of a man in the act of copulation, leaving him flat. She swung her body urgently round, raised herself up and lowered her opened sex on to Raoul's rock-hard shaft. Sitting astride him, she let herself descend so that he filled her full. She felt Lucien jump on the bed, then he too was astride Raoul and he was rubbing his cock against her back, masturbating against her flesh even as she began to ride Raoul.

Curiously, Raoul made no objection. Kate opened her eyes and looked down at him. His eyes were open and his lips drawn back into a half-snarl of passion. There was a sheen on his forehead. His hands came up and convulsively grasped her swinging breasts. He was beside himself with lust and no doubt an entire regiment of Scots Highlanders could have marched through the room without affecting the strength and determination of his lust.

Lucien came round beside Kate, kneeling on the bed. She turned her head to see what he was doing, and he thrust his cock into her mouth.

She wanted to laugh hysterically. They had both been inside her, one straight after the other. A second ago she had held Raoul's cock in her mouth. Now Lucien's sweet firm member was there. She shut her eyes, closed her lips, sucked and let him do the rest. It could not have been easy. She was mounted on Raoul and swinging herself up and down, squeezing his cock as hard as she could, dragging him to climax, fighting his iron self-control.

Raoul caught her by her hips, held her above him and began to slam up into her. He twisted slightly as he did it and it was an effort to keep her mouth tight around Lucien's throbbing member and not cry out.

Her breasts burned. Her lips trembled. She tasted semen and felt herself climax in response, violently convulsing around the man thrusting into her body. Even as Lucien released himself, so she came and in doing so, forced Raoul to come, unable to withstand the exquisite ripples of her ogasming vagina.

Moments later she lay in an exhausted tangle of sweaty limbs, unable to tell one man from the other and not greatly caring.

This then was Nirvana. She had gone over the threshold. This was maximum pleasure. She knew now the peace of complete satiation. If she had had the energy, she would have wept with happiness. She adored the men who had made it possible. She worshipped them. She wished John Sorrell could see her so that he would know she didn't need him, couldn't want him. She had enough.

This thought acted like a cold douche. Two men and she fantasised a third. What was happening to her? Why did she wish to display her sex-sodden body to the man who had left her in Paris? What hold had he gained over her, that she had not previously acknowledged?

She opened her mouth and carefully rolled over, making sure she did not hurt any part of the two men she lay with and upon. She found Raoul's mouth and kissed it sweetly. Then she nuzzled over to Lucien and kissed his mouth. She kissed them both again; it was a wonderful game; she adored kissing and both these men were intensely sexual. She fell asleep.

Deep in the night she woke, lying on her side. Peace slid all through her. A man held her hips and from behind he had slid his penis into her and gently, with a rocking motion that was infinitely soothing, infinitely sexy, he rode into her.

Facing her was another man. As the one penetrated her, so this one touched her breasts and kissed her mouth. She reached one hand down and found his erect cock. She masturbated him as he kissed her, as she was fucked, and knew she was in paradise.

Kate woke alone, late and stiff, the sun slanting through her partly drawn curtains. Laughter floated up from the terrace outside. She peered at her watch and saw half the morning had gone.

She rolled on to her back and let her mind make a lazy exploration of how her body felt. Used. Undoubtedly she felt used. She giggled quietly to herself. She had lost count of the number of times she had been entered, lost track of which man had done what, when. That in itself was a voluptuous and special pleasure. She had worked so hard to please Paul, to please her lovers before him. She had been so considerate of their egos. She had controlled and managed her own pleasure in an effort to enhance and protect theirs.

Last night had been for her. Both men had subjected themselves to her, pleasing her, teasing her, making love to her with mouth and cock and hand till all her body was a thrilling vessel, a recipient of the glory of sex in a way she had not believed possible. Was this why men went to prostitutes, so that they culd buy this total attention to their needs? If so, women had been foolish. It was an unearthly pleasure, not to be missed on account of any cod morality, changing with the seasons as sexual fashions came and went.

Kate rang the bell by the bed. When Anna came she brought a tray with coffee and croissants fresh and warm and sweetly flaky. Kate ate and drank hugely.

83

She felt marvellous, almost fit enough to tackle those damned mountains.

This thought made her laugh. She would not believe it if Lucien said he had risen at dawn once more to go off on an expedition. She did not believe she had left him with enough strength.

Later, bathed and dressed decorously in a swinging silky skirt and a matching vest top, her hair in an elegant knot atop her head and gold earrings swinging from her ears, Kate descended regally to take her place among the company.

Raoul and Lucien were out, it seemed, in the car. Jean-Marc, Pierre and Emil sat together on the terrace, reading from the collection of newspapers and magazines that Raoul and Emil had brought with them from Paris. Kate was greeted courteously, indeed in a friendly fashion, with no subdued sniggers or sidelong glances from the men. If they knew what had taken place, they had too much sophistication or their manners were too good for them to make any allusion to it. She need not worry about vulgarity.

The sun was warm, the air soft, the breeze delicious and the drink at her elbow long and cool. Kate read without paying much attention through a couple of articles in *Time Magazine* before she recalled that she had bought a copy herself at Heathrow. No wonder it had seemed familiar. She began to look for an article she had already half read on sunbathing and skin melanoma, when she came across a missing section.

Kate flipped again through the magazine. Someone had removed some pages. Sleepily, she wondered why. She went back to the contents page and looked to see what was gone. An article on archaeology had disappeared.

She shut her eyes and lay back in her lounging chair. She felt the sun, warm on her legs and shoulders, and sighed pleasurably. Did she really care so very much about the precise risk of sunbathing? She was a north-

84

ern, sun-starved European and she didn't believe that this bone-deep soaking was doing her anything but good.

Who would pinch an article on Albanian archaeological treasures? It was rude of them, since current news was at a premium and they were all sharing the same material. But then again, maybe there were pretty pictures with the article and Pierre or Jean-Marc had a scrap book . . . Kate fell asleep.

She woke hungry, having skipped lunch. She wandered inside and found a fruit bowl, helping herself to a peach and an apple. As she did so, she heard the buzz of a boat engine and knew with a tinge of anticipation that her two lovers of the previous night had returned.

Lucien was playful and invigorating. His zest inspired the company and Raoul watched with a cynical and benevolent eye. When their parcels were unloaded and Ann had served drinks, they sat down to decide what they should all do. Kate controlled shivers of anticipation. Lucien had greeted her by kissing her hand and his bright eyes had locked briefly with hers. Raoul, more formally, had kissed her cheek; she had found just the touch of his body as she laid her hand flat to his chest sufficient to reawaken the fires of the night.

It was decided after some fierce and mock-dramatic argument that they should play at archery. The straw butts were brought down and set up on the terrace. The bows and arrows were also brought down from the gallery and the stringing of the bows became the subject of intense masculine debate. Kate wanted to just watch, having little of the competitive urge outside her working life, but this was not permitted. Raoul discovered she had not fired a bow since the approximate age of ten, and took it upon himself to teach her.

He stood with his body turned sideways, hers against his, their left arms extended to hold the bow, their right arms crooked as he demonstrated how to notch the arrow and how to hold it so that it would release

cleanly. Her hair must have tickled his chin. Kate tried
frantically to control her sexual urge. She was behaving
like a teenager. She gasped, laughed and released her
arrow so that it flew gracefully into the water.

Kate groaned and apologized. Lucien darted forward.
'I will rescue the arrow,' he said dramatically.

'I expect there'll be others if you make me try again,'
Kate said, stifling guilty laughter. 'We should do this
round the back of the house where there are only
brambles a long way off to contend with.'

Jean-Marc released an arrow so that it struck the
target with a satisfying thuck. 'No, no,' he said peacefully. 'It is better here.'

'I should take out the boat and rescue my arrow,' said
Kate, who doubted her competence to pull the cord that
started the outboard engine firmly enough.

'No need for a boat,' Lucien said. He stripped his
clothes off completely, taking even his underwear off,
climbed the balustrade and ignoring the amused glances
of the men and the rising horror of Kate, he did a
perfect dive into the black waters of the lake.

He hit cleanly with little splash. Moments later he
surfaced and struck out strongly for the floating arrow.
He reached it easily and held it aloft, rolling over in
triumph. There was a round of applause from the
terrace and he swam back to the steps at the far end.
He came back among them, ignoring his own total
nudity, shaking himself like a dog, and presenting the
arrow with due ceremony to Kate.

He remained nude, taking his turn at the butts and
proving himself a fine shot. Several arrows made their
watery baptism and each time Lucien dived in after
them. He ignored Anna when she brought out a tray of
hors d'oeuvres and fresh drinks, and she ignored him.
Kate, who had until then forgotten his cavortings upon
her first night, suddenly and belatedly wondered what
Anna thought of it all. She would be inhuman not to be
jealous. Kate was a favoured guest; Anna was the maid
of all work. It certainly wasn't fair.

Nothing of this showed in Anna's rather heavy-featured face. However, Kate found the opportunity to ask Raoul something of her.

'It seems a great deal of work Anna has to do here,' she said when both she and Raoul were sitting out from a round of archery. Emil had suddenly sharply improved and had become correspondingly more enthusiastic.

'Indeed,' Raul said a little indifferently. 'I pay her well.'

'Wouldn't more help make it more companionable for her?' Kate persisted. 'She must be lonely.'

Roul looked full into Kate's face for a long moment. 'She is no English servant,' he said softly. 'She has her duties, but her behaviour need not be "correct" in the sense you mean. Do not think she is lonely, *chérie*. She has a boyfriend in Luz, I believe, and here she does not lie alone at night.'

'From choice, not duty, I presume,' Kate commented acidly.

Again it was a moment before Raoul answered. 'You allow your imagination too free a rein,' he said, still in that soft, intimate voice that only Kate could hear. 'My house may be mediaeval but my actions as an employer are not. Anna wants no help. I pay her all year and only twice or maybe three times is there anyone here, so her work is easy taken overall and she knows this. Morover, she is too jealous to want to share the work. She feels pride in being responsible alone for the Maison du Lac. And if she wishes to disport herself with my guests, that is her affair. The villagers of Luz, they are country bumpkins. Here she can enjoy a man with some wit and expertise. No, my dearest Kate, I do not force Anna to have sex with my friends. I have to restrain her and tell her she must wait to be asked.'

'She is a fine cook. Couldn't she leave here and go to one of the towns? I can see that life in Luz would be limiting.'

'Ah. Now you touch upon a sore point. Anna is

Cagot and will not leave here. She belongs to the Pyrenees and would not be happy anywhere else.'

'A Cagot. Is it a family name?'

'No. It is her race, her people. The Cagot have been here in this part of the world since the eleventh, twelfth century, an ancient and proud people descended, it is believed, from the Visigoths. They were persecuted for centuries, not allowed to outmarry or to worship with the Catholic community. You will see if you investigate the country churches of this area that there are low Cagot windows and little Cagot doors through which services could be watched. They survived all this, and Anna is one who claims pure descent. I believe her. Certainly she is strange and unlike such as you and me. Almost she has no speech, though she understands what I say to her. I do not believe her to be fertile, either. She has served the men in my family for two generations without any sign of progeny since she was thirteen and my father took her virginity.'

'I call that mediaeval,' Kate blazed, truly shocked at last.

'My arrogant little Puritan,' Raoul said fondly. 'You would have it that all should behave just as you do. I tell you, nothing will make Anna behave as you do and you insult her to think she is not happy. She does not want an office job and a car and a house to live in alone, as you have. She wants good lusty men between her thighs, and good food to cook and a new dress every so often to flaunt on Sundays when she goes to Mass. The clod she goes with in the village worships the ground she walks on because she was had by *monsieur*, my father. He was benefactor to the village and they all know this. It was he who provided the underground warehouses where the cooperative stores its produce before it is taken to be sold in Tarbes. You British associate sex with sin and disgrace unless it is with your lumpen husbands. For Anna it is the conferral of grace and a great pleasure. I happen to think that she has the right of it.'

* * *

In her room, Kate sorted idly through the reading matter she had brought with her. She found the copy of *Time* and as a matter of vague interest looked up the article on Albanian archaeology. It was unexpectedly interesting. Apparently there was and had always been a thriving trade in stolen artefacts in the archaeological world. Greece had at long last clamped down and got its borders under control. Even Latin America was beginning to halt the outward flow of pre-Columbian art. The thieves and smugglers were looking to the lowering of the Iron Curtain to provide new sources of material to serve a greedy world intent on buying ready-packaged heritage. Albania had been part of a rich Classical world: Macedonia, Illyria, Thrace. The predators were gathering as it struggled with its new social and democratic order, trying not to descend ignominiously into anarchy and far too busy to guard its treasures.

There was talk of life-size golden statues; wild claims of immense treasure to be found. It was just what the beleaguered government needed, but as to whether such stuff existed, or who would get to it first, that was quite another matter.

Pierre went off in the car that evening though no one said where. The evening meal was once again the superb experience Kate was coming to expect. Aware that travel was undoubtedly broadening her mind, she spent some time playing chess with Jean-Marc. She had no idea what would happen that evening and she no longer had any idea of what she wanted. She was, she knew, among stronger personalities than her own. Raoul at the very least was a man too used to getting his own way for one such as her to thwart. If ever there came a clash between them, her only recourse would be to leave. Under his lazy manner, his well-bred charm, lay an arrogance of spirit she had not come up against before. She did not understand him and knew he would be insulted to think that she might. This effortless paternalism would irritate her in the end. She must take what she wanted from the Maison du Lac and depart with grace and good humour when the appropriate time came. Nothing had been said; the invitation was open-ended. That was as well. She could leave when it pleased her.

She was aware when she went up to bed that she was suffering faintly from claustrophobia. She flung her window open wide and leant out to smell the night and enjoy the cool air. The island was small, the company limited and everything she could do was both public and constrained by lack of resources. It would be nice to be away for a few hours. She needed exercise, too, because apart from bedroom exercise she was doing nothing but lying about eating and drinking. She was getting fat and lazy.

She went to sleep alone. Deep in the night she was woken by Lucien.

He kissed and caressed her awake. She felt the excitement thrumming through him. Raoul was not in the room at all.

She wasn't quite sure how to take this. Had Raoul passed her on? Was she no longer officially 'with' him? Lucien was a lovely boy, but she was not a toy to be got rid of when she palled.

Meanwile Lucien was urging her out of bed, giggling slightly with excitement, his eyes glittering in the subdued light. He wore jogging pants and, as far as Kate could tell, nothing else at all.

She climbed out of bed and slid her negligée on. It matched her long nightdress and made a delightfully sensuous noise as the garments rustled silkily together.

'Come with me,' Lucien whispered. 'Come, sweet Katya. You will not be disappointed, I promise.'

'What is it? Why won't you say?'

'It must be a surprise.'

'What must be?'

'You will see. Come quickly. *C'est fort intéressant.*'

She followed him through the dark corridors, her gown billowing pale behind her. He held her hand, urging her on, and she caught the childish sense of adventure that impelled him. Neither of them wore anything on their feet and so their passage was soundless through the sleeping house.

The corridors twisted and several times they went up or down little half stairs, curving between landings, secret stairs that took one to tiny private landings, low-ceilinged and dark. Kate became thoroughly disoriented, so lost she wondered if she was taking part in some elaborate game and she was being deliberately led on a circuitous route.

They carried no lights and used none of the house lights which were supplied by a generator located down by the boathouse. All the time a great moon rode high in the sky and as they walked moonlight spilled in cold rectangles at their feet. The slanting bars of lights, irregularly spaced and irregularly shaped, interspersed with sinister voids of complete blackness, began to get on Kate's nerves. She tugged at the hand that drew her ever on, feeling like something out of *Alice in Wonderland*, so strange her companion and so mad their rush through the magical terrifying night.

He stopped obediently but she could feel his reluctance. 'What is it?' he whispered.

She too replied almost under her breath though there could be no serious reason why they should not speak aloud, unless they were next to one of the occupied bedrooms. But the mystery of this crazy voyage through the silver and black night had got to her. She was possessed of an inexplicable feeling of apprehension.

'Tell me what's happening,' she said. She shook Lucien's hand. 'What is all this?'

He closed with her instantly. His face was not much above hers and as he stood breast to breast with her, Kate felt his heart beating steadily against the irregular tumble of her own ill-managed organ.

His arms were round her. 'Are you afraid?' he whispered, his lips so close to her ear that his words were like a lover's caress.

'A little.' Kate shivered. 'Where are you taking me? Where is Raoul? Is this a game you're playing with me? Am I about to be fooled?'

For an answer he gently laid his lips against hers. He drew her head up and back, kissing her more firmly, and she was reminded how much she adored being kissed by an attractive man. His confidence and his expertise seemed inappropriate to one of his years, though he was only about five years younger than herself. Kate wondered somewhat dizzily what he did for a living. He seemed very fit. Was he a sportsman, or was that just a hobby, a pastime with him?

'Kate,' he murmured, nibbling her ear. 'I want to make love to you here but there is not time just yet.'

'Why not?' she asked, not meaning to sound crudely greedy for sex but wanting to understand what they were doing.

'You will see.' He choked suddenly with laughter. 'My English is very good, *hein*?'

'Your English is terrific,' Kate said weakly. He caught her hand and they were off again.

Suddenly she was aware of bare boards beneath her feet. Lucien slowed his mad rush and she was grateful, not wanting splinters in her toes. He stopped and for a moment held still, plainly listening. Then he led her through a doorway.

He walked in delicate as a cat. The room was unfurnished, small and with an angled ceiling. They were high, then, under the roof. The moon flooded passionless and cold through the attic window, filling the room with a cold dim light.

Lucien released Kate's hand. He knelt with exquisite gentleness on the floor, and now Kate saw that the wooden floor was discontinuous and that within its planking was a square area. This had a ring bolt set within it. Lucien lifted this with infinite care. Then he removed the whole piece, some eighteen inches square.

Despite herself Kate edged forward. Below the missing piece of floor were the joists that separated the floor of one storey from the ceiling of that below it. Most of this area was in total dusty darkness. Some, however, was lit by a dull yellow gleam. Part of the ceiling below was also missing. At first Kate thought it was missing completely, but after a moment or two she saw that it was glazed and she could see through it. She could see through it to the room below.

She felt Lucien's arm rest lightly over her shoulders. She drew back her flowing garment where it lapped over the hole in the floor and threatened to get mixed up in the dusty mess surrounding the joists. She leant forward, steadying herself with her hands, aware of the excitement in the man beside her.

The room below was lit and occupied. Her curious viewpoint delayed for a moment Kate's realisation of what she saw. It was strange how a new perspective hampered understanding.

The understanding, when it came, was like a sickening blow to the stomach. Kate raised her eyes and looked at Lucien. His face shone with pleasure, and it seemed to Kate no little part of this was malice.

She looked back down through the glass. She couldn't help herself. She had been told, of course, but she hadn't taken it in or realised its significance. Now she did.

'Why did you bring me here?' she asked hoarsely.

Lucien snickered. 'You had to see. You understand, English Miss. You had to see.'

Chapter Six

*P*ain. She knew about it, of course. Who didn't? Her nature was sufficiently eclectic for its milder manifestations to have some slight appeal. That is, the idea of pain and sex was stimulating and she had been aware during the sexual act on more than one occasion of an urge to sink her nails in and tear pleasure from the back of the man penetrating her. As pleasure reached its extremes, teeth-baring and biting came closer and closer together.

This that took place below her bore no relation to her own slight fantasies, her own vague interest. She could not hear through what must be thick glass, but she could see enough to know what was going on.

Raoul lay spread like a starfish on the bed below. She saw his dark face, thin-lipped and sensual, hawk-nosed. She saw his wide shoulders, his broad chest dusted with dark curling hair making a vague sign of the cross. She saw his flat belly; she knew it to be hard from her own congress with him. She saw the jut of his hip bones, his strong-thewed legs, long and spread wide apart. She saw his sex in its dark cloud, hard and jutting up.

Walking round the bed on which Raoul lay was an astonishing figure. Squat and heavy-breasted, it wore a species of leather armour which caused belly and breast to project in a gross exaggeration of sex. The buttocks were also bare and although the foreshortened view made certain details hard to see, Kate had the impression of an immensely hairy sexual mound.

Anna, for there was no doubt in Kate's mind as to whom she was looking at, carried a whip and, unbelievably, from time to time she flicked the man lying supine on the bed. Each time she did it, and she did it across his inflamed genitals, he jerked as though an electric shock passed through him.

Lucien tittered.

'Why do you show me this?' Kate hissed in fury.

'It is entertaining.'

'To you, maybe. Not to me.'

She jerked violently. Lucien's hand had moved swift as a snake and suddenly she was penetrated by his fingers.

'You are wet,' he said calmly. 'Why, if this is so distasteful?'

Kate pulled off him and stood up, trembling. Her clothes slipped and slid till she was covered by their discreet sensual elegance once more. She backed away across the room.

'It's disgusting, to watch,' she said, licking her lips.

'Aren't you interested? Is it not fascinating, this that Raoul does with Anna?' Lucien laughed again. 'It is not my fun, you understand, but I am very entertained to see it.'

'It's private. We shouldn't spy.'

Lucien moved close to her. A cloud must have obscured the room because suddenly it was pitch dark. Kate could hear him breathing, feel the warmth from his body in the dark close to hers. 'Nothing is private in the Maison du Lac,' he whispered. 'Don't you know that yet?'

The revelation was almost banal. Raoul, the sensualist, used his rich and pretty little inheritance to explore the darker side of his nature. He accumulated like-minded friends and several times a year they came here to disport themselves.

'I'm not like this,' Kate said with a gasp. What on earth was she doing here? What did Raoul think she was?

A hand lay gentle on her breast, kneading the soft flesh through the lace of her garment. Lucien stood against her, their bodies just touching. 'You are so beautiful,' he murmured. His lips touched her ear, her hair. The moon returned so that his dark body was outlined in silver: cold and dimly brilliant. His lips were on her neck and, unable to contain herself, Kate lifted her head so that he could kiss down her neck and on to her shoulder.

He swayed against her, his sex pliant and firm through their clothing, pressing into her. 'You are what you are,' he whispered into her hair. 'In these mountains anything is possible. Time itself stands still. Things here are true that are not true anywhere else.'

Kate pulled free and stumbled out of the room. In the corridor she stood dazed at the narrow window. The moon sailed once more behind a cloud and the whole world switched off. In the darkness, on naked velvet feet, came the man and now she knew he wore nothing.

This was it, then. The strangeness was everything. The beautiful male creature was something from the night come to pleasure her. It was no one's concern but their own. He came from her own nature, he was her own deep imagination made flesh here at the Maison du Lac locked in its bowl of rock floating on the dark waters of the earth. Their joining was elemental. She could no more deny it than deny her own essence, her own profoundly sexual nature. She was one half of humanity and he the other. Evolution was fired by sex, sex shaped the world, for the world was no mere dead rock floating in sterile space. Space lived. Life was everywhere. The very rock itself evolved, driven by heat within and weather without, the whole made possible by the living web that coated it and she was of that web, that rock, that space. Simply, she wanted the boy in her. He wanted to come and she was willing.

She arched back in the black cool corridor feeling his arm support her as he lifted her clinging slippery garment. She felt him curve over her and kiss her belly. His lips touched her own springing hair and then his fingers entered her vulva and gently he teased apart her swelling flesh, opened it, aroused it, stimulated it until Kate felt all her swollen sex pulse with slow deep desire.

He moved to support her better, his two hands now linked behind her back so she could lean back and open her legs. He came between them, keeping his own balance by leaning back, but his long wonderful wand of flesh bridged the gap and as he came closer and closer, Kate felt it nuzzle and then penetrate her waiting cleft.

The Vermilion Gate, the Sung Chinese had called it. Tao. The way. Yin essence and yang. Infinitely healthful. Infinitely wonderful. Kate hung in space and felt the man-thing fill her and move within her with slow assurance and ripe promise. They swayed, locked together by their dynamic balance, and Lucien drove sweet and sure and steady into the heart of her need.

He became more urgent. Kate found the wall behind her and leant against it. Lucien drove more firmly and, as the moon spilled radiance once more to soak their coupling in silver, Kate saw him as some species of statue, a living silver god of sex, ancient, Classical, mythological, but now made manifest because her own sexual urge had called him up.

A tremendous roar filled the house and echoed in booms and cracks so that the floor and walls vibrated. Lucien gasped and climaxed sharply. The light from outside flickered madly, stroboscopically, and after a dazzled shocked moment Kate realised there was a storm.

Lucien pulled her against him and bit her shoulder gently. Then he came out of her body and they turned to the window.

The lightning lit the sky in great sheets above the wall of rock on the far side of the lake. Kate could have sworn she could smell the sizzled air, but she was so deafened by the reverberations of the thunder as it roared around the rim of the bowl that it was hard to analyse any other sensation.

'Quick,' Lucien gasped, grabbing her hand.

Once more they were off, Kate following, desperately trying not to trip, her clothes billowing behind her and all the time conscious of the warm ooze between her thighs. The naked man ran primaeval as her imaginings so that she would not have been surprised to see wings on his heels. They flew along the bare boards of the corridor and plunged down a narrow staircase. They came to the richer part of the house, and still in darkness ran along the broader carpeted landing until they found a main staircase down. Constantly, they were brilliantly lit as the lightning played madly above the house. The thunder roared and shook furiously and before she had fully realised what he was up to, Lucien had drawn Kate to the main door which he tugged open.

They spilled on to the terrace into the night. Kate was frankly terrified. Lucien released her hand and began to dance across the terrace, his hands flung up and his arms flung wide. The thunder shook and roared so that Kate thought the rock itself must give way. The lightning flashed and quite suddenly the heavens opened and the rain fell.

This then was what Lucien had hurried for. He held his hands up to the deluge and allowed the water to cascade over his nakedness.

Kate was instantly soaked. It was not particularly cold, but in a mere second or so her filmy nightwear clung like a second skin to her soaked body. She caught something of Lucien's crazy mood. She began to laugh, it was all so outrageous, and when Lucien grabbed her to dance she went with him, whirling along the terrace in the rain as the heavens exploded and roared and drained themselves on to their madness.

Lucien was shouting and singing as he danced. It was some time before Kate saw they were not alone. Jean-Marc was there and the gauche Emil, laughing and clapping. She saw Pierre, his head thrown back in the thunder of the night, and she knew how they all were bound by a reaction so all-commanding, so primitive, that the centuries were stripped from them and there was nothing to choose between themselves and their Iron-Age forebears.

As she danced she became aware that all the men had stripped in the rain. She laughed harder. This was one to tell Sadie: dancing in the small hours to the heavenly orchestra naked in the rain.

Raoul and Anna were there now. How foolish she had been about that. It was no odder than everything else in this oddest of places. She saw in the occasional flashes that Anna still wore her extraordinary costume, the leather now wet and seal-slick in the rain. Her hair flew in wet snakes about her head and suddenly Pierre picked the peasant girl up bodily from behind in a great bear hug that lifted her feet clear of the ground. She squealed and wriggled and in a moment Jean-Marc was at her, between her flailing legs and pumping hard.

Kate whirled with Lucien. The lightning came at irregular intervals giving a frozen snapshot of what the others did. Her dazzled eyes saw nothing in the blackness between. They were glistening statues rearranged every time the turn of the dance and the flickering light gave her vision.

She was pulled out of Lucien's arms and found herself confronting Raoul. His hair was plastered wetly across his forehead and his greater height and physical presence were exaggerated by the wildness of the night. He looked down her, holding her hand, and when her eyes followed she saw her own body was outlined by the clinging thin material so that it was as if she wore nothing, except that her edges were blurred. The planes

99

of her stomach, the thrust of her breasts, the shape of her nipples, the hardness of her sexual mound, were all displayed.

Raoul took the material of her nightdress and tore it. Kate backed from him, frightened by the black pits of his eyes, but he followed her and suddenly the roughness of the stone balustrade was at her back. She saw Raoul's sex standing forward as she arched over the rail. Her legs came apart, he knelt slightly to enter her and in all the wild night she felt his heat within, pulsing through her body as he shafted her.

It seemed to her in her madness that her body shook not just to the vibrations of the man thrusting into her but also to the vibrations of the roaring night as the thunder reverberated around the bowl of rock in deafening mind-numbing cracks and explosions of sound. The rain sheeted down. In the corridor above a man had also taken her in this mad cacophony of noise and flashing light. Now she was taken again somewhere else, and all the time she was being taken she heard a great hissing roar as the lake waters boiled in the blackness behind and beneath her head.

Raoul stopped and she would have fallen into the bubbling cauldron below had Lucien not caught her. She slid helplessly, leglessly against his slick-wet skin and now Raoul held her as well and both men supported her.

In the flashes of light she saw that their faces were not kind. Lucien's blazed with its own strange light. Raoul's was set and taut. This mattered to him. He needed this madness, this abandonment to the elements. Something in him was incomplete unless this total unleashing of human sexuality could take place.

They lifted her. Each caught her under one leg so that her thighs were held wide open. Her head fell back so that rain streamed over her face and into her thirsty mouth. The rain striking her exposed sex was very good and it was a moment before she realised it had stopped.

Raoul put her down, forcing her to her knees. She

looked up and saw his sex streaming water like a fountain. She opened her mouth and he entered her. She began to suck him as he plunged into her. The rain poured down his body in cataracts; she was drowning in the thunder of his sex.

Something was happening behind her. Her rear was being lifted till she was on all fours. She sucked at the rigid column of flesh in her mouth. She felt her sex open. Rain poured between her buttocks. She was entered, possessed.

She drew the lifeforce from the man before her. She felt the ground tremble; her eyes were dazzled so that she didn't know whether they were open or closed. Her ears were numb with the noise. Her rear shook. Her sex was lax and soft, full of male juice, full of male sex. She felt it vibrate as she was taken.

Both ends. She moaned, lost in the vastness of the night, of the experience.

Her mouth was suddenly full. She felt Lucien climax inside her. She hung suspended between the two men. They picked her up as they had before, one of her arms round each of their necks, her legs held wide, one by each man. Her head lolled back. The rain caressed her throbbing vulva.

Lucien staggered suddenly. There was pressure between her thighs. Her head came up heavily, like a drunk's, and she found that Pierre was thrusting into her body.

She tried to wriggle away, but she was held fast. Raoul's face blazed now but Lucien was laughing hectically. Pierre was serious as he thumped into her, the two men supporting her staggering now and again at some extra thrust, and ecstasy became dream.

Pierre was done. Kate could hardly feel him except for his warmth. She moaned and rolled her head as he moved away and she felt herself lowered to the ground.

She couldn't support herself. Her legs were jelly, soft and rolling. She fell forward on to hands and knees. A moment later she was lifted again, this time so that she was almost upside down, on her hands but with her hips raised up and her legs held wheelbarrow fashion.

She cried out helplessly, rolling from side to side. She felt the thrust of manflesh again and knew she was being used. Her wet hair stuck in her eyes, in her mouth. The rain bounced up from the terrace, so hard did the drops strike the ground, stinging her face. Her torn clothes clung and threatened to engulf her so that she could not breathe. With no remission, the terrible thunder continued to assault her ears so that she was tired of hearing and would have given anything for silence.

Now she could see nothing in the flashes save for the grey spears of rain and her own hands. Her body jarred and jerked to the man in it. She was lowered to the ground and she rolled over and saw above her, caught, frozen in the lightning, Jean-Marc, his face sharp and intent. He was opening the front of her nightdress, intent on finding her breasts. She saw his penis hanging down between his legs like some old image to an earlier, more priapic time.

As he fumbled, she tried to hit him. He caught her hand and twisted it palm up and kissed it. Then he moved over her so that the terrace was rough and wet under her body as he pressed her down. He kissed her face, her neck, her wild rags of hair, and she heard him moaning to himself and knew that he was transported with pleasure at the violence of the night and his own exploration of her body. The man shook and trembled with emotion. The storm was a drug, a sexual drug, and the men were crazed.

The fear went cold through her. She was trapped on an island in remote mountains with the weather gone mad and five powerful and sexual men who believed they could do what they wished to her body; who treated her as a willing accomplice to their orgy. As Jean-Marc kissed and licked at the wet silk stuck to her skin, she knew real fear, gut-deep. Her mind struggled to work. Emil had not had her yet. Would the others come round again? Someone was fiddling with her now even as Jean-Marc kissed her and made love to her trembling body.

Kate was now quite detached from what went on below her. She was detached also from the storm which was but a climatic exuberance common to these parts. With fear had come common sense. Things had gone too far. She wanted out.

Her body juddered. She did not know who it was. She no longer really cared. They mustn't turn violent. They were all mad, drunk maybe, and she mustn't cross them too obviously.

She had come with Raoul. He was the most intelligent, the dominant one among them. Would he save her now?

She was aware of a disturbance above her. Jean-Marc twisted and looked up. In the occasional light Kate saw a termagant standing above her.

Fear, cold and an excess of emotion combined to drive Kate into near-hysteria. The situation was degenerating into farce. Anna was feeling left out, was she? That had to be a good thing. Let the men do what they wanted with Anna. As for herself, she had had quite enough.

With attention focused elsewhere, for Anna was striking at the men indiscriminately, Kate found herself free enough to crawl out of the way, Shivering in her torn, sodden clothes she came up against the balustrade and huddled against it. Anna was shouting so that she could be heard even over the storm. Evidently, she was enjoying herself.

The storm had lasted for ever. Without having noticed it, Kate found that the lightning had reduced, the thunder was easing and moving away and the rain was diminishing. She pulled herself up against the balusters and wiped the hair out of her eyes.

Anna was lost in a vortex of men. Occasionally Kate saw her head thrown back with her mouth wide open in shouted triumph and the men held her and entered her body as they wanted. A cold wind circled the rock bowl and Kate shivered. The sky was paler than the earth. Dawn was coming.

Lucien was upside down, balancing on his hands and his head. Anna was supported between two men even as Raoul and Lucien had earlier supported Kate. Only it was Lucien who penetrated her as she was held in the sitting, and it was the men who held her who supplied the necessary motion.

Dispassionately, Kate observed to herself what an awkward position it was. Lucien would hardly be able to come in such a mode, but then they were all beyond caring. It was the experience rather than the gratification that mattered to them now. They were given up to excess. Their bodies might not be able to follow where their minds led, but that was not going to inhibit anybody at this stage.

She should get herself out, get to the safety of her room. Apart from anything else, she needed to get dry and warm. A cold would be a fittingly absurd climax to the sexual frenzy of this extraordinary night.

She limped away, into the house and up to her room. Kate locked her door for the first time since entering the Maison du Lac, and ran herself a bath.

No real harm done, she thought. Maybe the men would be ashamed the next day. It was going to be hard to carry this one off. She would rather meet privately with Raoul and explain that life here was a little too strong for her and she would like to leave. She would be more comfortable with herself when the events that had occurred here had reduced to an astonished memory.

Before she climbed into the bath, she looked out of her window. They were all still there, on the terrace. Anna lay full length on the table they dined at. The men were arranged round her. They bent over her as if she were food, as if they had no hands. They bit and kissed and sucked her flesh. Then they touched her. They must all have been too far gone to penetrate her.

Instead they felt her, possessed her with fingers, mouths and tongues. Between them Anna lay like a queen, revelling in the grossness of their mutual behaviour. She was like some great insect, queen of the hive; they her workers serving her, endlessly serving her.

Kate went to the bath.

She woke from disturbed and battling dreams late the next day to weather so peacefully beautiful that the night became as unreal as the events that had taken place in it. She drowsed in the animal warmth, hearing the lake-birds call, wondering what to do. She had never even been for a walk since she arrived. She had eaten, drunk, slept and screwed.

Kate blushed for the night. It was impossible to face the others, even Anna. She slid from her bed and crept stiffly to the window.

She was in luck. Raoul was alone on the terrace, standing with his back to her, scanning the far rock wall with binoculars. Kate opened her window wide and called down to him.

He turned abruptly and stood squinting in the sun, looking up at her.

'Can you come up?' Kate asked. He nodded and walked swiftly into the house. Hurriedly, Kate brushed her hair and unlocked the door.

She was shocked at his appearance. His face was cold and closed and she wondered suddenly how she could ever have trusted her safety to this man. He looked like a tiger: poised, beautiful and deadly.

She sat curled amid the tumbled bedclothes. 'I want to go,' she said abruptly. She hadn't meant to be so brutal – she had intended to prettify her request – but Raoul looked so cold and distant she was unnerved.

'Why?'

'I'm embarrassed about last night. I didn't enjoy it. I don't want to meet the others. I gather you are all intentionally here as a sex party. I don't understand this. You should have with you women who understand, who want what you do. I'm afraid I'm too suburban. Too bourgeois.'

'Who told you this about the sex party?'

Funny how she had missed the resemblance to a snake before. She shook herself impatiently. 'What does it matter? I don't belong here. I'm out of place. You've been very good having me, but now I'll take myself back home. Perhaps someone would drive me to Luz. I can get a bus to Tarbes from there.' Piercingly, she knew how wonderful a hotel room in dull Tarbes would be. Her heart was hammering. She was really scared.

Raoul smiled, a slow contented smile of malice. 'But we need you, sweet Kate.'

'Need me? I don't understand.'

'You must not go yet. You have not served your purpose.'

'I don't think I understand you.'

'You will.'

'Raoul, you can't hold me here against my will. Maybe I haven't made myself clear. I wish to leave. I'm not complaining. I won't say anything. I'm hardly like to, after all. No one's done anything wrong. But things aren't to my taste here. I'll spoil the party if you keep me. I'm going to pack and go, Raoul. You can hardly prevent me.'

'But I can. I can do precisely that. I can prevent you from leaving for as long as I please.'

'Don't play cat and mouse, I'm not in the mood. My friends have my address. You aren't insane, Raoul. You have a job, a position, a place in society. If you are difficult, I'll go to the police. You will be embarrassed and your right to work in my country will be threatened.'

'You talk nonsense, *chérie*. You know nothing of the business. Be a good girl and stay here for now. Anna will bring you breakfast. Your time will not be unpleasant unless you wish it to be so.'

'Are you seriously planning to keep me a prisoner?' Kate choked over the words.

Raoul stood up. He walked over to the door and casually removed the key. He blew Kate a kiss and left the room.

After several rigid seconds, Kate got up from the bed and tried the door. It was undoubtedly locked. It was also a solid, massive, panelled affair in oak. Short of taking it off its hinges, she was not going to get through it until it was next unlocked.

She went to her window. The sun shone benignly on a clean soft world. Birds floated on the lake. Insects hummed in the sweet fresh air. It was a sheer drop to the terrace, however, and Kate really didn't fancy falling on to the hard paving slabs.

She couldn't believe this. She had strayed into the pages of fantasy, of melodrama, with Raoul a copybook villain and Pierre and the others his henchmen.

Kate shivered at this thought, though it was warm. As it happened, Raoul fitted the picture her errant mind had drawn rather too well. It wasn't precisely that he had changed. She had always been aware that ice lay under his charm, steel within the velvet – indeed, that had been part of the attraction. Playing with fire. But he had seemed an eminently civilised man and far removed from the excesses the villains in slasher movies got up to.

She came back to the facts. The incredible facts of her captivity. It had to be an elaborate (and tasteless) joke. Maybe she had offended the man's arrogance in some way during the glut of the night, and spitefully he sought to make her afraid in revenge for the imagined slight. Only this was insane. Undoubtedly she would go to the police. Only a fear of looking foolish would prevent her, unless Raoul had her eventual death in mind.

Now the terrible thought was out and in the open, Kate attempted to examine it as dispassionately as possible.

She could see no benefit to Raoul. Her death and the subsequent inevitable investigation could only be a threat to his way of life and permanent well-being. True, he could easily dispose of her here. Moreover, Kate had the uncomfortable notion that henchmen rather precisely described the relationship between Raoul and the others. There wasn't the equality of friends between them. It was all rather *de haut en bas*. Only Jean-Marc had at all the air of being Raoul's equal, but it was more the air of the firm's accountant than its managing director.

Hold on here. Lucien had as good as told her this was a sex party. Maybe these men belonged to a perverts' club in Paris or something and Raoul was the big man, the one in charge, the fixer. It might please them to pick up an innocent (if she could describe herself as such a thing) and play increasingly horrid games. Perhaps all they had in mind were more elaborate sex orgies involving the willing and mentally defective Anna and the unwilling and all too aware Kate. Perhaps that gave spice to the thing. After it all they could let her go, secure in the knowledge she would condemn herself as well as them with incredible and unprovable tales of sex. She would be notorious afterwards, if she attempted to get them locked up. She could just imagine Raoul's urbane and amused denials, Lucien's incredulity, Pierre's stolid and contemptuous denials, Jean-Marc's icy disapproval. . . Moreover, she had come here willingly and no one would believe that some sex hadn't been on the agenda. There would be witnesses to her relationship with Raoul in England. She would come over as an hysteric and they would snigger at her discomfiture in the press.

Would they go so far that they needed to kill her? How mad were they? How perverted? Would she be mutilated? Beaten? There had been no sado-masochistic signs so far, except for Anna and her leather outfit playing at hurting Raoul. And if they killed her, they would share an uneasy secret. Raoul didn't seem the sort to put his life into the hands of others. Emil certainly looked unstable.

Emil. The weak link. The odd one out. If he turned up on the terrace alone, she must talk to him, persuade him to help her. Except that she couldn't: his English was almost non-existent.

There was a noise at the door and Anna came in. Kate rose to her feet and advanced, but then she saw that Anna was grinning and behind her was Lucien, dancing on his toes, waiting for her to try to get past.

She ignored Anna and the tray. 'Lucien,' she pleaded. 'We are friends. Lovers. You mustn't be a party to this.'

'Enjoy it,' Lucien said exuberantly. 'I am.'

'No, this is no joke. You mustn't do things like this. It is against the law.'

Lucien spluttered with laughter. 'I hadn't thought of that,' he confessed. 'I must tell Raoul. He will find it very funny. Against the law!'

'Anna,' Kate cried. 'Tell them they mustn't.'

Anna's dark eyes were wells of malice. She grunted something unintelligible and backed out of the room. Kate was alone once more.

Her mind worked coldly as she ate the food. The physical conditions of her imprisonment were excellent. Since the men required her to have some minimal attraction, this was perhaps to be expected. Plainly she was to become some sexual toy. She must not mind too much what they actually did. It didn't matter. It was of no consequence in the long run; it in no way diminished her or altered her as a person. It was something that would be inflicted on her and she must bear it and remember it was separate from herself as a person. Real pain was something else, but at the moment she had no need to believe things would go that far. She would be affronted and abused, but it was by no means certain there would be any physical damage.

Kate trembled and spilt some coffee. There were disadvantages to thinking clearly. A little self-delusion might go a long way here, as an aid to keeping up her spirits. In a day or so this whole thing might be over, the men's appetites slaked, their perversion satisfied.

And never never again would she allow herself to get in such a vulnerable situation.

Kate made her bed and dressed carefully. The trouble was, she needed the boost of looking calm and attractive, but it would only succeed in making things worse. That is, unless they wanted to witness her mental and physical degradation and were looking forward to screams and panic.

Kate shuddered. She would hold herself together as long as she could. Her self-respect demanded it.

The long weary day wore slowly away. Kate paced her room and her bathroom, did exercises, considered the chimney as an emergency escape route, tapped fruitlessly at the panelling and thought about dismantling the door lock with her nail file. She also thought about what she would do if she did get out of the room. She was on an island. She could swim, but she would be vulnerable and exposed while she did it. That made a night-time escape more practical, though the idea of swimming in the black cold waters was extremely unattractive, not to say dangerous.

Then what? She was miles from Luz which was, as far as she knew, the nearest point of civilisation to the Maison du Lac. She certainly couldn't go up that towering wall of rock and over into Spain. But if she headed for Luz and they found her gone, they would know precisely where to look. It was the obvious route. She didn't even know if she could manage it in the dark.

With a sensation of horror, she recalled Lucien's fascination with hunting. If she escaped, they would hardly allow her to turn up bedraggled and without luggage at a police station. It would give her story the credence it would otherwise lack. No, there would be no washing their hands of her if they found her gone. They would come after her hotfoot. Lucien appeared to be as comfortable out in these mountains tracking some innocent beast as he was in the sitting room downstairs. She didn't fancy equating herself with some creature of the wild. They might get quite a sexual tingle out of a manhunt (womanhunt) done for real.

At intervals, she saw various members of the party on the terrace. Then the time came when they decided she must come among them.

Pierre came to get her, the thug in him that she had seen from the first well to the front now. He grasped her roughly by the arm and pushed her ahead of him down the stairs and out on to the terrace. Kate saw the table had been laid for dinner alfresco. She noted there were only five places set. She was hauled roughly, vigorously protesting, so that she was in a genuine fury by the time she arrived.

'There is no need for this,' she shouted at Raoul who was sitting with an apéritif calmly watching.

Pierre shook her. Her arm hurt and would certainly bruise.

'What have I done to deserve this, you animal?' she screamed. 'All of you, you must be mad. How can you possibly think you can do this sort of thing in this day and age?'

'This day and age?' Raoul said lazily. 'My dear Kate, do not make the mistake of thinking that this day and age here at the Maison du Lac are the same day and age you left behind in London. Or even Tarbes, for that matter. At least a century separates us from Tarbes, I should think. Maybe more.'

Lucien sniggered.

'Don't delude yourself with sophisticated double-talk like that, you squalid man,' Kate hissed. 'You are behaving like a vulgar boor, you are a vulgar boor, and these men who are playing willing assistants might find the smiles wiped off their faces when the consequences come home to them. I cannot be kidnapped like this. You will not get away with this. People know where I am and I will be looked for. If they don't find me safe and in one piece and at liberty, you will find yourself behind bars for a considerable portion of your life. You won't find prison so elegant, Raoul Martineau. Even in French prisons I believe the general standard of the amenities is considerably lower than anything you would consider acceptable.'

Lucien was translating in an undertone to Emil who nodded thoughtfully. Kate was beyond psychology and the plans she had carefully thought out concerning not antagonising her captors. She was plain bloody furious, and was relieving the accumulated tensions of a dreadful day.

'Tie her up,' Raoul said.

Kate couldn't believe it. Pierre and Lucien came together and Kate saw to her real horror that they had a chain. She began to struggle violently. She was completely ineffectual. Moreover, part of her was scared she would excite them sexually as she fought. They succeeded in any event at chaining her neck and fixing it to the stone balustrade.

She had her hands and feet free and there was nothing she could do with them. The metal sat round her neck; unbreakable, immovable. She was chained like a dog and must remain within its length.

They all sat down. Anna lit candles and the white linen and napery gleamed as dusk fell. Silver and glass shone. It epitomised civilisation and gracious living.

The lake was glassy smooth in the quiet evening air. Raoul had put something classical on the stereo in the house and an external speaker sent the calm and dignified music swelling through the clear reverberant air.

Opposite, dour and forbidding, the great curving wall of rock reminded Kate that her captivity was more than symbolic. Anna served the food. A tray was put by her, even including the rolled linen napkin in its silver holder. There was wine for her, a glass and a small decanter.

For all that, she was a dog on a chain. She began to pace, deliberately rattling her chain to cut across the message sent by the ordered beautiful music, the aromatic food. She could think of no means of escape whatsoever.

She paced and rattled and it was some sort of a small triumph when Raoul turned his dark head. 'My dear, you seek to irritate us. Is that wise?'

'You think I think you'll let me go if I'm nice, is that it?'

'I think you would be wise not to antagonise us unduly. You are so very far from your friends.'

Kate stood stiffly, staring at him. 'How dare you threaten me, you cheap thug.'

'I tell you,' Raoul said, and Kate heard unmistakably the note of real menace in his voice. 'I tell you, be quiet foolish woman.'

Kate bent to her tray. She had no knife. She picked up her empty wine glass and flung it as hard as she was able at Raoul. He jerked back instinctively and she laughed as the glass shards scattered over his food. She hadn't known her aim was so true. She bent swiftly a second time and picked up her decanter. She flung this after the glass. The effect was even better. The sturdy vessel hit Raoul in the chest. The stopper came out and wine shot everywhere. He leapt to his feet and gripped the back of the chair next to him. 'Emil,' he shouted 'Now. *Maintenant*. Do it.'

113

Chapter Seven

*E*mil came towards Kate and for the first time she realised what sort of a man he was. The dullard, the misfit, had disappeared. The young man before her was bouncing on his toes and practically rubbing his hands in anticipation. Delight filled him. The blank brown eyes were alive, even glowing, such was the transformation.

He moved to hit her sharply across the face and danced away at the last moment, giggling.

Kate's head snapped back in alarm. She stared at Emil disbelievingly. He was a hired goon.

He feinted at her again. The metal collar bit into her flesh as she jerked back. She made a small sobbing noise and instantly controlled it.

She didn't hear Raoul order Emil off, but he must have done because the boy's shoulders drooped ludicrously with disappointment and he turned away, a sulking fit evident in every line of his heavy young body.

Raoul had wiped his face and shirt front and faced her across the terrace. The light had drained a little more during the exchange, or Kate's sight had darkened, and the candles lit his face from underneath

114

giving the hollows of the eyesockets and the cheeks an alarming depth. His face was skull-like.

'This time,' he said in a shaky voice, 'you will not suffer in proportion to what you deserve. I am not a cruel man. But be warned, my dear. If you dare to play such tricks again, your punishment will be severe. Emil longs to get at you, and it is not in the sense that I or Lucien or any of the others have enjoyed you. Emil only has one pleasure and he has just demonstrated it, quite effectively, I think. I will give you time to think for yourself of the danger you are in when you attempt a useless resistance to my wishes. Perhaps your own mind will frighten you sufficiently. For your own sake, I hope this is true.'

'What is the plan, Raoul?' Kate asked. Her voice was marvellously steady and in no way a reflection of how she felt inside.

'Ah. Not yet. I trust all will become clear in time.'

'Perhaps if you explained, there would be no need for all this,' said Kate, gesturing at the chain that held her captive. She tried very hard to keep the wobble from entering her voice and almost succeeded. She was beginning to get a reaction to what had just occurred.

'I prefer it this way. Now behave. You will suffer, I assure you, if you do not. You have no friend here and don't be so misled as to think otherwise.'

He left them, no doubt to change his shirt. The others turned back to their meal as Anna cleared up the mess caused by Kate. From time to time she shot malevolent glances at Kate. Kate wondered what she could possibly make of all this. Could Raoul do as he liked in front of her? Had she no sense of the law or did she merely consider her master to be above it?

She didn't know. She was tired and frightened and she wanted very badly to be away from here. She wanted to be bored and safe with conventional dull people. She wanted ordinary scenery, flat, cut by motorways, covered in housing estates. The gloomy grandeur of her surroundings was not helping her one bit.

She sat on the terrace, resting her back against the balusters, and tried not to cry. That was a humiliation she could do without. She ignored Raoul's return and he ignored her.

The next day was also spent on the terrace ignominiously chained. No one physically hurt her, though Emil lounged near at hand. She was fed. When she requested it, she was taken indoors and allowed to use her private bathroom before being brought back down. But her subjection was total. Her loss of self, of dignity, of ability to think properly – all were part of the awful experience of being chained and under another person's arbitrary will.

She became so mentally wretched that she had to do something. She simply could not endure the status quo. Without proper planning, without real forethought, Kate took the one moment when she was freed, when the neck chain was off and before she was hustled into the house by her guards, to make her gesture, her necessary obeisance to the gods of liberty and self-respect.

She threw herself over the balustrade into the lake.

She hit the cold waters with an ugly awkward splash, unbalanced and ill-prepared. Her arms were up sheltering her head rather than being used to dive cleanly and for a moment she rolled under the water, controlling panic, unable to tell which way was up.

The water was peculiarly black. She couldn't account for the terrible darkness and just as she got up and down sorted out, she saw to the paler, lighter side of her, a disturbance in the water.

Looking up she could see the membrane that was the interface between air and water. Despite the darkness to one side of her and the light to the other, fuzzed with the swirling silty cloud she had stirred up in her threshings, she was none the less able to see that she had been joined in the water and would shortly be recaptured.

Blindly, she retreated to the dark. Her lungs wouldn't hold out much longer. Her hands hit the dark and she felt its disagreeable slimy hardness.

It was the wall supporting the terrace, part of the foundations of the house. Kate slithered along it, needing air but delaying coming up and being tamely recaptured. She went in suddenly. She groped, she was in an archway and if only there hadn't been this problem about breathing, she could have stayed there, hidden, till the searchers gave up.

She clutched vainly at the horrible wall. Again there was nothingness. Kate flailed, banged her head, gasped out some precious air, and came up in total darkness.

Her head was out of the water and frantically she began to suck air into her lungs. Her head hurt quite a lot and the air tasted funny even to her oxygen-starved lungs. What consumed her mind though and blotted everything else out was the fact that she was blind.

What had she done? Why couldn't she see? She was sure her eyes were open and yet the darkness was absolute.

Was she dying? Were these the last thoughts of someone going unconscious? She believed she was breathing air, but perhaps she was hallucinating and really the cold water was rushing into her lungs and this was the pleasantness of death.

If she was dying, it was a damned cold and uncomfortable business. Her skirts were winding round her legs, she had lost one sandal, she was tired of keeping her head above water and her ears were echoing horribly.

Yes, her ears. It was as though she were in a hollow place and the water around her glup-glupped with tinny reverberations. Dank. Cellar-like. Dripping.

Kate's brain woke up. She was under the terrace.

Cautiously, she began to explore her inky surroundings. Almost immediately her feet bumped into something and with some painful scrabbling she found she was climbing a horrible half-submerged stairway, encrusted and slimed.

She went up on hands and feet as soon as her upper parts were safely out of the water. Once again her poor sore head struck a hard surface and she slid back several steps before she was able to stop herself.

She dragged herself back up dizzily. This time she spared a hand to feel above her. The undersurface of whatever it was that roofed this semi-submerged chamber was utterly disgusting, dripping with strands of clinging slimy stuff, but she explored it with numbed wet fingers as best she could.

Was she trapped here, to die slowly? Why were there stairs if they led nowhere? In a feeble fury Kate battered at the roof and was illogically cross when it gave way, as though it had initially resisted her from spite.

It was heavy, some sort of trap door in a material she couldn't identify through the ghastly chill jellyish foliage hanging from it. Kate heaved with two hands and then half-stood so as to get her shoulders to the business.

Dim light filtered through. Kate gave a sob of relief. She gave an enormous heave, the slab slid to one side with an unpleasant grating noise, a shower of dry grit and gravel fell into her eyes and she was free.

At this point, as she put her head and shoulders into the chamber above her, she remembered that it must be in the house and could well be occupied. She could be coming up under the dining room table for all she knew. She had made enough noise to attract everyone's attention and now they could all crow as she made her sodden, slimed reappearance into their midst.

But it was not the dining room, nor any room she recalled. It had a dirt floor over stone slabs and corners so dim she could hardly make them out. The light came from above and was dull, though her eyes received it gratefully.

It was a cellar. No, it was the dungeon. She was at

the bottom of the tower and she had entered via the water gate.

Carefully, Kate replaced the trap and covered up its edges as best she could so that the floor was uniform again. Wet marks made her every move clear, but they would dry and disappear in time. Her mind was working with cool efficiency at last. Her need to assert herself had unexpectedly paid off. She had eluded pursuit, unless Raoul knew about his underwater architecture. They must think her drowned and would be frantically searching the lake all around the island, and the island itself in case she had come ashore and was hiding in the scrub. In a limited sense she was free.

Her first need was to get dry clothes so that she kept her health and didn't give herself away by sneezing. She mustn't drip. So it was with a horrible reluctance that Kate removed her clothing. Her body was goose-fleshed and damp, but she wrung out her hair as best she could and prepared to make her way to her room. She need not wait till dark. They would all be occupied outside. Now was her chance, as long as she took good care not to meet up with Anna.

She crept up the ladder, through the room above and up the steps out of it. As she reached the door into the main house, she remembered it had been locked. Dear heavens, if it was locked now she was sunk. She had exchanged one imprisonment for another. Cautiously, Kate tried the door.

That last time Raoul had pursued her in amorous dalliance – she had fled giggling and he had come running after. He had shut the door (or Anna had subsequently) but no one then or since had bothered to lock it.

Kate slid her naked person on to the landing and shut the door behind her. Carefully she slunk into a room that overlooked the terrace. The boat was out, she could see it. Raoul stood on the terrace with his back to the house, grimly watching. The other men must be deployed about the place, hunting for her. Ah, there was Anna, coming to stand by Raoul.

Kate had her opportunity. She fled on winged feet to her room and hastily pulled on jeans and shirt and jumper, her shivering flesh welcoming every addition, though the day was warm. She caught up her handbag; she daren't take it intact, but she retrieved her bank card and some money. And a comb.

Now she found socks and trainers. Hastily she made sure her rummaging didn't show. There were biscuits and fruit in the room; she took some of each. Belatedly she remembered there was no water in the tower. She took a bottle of mineral water and the only waterproof bag she had: a plastic-lined shoulder bag for beachwear. Now she had to make it back to the comparative safety of the tower. There she would have a chance to plan her next move.

As she went past it, Kate helped herself to the key from the alcove next to the door to the tower. Inside she locked the door, probably a frail barrier between herself and the madmen who sought her, but cheering psychologically. What was of greater significance was that there were bolts on the inside. Kate worked these carefully across, damning their stiffness and noise. The door itself was solid. Now, even if the lock was broken, she still had some protection.

Kate went up. She remembered the dead thing near the top, but she had to be up rather than down. She wanted to be nearer the light and air; nearer the sun. Down below had been terrible, and she was no longer quite satisfied with Raoul's explanation of the provenance of the implements of torture. If he was a typical scion of his family, then they had probably gone in for that sort of thing in previous ages.

Moreover, if she made any betraying noise that could carry through stone walls, it would be better made here on the attic level than lower down where everyone lived.

Kate ate some fruit and biscuits, drank some water,

and surprisingly managed to doze. She was exhausted. As warmth gently filled her body and sleepiness overcame her, she began to wish she had stolen a blanket and to wonder if it was worth risking a return journey. She might even sleep on her bed. It was the last place they would look for her.

What were they doing? If they were going to report her death as an accident, then they had better get on with it. There was no telephone link to the mainland so they would have to use the boat and the car. Kate supposed they would rather continue the hunt until darkness closed in, just in case she had somehow slipped through their net. What would she do if they found the submerged chamber and came up the tower after her? Should she have left the door unlocked to indicate she had got away into the house? Would she be better off hiding in the attics than trapping herself in the tower. If they found the tower locked and assumed she couldn't get into it, then the attics were more dangerous.

Kate was too tired to work through the permutations. She fell asleep.

It was a blessing her watch was waterproof. The light was fading but by holding it to a window slit Kate was able to read the time. It was very quiet outside except for the faint moan of the breeze. They had had time to search the island from one end to the other. They might still believe she was under the surface somewhere breathing through a straw, but each passing hour had made that less and less likely. They were patrolling, however. From time to time Kate caught a glimpse of one of them, and she could also see the boat slowly and repeatedly circling the island.

Kate ate her food and drank her water. She rested, making sure she could not be seen from the windows at any time. She had to decide what to do.

Caution urged her to wait. The only way they could make themselves safe was to report her death as an accident. It was so close to the truth that they would be convincing, and all would tell the same story. There would be no come-back. If they did report her, the police would turn up eventually and no doubt the lake would be dragged. She supposed the retrieval of her body was that important. All she had to do was wait and then appear in front of the police.

It was dull. It involved waiting. It was the safest thing to do. When she had gone to her room she had anticipated a midnight swim with her clothes held in her bag on her chest. Now she had had time to think, that seemed quite unnecessary. Even if she made it to shore and dressed herself in dry clothes and took off into the countryside, the thought that Lucien might be on her tracks made her shiver with apprehension.

They patrolled the island all night. They also patrolled the shore. She caught occasional glimpses of a light there. Would she be capable of breaking into the garage and hot-wiring the car? She didn't think so. A pity. That would have been escape in style.

She dozed uncomfortably. In desperation she let herself out and slid through the silent house to her room. She refilled the bottle of mineral water she had taken before from the tap and replaced it on the shelf. Now she could take another one and feel relatively sure no one would notice one was missing. She cleaned her teeth. She stole two blankets from a cupboard and a cushion from the armchair, not daring to make off with a pillow. She crept back to the tower and found that however she tried, she could not shut the bolts quietly. In the silent house they made a terrible noise. The door was locked and that would have to do. Kate put the key in her pocket, went up the steps to the chamber above and tried to sleep.

When the noise started, for a delirious moment Kate thought the police had arrived and her suffering was over. Then she heard sharp cracks and realised with horror that someone was shooting. There were shouts

122

from outside, lights blazed and for a time people seemed to rush about all over the place.

The noise quietened. They must have gone indoors. What on earth had happened? It couldn't be the police unless Raoul had completely flipped his lid.

Who were they? What were they up to? Kate could find no explanation for their behaviour.

The stone walls of the tower were very thick. Kate heard nothing from the house and the long hours stretched until dawn. Kate's thoughts were as uncomfortable as her aching body. They hadn't gone for the police. They had been shooting at someone or something. They appeared to be criminals.

What part in all this did she play? Why had she been brought here? Perhaps they had already faked her leaving and were untroubled by any problems her disappearance would bring on their heads. But why, why, why, had she been brought? Raoul had met her by chance. She couldn't believe he had planned all this for the sake of her *beaux yeux*.

She became fully alert in a moment of pure horror. The room she lay in was grey and gloomy with dawn light filtering through the window slits. Someone was trying the door in the chamber below her.

A sickening sensation of failure swept instantly through her. She could have got away. If she'd left in the night, swimming silently on her back, she would have made it to the shore. She could have crept off in a circuitous route. She wasn't in the desert. She would have stumbled across civilisation in the end. She was a healthy young woman and she could have survived some time, even in this remote and mountainous district. But she had sat tamely here, believing the police would come even though she knew she didn't understand what she was up against. Still, she had continued to believe she could think logically and that the men who had taken her prisoner would act with circumspection. All the evidence was that they didn't care. They must have been going to kill her all along. They were perverts; they probably made snuff movies, those videos where sex and death mingled for real. She was the victim and she had hung around long enough to sign her own death warrant.

Kate backed against the wall, terrified and incapable of hiding it. The noise below grew. There was some remote angry shouting. Time passed. They were going to break down the door. She didn't know what to do. She couldn't go up, there was no point. She couldn't go down past where they were breaking in. She was frozen with fear, trapped by her own stupidity and mental arrogance. Instinct would have guided her more safely. She should have got away while she could.

She heard the door open at last. There was probably a second key. If she had shot the bots, if she had darted down and gone through the trap even though she would have left clear traces of her escape route – it was all too late. No doubt they had found the way in under the tower and this was the result. Kate drew herself upright and tried to give herself a ghost of dignity.

There were male voices raised in anger. She heard Raoul's amused drawl and one of the others, Pierre perhaps, snarling angrily. A voice she didn't recognise answered. The door shut and silence fell.

Kate stood very quietly hearing little over the thundering of her heart. She had no idea what was happening. After a little while, she heard noises below her. Someone was there, either alone or not talking.

Time passed. Whoever it was tried the door. She heard their feet scuffling as they moved about.

Kate dropped to one knee and took off a shoe. She walked on velvet feet across the floor. She knelt by the square opening that led down in such a position that someone coming up the steps would be facing away from her. She raised the shoe in her right hand and wished it was a baton of wood or a poker. She felt murderous.

Whoever it was began to ascend. The top of his head

came into view, then his shoulders. As soon as his head was properly clear, Kate struck with all her might.

He fell with a grunt. Kate knew almost at once she had failed to knock him out, the hard-headed bastard. He scuffled around the floor below her and groaned.

'Who's up there? I didn't know this prison was tenanted. For Christ's sake . . .'

She had no idea who it was. She backed slowly away from the hatch and waited.

He came up cautiously, looking all around him this time. As he emerged, a shaft of thin sunlight struck across the room as the rising sun broke free of the surrounding moutains. It was pink, blood-tinged, and in the peculiar light Kate saw who it was she had assaulted.

She dropped the shoe. She felt the shock wipe her face free of colour. 'You,' she gasped.

He came up the last of the steps and turned to face her properly. 'That's no way to treat a friend,' he reproved gently. 'You lack femininity, Kate. The soft sort, I mean. I thought so before in Corfu. I'm damn sure now. Has anyone ever told you, you're no lady, Kate. No way.'

They sat together on Kate's blankets, John Sorrell and herself. In the bizarre world she now inhabited, it seemed no odd thing to Kate that she should sit thus with a man who had used her to escape justice, not just in hot blood when they had met on the path on Mount Pantokrátor, but for some time afterwards when she had accompanied him half across Europe, giving him the protective cover of her presence.

Once more he was tired, dirty and wounded. This was the victim of the shooting, but it had resulted in no more than a graze over his hip, he said. Kate could see the blood on his shirt.

'What are you doing here?' Kate asked.

'What are you doing here?' he said.

'I met Raoul in London and he invited me to accompany him on holiday. He says he owns this place.' Kate shivered. 'I believe him. It suits his personality.'

'You met him by chance?' John asked politely. 'Or perhaps you knew him already?'

'By chance.'

'You didn't meet him in Corfu?'

'Corfu? No. Should I have?'

'He was there, Kate. So were you.'

'So were you. You know him. Who is he? What is he?'

'You don't know?'

Kate was nettled. 'Obviously I don't know.'

John hesitated. 'You see,' he said eventually, 'I just can't tie you into this. I walked into a trap. You were the bait. But was the bait entirely innocent of the role she was playing? That's what I want to know.'

Kate stared at him. He gazed limpidly back. 'I suppose finding you imprisoned here says something about your innocence,' he added.

'I'm not imprisoned. I escaped them. They don't know I'm here.'

'I'm in prison and you're not?'

'No. I mean, I got here by myself. They think I'm out there somewhere. In fact, they must think I'm dead.'

Something prevented Kate from rushing to tell this man just how she had got there. She found his presence incredibly suspicious. However attractive he was, he was undoubtedly one of the bad guys. That made Raoul one of the good guys. This was plainly absurd, and so either there were several sets of villains around, or John was really in cahoots with Raoul. Maybe he had recently fallen out with him. Thieves proverbially fell out with each other. Yes, that was it, they were thieves. They were crooks. She had them placed at last. Well, she might not understand her own place in the scheme of things, but she could bet that if John found a way of using her to his advantage, regardless of her own, he would do so. She had better keep private that particular piece of knowledge: that she knew a way out of here.

She had a cold thought. Perhaps they knew she was in here and John had been deliberately scruffed up and sent in as if he were a prisoner to find out what she knew.

She didn't know anything. They just thought she knew something.

'You'd better let me look at your wound,' Kate said cunningly. She wanted to see if it was real. 'I've got some water. We ought to wash it.'

'You're very well appointed,' John said. He smiled and cocked his head sideways enquiringly at Kate.

'I snuck out in the night and helped myself.'

'You've been here a while?'

'Too long.' Kate leaned forward and began to pull his shirt loose from the waistband of his trousers.

He winced and she realised she must have broken the scabbed surface of his wound. He lay down on his side, propped on one elbow, watching her as she edged his trousers down a little and she was suddenly acutely aware that she had been intimate with this man's body. They had been lovers, and it was not time and boredom that had parted them, but circumstance.

She made a pad with a tissue from her pocket and soaked it with the mineral water. She began to wash the graze on his hip quite gently.

'Why are you here?' She asked quietly.

'They told me they had you and they would do a swap. Or they would kill you.'

Kate stopped what she was doing. 'Swap me for what?'

'Something I had.'

'You came here to get me out?'

'I came here to see if they really had you. I didn't intend to get too close. How did you meet Raoul?'

'He pulled me out from under the wheels of a car.'

'In Corfu?'

'In west London, near where I live. He works in London.'

'Does he now. Have you been there?'

127

'Where he works?'

'Yes.'

'No, but . . .' Kate stopped. She had accepted that story at face value: the geologist background, the aerial surveys. It had authenticity. She hadn't checked it.

It Raoul had lied to her from the start, he had nothing to lose, no respectable life, no decent job.

'You say Raoul was in Corfu,' she went on slowly.

'He and his pals. Minions. They followed us, you know. I lost them in Paris. I didn't realise they would go on after you.'

'You mean Raoul engineered that meeting with me?'

'I guess so. Took you to bed, did he?'

Kate stared at him in stony silence.

'I guess so,' John said softly, 'or you wouldn't have come here. That is, assuming you are the innocent you make yourself out to be. Good-looking kind of snake, isn't he?'

'Aren't you all?' Kate said bitterly.

He reached out and took a handful of her hair. He pulled her towards him and rolled on to her. His mouth was as she remembered: possessive, promising, offering.

He released her before she had time to pull away. With their faces very close together he looked into her eyes. 'You're tasty, Kate. I can't blame the man.'

Very carefully, as if he might bite, Kate moved as far away from him as she could.

'The thing is,' John went on conversationally, 'how far in are you? Has the sexy Raoul persuaded you to play along? Are you going to bed me and get a little pillow talk going, so that I tell you what you want to know? What Raoul wants to know. I mean, you might pounce on me again. You're the lady who leads the way, I distinctly remember. You're good at it, too. I can recommend it. Will I be able to resist a second time? Should I resist, I ask myself? Are you the hearty breakfast traditionally offered to the condemned man?'

'You've got a mind like a gutter,' Kate said. 'Because

you are dishonest, you can't imagine other people might be different.'

'People near Raoul generally aren't.'

'I didn't understand what he was.'

'You mean you do now?'

'No. That is, things got out of control. I got frightened. I wanted to go. Then it became clear I was a prisoner.'

'Chained on the terrace.'

'You know that?' Kate's voice rose dangerously.

'I saw. From a distance. I guess I was meant to.'

'Then you know this is for real.'

'Do I? Raoul is a subtle man. And you are a lady, a female I should say, who is willing to forget all about moral scruples and honesty and the law and all that, if she can get a good fuck. Who should know better than I? And you fuck beautifully, I've got to hand it to you. I bet that smooth bastard does it even better than I do, too. Given what you did for me, what the hell might you not do for him?'

Kate stared at him, aghast. She was so angry she wanted to tear his eyes out. Now she had not only to escape from the appalling and terrifying Raoul, she had to get away from this half-pint villain who insulted her at every turn.

Could she use him? Could she use him to help her escape, and then ditch him? She would have to sell up and move when she got home. Kate started to shiver. Raoul knew where she lived. He had enticed her here. Now she knew things about him, not much admittedly, but enough to get the police interested. But if she escaped, who would get to whom first? The police to Raoul, or Raoul to herself for revenge; for his own protection; to eliminate her as a witness?

'What's the matter?' John said in a changed voice. 'You look like you've seen a ghost.'

'He'll follow me. Even if I get away, he'll follow me and kill me. He must have meant to do it all along. When I fell in the water, I thought he thought I must

129

have drowned. I thought he'd have to get the police, say it was an accident. When they arrived I could show myself and I'd be safe. But I'll never be safe. It'll be my word against his and he's so smooth. He's somebody here, too. Anna treats him like he was the king or something. Like she was his slave.'

'What did he do to you?'

'He chained me up. When I wanted to leave, I mean. Emil hit me, too.'

'Why did you want to leave?'

'It went too far. It was fun at first, but then I didn't like it. The storm and all that. It was over the top.'

'What was?'

Kate stopped. She came out of the trance of horror she had been in. She looked at the creature across the room and her lip curled with disdain. What on earth did it matter, what he thought of her? She wasn't dependent on his good opinion. His opinion meant nothing to her. She had helped him escape in the past, when they were in Greece. He owed her for that. He must help her now.

'The sex.'

'The sex?'

'Yes, of course. I came here as Raoul's bedpartner. Obviously. He's terrific in bed, just like you thought. Superb. His friends were very nice to me at first. Then they got too friendly.'

'They all wanted a little slice of the action?'

'They had Anna, of course. The storm was unfortunate.'

'The other night?'

'You were around then?'

'I heard about it. What happened in the storm?'

Kate's lips twitched sardonically. 'What do you think?'

'You bitch,' John said softly. 'You bitch on heat. Come here.'

'What do I get out of it?'

'What do you want out of it?'

'You screwed me before and I helped you get away. Suppose I screw you now. You help me get away.'

He sat up stiffly, his face closed and set. 'You don't set much store by the niceties, do you?' he said.

'You know already I'm no lady.' Kate got to her feet and came slowly across the room. She had no doubts about what she was doing. She needed all the help she could get. She needed a man on her side and she needed a man's strength. She particularly needed a man the people after her wanted more than they wanted her, so that if it came to a choice they would go for him rather than her. As for using her sex, that was nothing. She had long since admitted to herself that, regardless of his character, she lusted for this man's body. The chemistry between them was the most powerful she had ever felt. She was glad of an excuse to ignore his insults, to ignore what he thought of her. Quite simply, she wanted him in her. She wanted to feel the press of his skin. She wanted his lips on hers. She wanted his strength wrapped round her, pressing into her, used to push his sex into hers and keep it there till she was full.

She knelt down before him as she had done once before, long ago, in a cave. She took his face between her hands and felt the rough graze of stubble on his unshaven chin. She felt his throat. How vulnerable he was, after all. She saw a faint twitch in his cheek. He was moved. He felt this as she did. He held her in contempt, but he needed to enter her as she needed him to do it.

She could see the crinkles edging his eyes now. His lips were parted and the white of his teeth gleamed slightly. His cheeks were faintly hollowed, there were smudges under his eyes and she saw a faint scar on his temple where his hair was pushed aside.

Kate ran a hand up into his hair from the back of his neck. His hands lay slack, unused. She brought her face down and laid her nose against his, rubbing it gently up and down, smelling him, feeling his warmth, feeling her heart judder in excitement.

131

Her own lips parted. She twisted her head slightly and brushed them dry across his cheekbone. His face lifted in her grasp. She kissed, still dryly, the very edge of his left eye, and felt his lashes flutter on her cheek as she did so.

It was his skin, the smell of him, that was driving her crazy with desire. She kissed the closed lid of his eye gently, nuzzling the eyebrow, sampling each exquisite sensation. Again the lid fluttered under her lips, alive, like a small bird, like a moth.

Kate wet her lips slightly and kissed the side of his nose. She rubbed her own soft skin against his stubble, finding the rough caress exciting. She had one hand under his chin now and she lifted his face – he made no attempt to resist her – and found his lips.

She kissed his lips again and again, soft kisses on the surface, along his mouth, at its edges, brushing her lips against his, savouring each exquisite touch. She felt his body tremble slightly and suddenly she opened her mouth properly and twisted into his, opening his under hers and kissing him deeply and fiercely as her need became so demanding it threatened to go out of control.

His hands were up her back now, pulling her into him as he responded. He forced her over, kissing her hard, and one of his hands came over her breast. He squeezed it hard and Kate arched her back and gasped. He wrestled in under her shirt and she felt the thrill of his skin against her ribs, against her breast. He got the nipple centred in his palm and began to rotate his hand.

Kate clung to him and moaned. She too was groping up under his clothes, feeling his body where it curved over her, feeling the taut muscles in his body. She unfolded her legs so that she lay on the floor and he could move on to her properly. His weight was heavenly. She rubbed herself against him and was shocked as he suddenly withdrew.

He was pulling off his clothes. Kate sat up and slid backwards a little away from him. She undid each button of her shirt instead of pulling it open and back so that her arms were trapped behind her as she sought to release herself from the sleeves. Her breasts thrust forward.

He watched her, his eyes narrowed and hard. Kate freed herself from her shirt and undid her jeans. She began to wriggle out of them.

She stood up to take them off, taking her panties with them. When she was quite naked she closed in against the seated man, putting a hand on his shoulder, standing by his face.

He looked up at her.

'You know what I want,' she said huskily. She lifted on leg and placed the foot lightly on his shoulder. He turned his face up. She closed her eyes, concentrating on keeping her balance. She felt his breath and then his tongue.

He let his tongue project into her sex first. He walked its warm wet strength along the cleft of her sex, stirring her torpid flesh, arousing her, opening her, preparing her.

One strong hand grasped her raised ankle. He knelt up slightly and she felt his whole mouth come over her sex. He kissed and sucked at her. She felt him take her labia between his teeth and gently pull. He pushed his mouth further in, kissing and sucking. He was fierce and Kate wanted him to be.

Suddenly she could no longer bear being denied his hardness. She came free of him, opening dazed eyes, and sank down on hands and knees. He was fully erect. She kissed his penis, kissed the side of the club-like head, kissed the soft ring of silken skin; she kissed the hard stalk and she bit gently at his balls. She rubbed her face in the hair of his groin and then she drew gently back and took his whole member in her mouth, as far as she could admit it, and she kissed and sucked deeply.

His hands were under her body fondling her breasts. They came up to her shoulders and he levered her gently off him. He rolled her over on to her back on the

133

blankets. He moved over on top of her, kissing her face and neck and breasts. His erect penis brushed across her stomach. Kate opened her legs and lifted her haunches. She caught herself behind her knees and pulled herself so she had her sex reared up to receive him.

Up on his arms he held himself for a second. They looked into each other's impassioned faces. He began to lower his body, adjusting as he went. Kate felt his sex press against hers. It slid slightly in her vulva. She pulled harder at her knees. His club-head met her entrance. He pushed, using the weight of his hips, controlling himself. Kate clenched her sexual muscles. She wanted to feel at the maximum the pressure of his fatness as he entered her.

Now he was entering her. Kate's sex came open despite herself, like a flower. Her lips swelled to meet and enfold him. Slick-wet and willing, her soft flesh squeezed warmly in welcome. His hard tube sank into her. She gripped at him joyfully. He lifted slightly and began to thrust: regularly, deeply, strong profound thrusts that seemed to go up into the very core of her being.

She wanted to cling to his back, to hold his body close against hers. At the same time, she wanted to be speared by him through and through. She clung to her own body, therefore, admitting him as deeply as was possible, maximising each thrust and moving to meet him and withdraw in a synchronous symphony of sex.

He was thrusting harder. She could hear him panting. He came down on to his knees, gripping her legs and pushed as hard as he could go into her. Kate felt herself slide along the floor and shouted with pleasure. His balls were slapping her. It was bliss. She was coming to climax – he wasn't going to leave her behind – and when she felt his balls harden and his cock swell and burst, she was with him, her own sex in spasm, gripping him convulsively again and again as she orgasmed around his climaxing cock.

He lay slack across her trembling body, for she refused to let him move his weight away. She felt his heart thump in his chest and caught its echo in her own. She was flooded with contentment. No matter what the circumstances, this man was worth the effort. He did things to her no other man could do, had ever done. It wasn't mechanical, it was chemical. Her body simply didn't react like this with other men.

'Noisy bitch,' he said gently. 'You'll have them in here wondering what's going on.'

She woke suddenly to her surroundings. 'No,' she whispered. 'They mustn't. They don't know I'm here.'

'Does it make any difference?' he asked lazily. 'We're both locked in. Or is it just that you're frightened they'll separate us and you won't have me to screw you.'

She ignored the insult, expecting nothing different from him. 'They'll take the key away if they find me,' she said.

He froze. 'The key?'

'Yes. How do you think I get in and out? I've got a key. It's in my jeans.'

He pulled out of her without ceremony after one incredulous moment. Kneeling naked by her clothes, he went through her pockets. Kate, still sexually dazed, propped herself up on her elbows and watched him. He mustn't realise how much her body adored him. She must hide from him the power of her feelings.

He pulled out the big key. 'They had an argument,' he said softly. 'The woman had to go down to the kitchens and get one. You had it all along.'

'I told you they didn't know I was here.'

He padded back over to her and knelt beside her. He held the key.

'I didn't believe you. The whole situation looked like a set-up. You're a honey-trap, like it or not. I couldn't assume you were straight. I can't assume that.'

'I couldn't care less,' Kate said viciously. 'We've got a deal, remember? You're going to help me get away.'

He began to get dressed. 'That's right,' he said

135

cheerfully. 'I remember. You're certainly a hot one. A man has trouble sometimes remembering it isn't the real thing. Heaven help the poor sod you really go for. I think I'll hang on to the key, if you don't mind.'

Kate felt herself go white. 'You wouldn't leave me here. Not after what I've done for you.' She meant what she had done in Corfu, helping him to escape the authorities. He chose to understand her differently.

'Is it easier when you don't care, or harder?'

'What?'

'To screw good. I mean, does it interfere if you actually have feelings for the man? Do they interfere with the performance, or do they help it? Or haven't you ever had feelings and so you don't know?'

The tears came despite her anger. Kate sat up and reached for her clothes where he had dropped them by her. She mustn't tell him about the water gate. If he ran out on her, that would be her only means of escape.

She wiped her eyes surreptitiously. She was damned if the cold-hearted callous bastard would see her hurt. 'Do you want to get out tonight?' she asked, keeping her voice light and steady. 'I presume you can swim. It would help if you could hot-wire the Renault. I can't, I'm afraid.'

He had drawn breath to reply when they heard the door below being opened.

Chapter Eight

John was across the room and at the top of the steps in a flash. Kate sat frozen, terrified. They had been heard. She had shouted in her lust and she had been heard.

'Are you coming down or shall we come up and get you?' It was Raoul, the insulting, supercilious, amused drawl very evident despite his accented English.

'I'll come down,' John said lightly, putting the key on the floor. He jumped.

Kate felt sick with relief. They still didn't know she was here. There was no reason for them to come up. She just had to keep very still.

There was some scuffling below and laughter. Someone grunted. Kate forgot about her own position and felt sweat prickle. They were going to rough him up and he knew it. He had known it when he went to them to stop them coming to him. When he had protected her.

She heard them all go down the steps into the chamber below. The noise continued. They must be descending the ladder into the dungeon. Thank goodness she had removed her wet bundle of clothes.

Kate's heart began to hammer. She heard noises, muffled conversation. Some time passed.

He didn't scream. All the time it went on, he didn't scream. He shouted and swore at the beginning. He groaned later on. Once or twice he called out in some ghastly extremity of pain. But he didn't scream.

Kate simply sat, her mind fizzing, her limbs trembling. She didn't even retrieve the key. She just sat, hearing the distant sounds of torture.

When they left, there was considerable laughter, but she heard Raoul's voice clearly, speaking angrily in French. He wasn't pleased, then. Whatever their object had been, they hadn't succeeded. No doubt Pierre and Jean-Marc and Emil and Lucien laughed because they had enjoyed their assault on the frail vulnerable tissue of the man at their mercy. But Raoul had not had his own way, and so was angry. Not a man to thwart, of course. She must remember that, Kate thought idiotically.

She stood up and waited for the tingling to stop as her circulation adjusted. She walked softly to the steps and went down them. Down again to the room below.

She looked at where the ladder led into the dungeon. No noise came up. She didn't want to go down.

Like a sleepwalker, Kate went over the ladder and climbed down it. Candles had been set in stone niches and they had not yet gone out, thought Kate could not have said whether minutes or hours had passed since the business in the dungeon had started. On all sorts of levels, her mind wasn't working at all.

He was hanging from manacles set high in the wall. His head was down so that his chin rested on his chest. He hung from his wrists, his knees buckled.

'No,' Kate said. He couldn't be dead.

She went over to him. His shirt was open and there was blood on his chest. She lifted his head – it was heavy – and he moved slightly as his eyes blinked dully open.

He tried weakly to pull out of her hands. 'It's me,' she sobbed. 'They've gone.'

Something like intelligence came into his eyes. He

frowned. Kate moved so that she supported his body, taking its weight to relieve his wrists. He lay against her, his head on her shoulder, and she felt him trying to take his own weight on his legs.

Pushing into him, Kate fumbled at the manacles. They were locked.

She put her arms round his waist and lifted him as best she could. Holding him, she whispered: 'I'm so sorry.' She felt the warm tears on her cheeks.

He stirred in her arms. 'There's a poker, an iron bar,' he said, his voice slurred. 'Over there. Prise these damned things out of the wall.'

She let go of him gently and was relieved to see he could stand, leaning against the wall certainly but on his own two feet. She groped across the cellar and found the bar.

She levered the ringbolts out of the stone walls without much difficulty. She helped him up the ladder, through the two rooms above and back into the one with her blankets. He leant on her as she took him across the floor and let him subside gently.

He lay back, his skin greyish with a dull sheen over it. He looked ghastly. He had bitten through his lip and there was blood on his mouth. Both his cheeks were grazed and bruised. There was blood coming from one ear. His chest was horribly marked. Kate could smell it. He had been burned.

'That's a new experience,' he mumbled, his eyes closed.

'I'll get you away,' Kate said, stroking his brow. 'We'll get away.'

'Give me a minute, hey? It isn't that I don't want to go . . .'

'It'll have to be tonight. We can't do it in daylight. What if they come back? I can't bear it.' Kate's voice rose in panic.

'Hey, hey. Stop that. I might think you care about me.' He stopped and, incredibly, he grinned, although rather faintly. 'Course you do. I have to help you. We have a deal.'

Kate propped his head on the cushion. Carefully she washed his face, relieved to find that the blood by his ear was from the lobe, not from within. She didn't dare touch his chest, which was raw and blistered. When she was done she arranged herself so that she sat propped against the wall. She undid her own shirt and gathered him in her arms so that his head was against the pillowed softness of her breasts. His dark scarred face with its roughness of coming beard lay against her white soft skin. She held him and he slept.

She slept herself and woke stiff and hungry. She had released her hold in her sleep and now his head was in her lap. A fly buzzed in the room and settled on his chest. She flapped it away and the movement caused him to open his eyes.

'Hi,' he said. His voice broke slightly. Kate reached for the water and held it for him so he could drink and ease his throat.

She looked at her watch. 'It's only five,' she said. 'I can't think why it's so gloomy.'

'I thought it was my eyes.'

'If it's not a silly question, how do you feel?'

'Really, I won't worry about hangovers in the future. How come you look so pretty?'

'You're a mess,' Kate said, and was horrified to hear her voice catch.

He sat up, going white in the process. Then he sat for a moment looking down at himself. 'Jeez, it looks bad.'

'It is. You need medical attention.'

'You think Anna's a nurse?'

'There are two ways out of here. One is through the door into the house. The other is through the dungeon. It's the way I got in.'

'The dungeon?'

'It has a trap door. It isn't solid under the tower or the terrace. There are steps down into the water. Somewhere, underwater I think, there's an archway

140

and you can get out into the lake itself. I came the other way. I jumped into the water, groped my way along the wall and fell through by accident. It was horrible. But once I found the steps I realised they must lead somewhere. The trouble is, if we go out that way, they'll see what we've done. If we use the key and go out through the house when it's dark, even if they recapture us they might put us back in here because they'll find the key and keep it. But we'd still have a second chance.'

'Good thinking, batwoman. It's a pity I'm physically a bit below par. Normally I love a healthful swim but at the moment somehow I don't really fancy it. Why are you crying?'

'You feel well enough to joke,' Kate sniffled. 'I thought they killed you.'

'I wished they had at one point. Not so hot, eh?'

'Why did they do it? What was the point?'

'Beyond a little sadistic satisfaction? Oh, they want to know what I know.'

'What do you know?'

'Well, I don't actually. They just think I do. That's my fault, of course.'

'I don't understand,' Kate said dully.

'I guess you really don't. Know anything about archaeology, child?'

'No.' Kate sniffed and wiped her nose. She had used all her tissues cleaning up John.

'I do, you see. They think I know where a rather fabulous hoard is hidden. The trouble is, if it exists, I don't know where it is. I wish I did.'

'Why do they think you know?'

'I let it slip. We are competitors, you might say.' John eyed Kate sardonically. 'We steal archaeological treasures. Raoul has a big organisation. I'm a freelance, a small-time thief. Only I've got a lead on to something big. Raoul wants that information.'

'You had something with you when I met you in Corfu?'

'Yes. I offered to sell it to Raoul and his friends. Then

it became clear to me he wanted what I had, but he wasn't going to pay for it. Dishonest, eh? I'm afraid so. Lover-boy is something of a bad lot, actually.'

'I didn't know when I met him,' Kate said desperately.

'A woman's intuition not working? You knew I was a bad lot, though.'

'Not as bad as him,' Kate said absurdly.

'He's threatened to kill you, then?' John said it casually, but he raised his eyebrows and waited for Kate's reply.

'You wouldn't have.' Kate's voice was husky. 'It was a bluff.'

'Tut tut tut. No intuition at all.'

'Why are you doing this? We need to trust each other; to help each other. We have to escape. Raoul tortured you. I couldn't bear it.'

He took her hand and turned it palm up. He kissed it, then her wrist, then her arm. He looked up into her eyes. 'What is it?' he said.

'You know,' Kate said painfully.

'Tell me.'

She turned her head away. Damn him. Damn the bastard. She must pull herself together. She turned back and grinned. 'Sex, of course. I go for you. Have from the start. I hope the chest stops hurting soon. A couple of days out there in the mountains with you might be fun. Maybe if I'd taken a potshot at Raoul I'd have felt the same way about him. You're the only man I've tried to kill. It's had this really weird effect on me.' She shrugged and smiled.

'Did they all have you?'

She didn't pretend to misunderstand. 'I was sleeping with Raoul and Lucien anyway. Both at once. The others had me in the storm. Certainly Pierre and Jean-Marc. I'm not sure about Emil. Some of them had me more than once, but by then I was protesting and I couldn't see.'

He hit her with the back of his hand, across her face.

She was astonished, and gratified that he was so strong. They would need his strength in the hours to come. She leant against the wall and smiled at him, her head ringing and her cheek sore. He cared, then. Despite everything he said, he cared. She had the power to hurt him.

He went to the window slit. 'There's a storm coming. The sky's pretty dark. It'll get lighter later on. I think we should go. I'm not sure I can take another session.'

'But they'll be indoors. They could be spread all over the house.'

'I'm sorry to appear so unheroic. I'd rather get out of here and be recaptured and shoved back in than I would stay here and wait tamely for them to come back with their pokers and their fire. I don't think it'll be my chest next time. My French leaves something to be desired and Raoul's English went to pot a bit when he got excited, but I gather the next stage is to bring Anna and let her select the juicier bits of me.'

'Right,' Kate said, feeling white and sick again. Was this horror never going to end?

He unlocked the door. There was no way they could find out if it was guarded since it was too thick to hear through. Kate kept back up one level so that if John was instantly recaptured, she might still escape detection. He was not, and he signalled her to come.

Out on the landing they went silently into a room and looked over the terrace. It was empty. The sky hung heavy with black clouds whose bellies seemed suspended over the bowl of rock. They were hideously in movement, rolling in a tormented fashion as if working up to some horrible climax. Of course they were. The storm was brewing nicely. Kate found the thought of swimming even more terrifying. But it would hide them. If they could just get out, the storm would hide them from the men sheltering in the house. No dancing on the terrace this time, Kate thought. The only problem was that they might take their enforced inactivity to the tower, there to renew their games with John.

They stole along the gallery, past more attic rooms. Suddenly Kate thought she recognised where they were. She took John's hand and led him into a room. She was right. Carefully, she lifted the square of wood. Now she was looking down into Anna's room. It would be useful, knowing where she was. The hope was that she was in the kitchens preparing one of her superb meals. But she might be here.

She was. Kate stared. She was not alone.

A frame, like a ladder, leant against one wall. A naked man was strapped to it belly-down. His face went through one gap in its latticing. His genitals went through another.

Sitting within the triangle formed by the frame between where it stood on the floor and where it rested against the wall, was Anna, open-legged and with her clothes pulled roughly open so that her bare breasts and splayed legs were clearly visible to the bound man. Standing in the room and also quite naked, was that superb physical being, the golden Lucien; the pretty boy, the lover, the athlete, the huntsman.

Lucien held a scourge. He raised it and struck the buttocks of the bound man. As he did so, Anna caressed the protruding genitalia just above her face.

Lucien struck again. Anna fondled and stroked and masturbated.

'Three down, three to go,' John whispered. 'Shortens the odds.'

No doubt Raoul was properly preparing himself for another bout of torturing John. Kate replaced the wooden square of floor. She was trembling. She had, after all, known Raoul was a pervert from the start. It was alarming to see it displayed so vividly when she was in the company of John. She wanted to tell John that she had taken part in no such games, but she was aware that she would sound at once feeble and a liar if she did so. The trouble was, it was the bourgeois instinct in her, her very sexual dullness, that had responded so gleefully to the deviance in Raoul. Had

144

she been more genuinely salty herself, he would have had no appeal.

Kate felt that the subtlety of this would be lost on the adventurer beside her. Anyway, it hardly mattered. She was bound for the police and civilisation. He was bound for the wide blue yonder. If all went well, they had a couple of days together at the most. At some point when they could talk she must reassure him that she would not refer to his part in this. She would pretend she had escaped alone. He need never be mentioned.

Back in the gallery, she tried to remember what she had done next on that previous occasion. Lucien and she had made it together out here in the corridor. Then they had gone downstairs.

They crept along, Kate leading since she knew more of the house. They came to the stairs leading down from the attic to the lower level, the bedroom level, where they might expect to find the other men. John carried the iron bar that had been used to torture him. It seemed fitting. Kate's only wish if they met someone was that John would get in first before too much noise had been made.

She remembered those half-stairs, those byways Lucien had led her up and down that mad night. They seemed to exist only in her imagination. She could not find them now.

They went down, sticking to the centre of the treads. Kate did not know who had what room where. Now they were entering the really dangerous zone. They had to get down and out.

There must be a second door leading outside from the kitchens. It was inconceivable that there was not. They knew Anna was safely occupied upstairs with her lord. Going away from the dangerous central hallway containing the main exit from the house on to the terrace, highly visible from many windows, they made their way to the back regions.

They entered the gleaming ceramic cavern in which Anna worked. John grabbed some bread as they passed and a hunk of cold meat. They wasted time entering the freezer room and the cold store, also finding a store where there were gas bottles. At last they found a door to the outside, leading into a kitchen garden, wild and overgrown. They went through and for a moment Kate fought the impulse to sob.

They stood in the heavy threatening air, the wind making mad little gusts through the overgrown herbs and waving carrot fronds. It seemed inexpressibly wonderful to Kate. They were outside the house, freedom lay before them, and she had John at her side.

They made their way swiftly through the garden and out of the gate in the garden wall. Now they had to cross open green and they did it at a crouching run. As they did so, the first heavy drops fell.

They were in the prickly scrub and Kate's mood soared drunkenly. They reached the lake edge and there for the first time her spirits quailed.

The water was grey-black, whipped into ugly little crests and crosshatched waves. The wind went round, first one way and then the other. The rain fell more heavily, flattening the threatening maelstrom but adding a horror of its own.

They were momentarily in shelter before the rain penetrated the foliage above them. John began to strip, pulling off his boots and making a pile of his clothes. Kate did likewise.

Her plastic-lined bag had a hopeless air about it. They packed their shoes in first and then the tight bundle of their clothes. Kate was shivering but John seemed untroubled.

'Can you manage?' he muttered doubtfully. They had agreed that he could not rest the bag's scratchy outer layer on his raw burnt chest. It was Kate who would have to hold it and swim on her back using only her legs.

'I'll have to,' she said, fixing the top in an effort to keep the rain out.

Entering the water was horrible. The sharp stones

146

were slime-covered with a coating of loose silt that oozed unpleasantly through the slithering, numbed toes. The water felt bitterly cold. Kate stumbled in, John holding her hand and leading her.

'That way,' he said, pointing across the lake to the rock wall where it rose first as a scree slope and then as the cracked and fissured base of the rearing rock itself.

'No. The shortest way. Over there.'

'No. Down you go. Take your time. I'll stay with you.'

The cold was alive and malevolent, its icy fingers entering Kate's flesh and bones. The bag was awkward. The flattened waves broke over her face from time to time. It was not actually difficult, merely vilely unpleasant. Kate swam and swam till her legs ached and her head hurt and her chest was on fire with the strain of breathing through waterlogged air. Sometimes she felt John supporting her head and partly towing her. Sometimes she did it entirely alone. He guided her and she swam and she swam till her head hit some rocks and John took the bag from her. Dazed, frozen and exhausted she crawled from the water over loose muddy scree. Again John guided her, and she found she was behind and partially under a rock, shivering and sheltering. For the first time, she heard the cacophony of sound in which they had made their escape. Her ears and eyes must have closed during the awful swim. The lightning flickered in pale evil sheets of ghastly greenish light. The thunder rattled maniacally round the rim of rock towering above her. The rain drummed ceaselessly.

'No point in getting dressed,' John shouted in her ear.

'Why here?' Kate said weakly.

'We're going to climb this and make it into Spain.'

'No.' It was a feeble cry of terror.

'They'll expect us to go the other way.'

'Because we wouldn't be stupid enough to do this.'

'You don't mind heights, do you?'

'I hate them.'

'Pity. It's quite an experience. We'll be going through the Brèche de Roland.'

'What's that? A tunnel?'

'A hole. In the rock. Direct route to Spain. You'll like it, you'll see.'

'I want to go home,' Kate said and sobbed suddenly.

'Don't we all.'

He sounded bitter. Kate raised her hand. The rain was easing. She might be able to dress soon and get warm. 'You can have no home,' she said cruelly. 'Not doing what you've chosen to do.'

'No.' he said mildly.

'It isn't as if anyone made you a crook. You've done it to yourself. Too lazy, too greedy, to go about things the honest way.'

'I expect you're right. Just plain natural badness, then. I expect I could be pulling down more as an honest-to-goodness archaeologist working from a university and discovering Chimú stirrup-spout pots than as an adventurer and crook scavenging about the countryside with innocent maidens.'

Kate opened the bag, took out her soggy shirt and began to dry herself with it. 'What are Chimú whatsit-spout pots?'

John took the shirt and began vigorously to rub Kate's back. 'Moche, actually, the people who preceded the Chimú. Andean. First millennium. They made these rounded pots and decorated them. Terrific stuff. They were very talented potters. They particularly excelled at the three-dimensional stuff.'

'So?'

'So they depicted sex. Not just any old sex. They really went for anal intercourse, if the pots reflect the society that made them. Men and women, boys and boys, they really liked it up the bum. They liked sucking, too. They liked it with animals. They just liked it full stop, I guess, and they liked making images of it. These were pots to drink out of, you understand. It

148

really tickled them to make the spout a nice fat penis, depicted with exquisite realism. You took a drink, you took a suck. Odd if you were a man, I guess. Mind you, some spouts were made like a vulva. I don't know if that's odd for a woman. You ever sucked a woman, Kate? I can recommend it. You're beautiful there, now I remember. What a piece of work you are.'

He rubbed her back hard. Warmth came from his roughness. 'Why go with me when you despise me so much?'

'I don't like Dali, but I know a fine painting when I see it. I expect Raoul enjoyed seducing you to get you to come here. What a blow for him if you'd been a dog. Mind you, he only took you as my leavings, so you wouldn't have been entirely hopeless. Not that I exactly chose you myself. You were what happened to be on the track that day. And of course, you did the pouncing. I only obliged the lady. And made use of her afterwards.'

'You go up the wall. I'm going to Luz.'

'Sweetheart, you're coming with me.'

The rain had stopped. Across the lake sunlight flooded across island and water in a thousand painful pinpricks of dancing light. They were in shadow, here under the cliff. Kate faced John.

'What do you mean?'

'I'm not offering you a choice.'

'You think I'll be recaptured? Why should you care?'

No, I'm thinking you might get away. You're a resourceful woman, Kate. What if you make it to Luz? Who will you go and see?'

'Oh. That. Look, I won't tell the police about you. You know that. I didn't before. Only stop insulting me. I hate it and it isn't true.'

'I insult you out of self-defence. I want you so badly, see. I thought you knew. And I don't want you telling the police about Raoul. Not yet, anyway.'

The burns on his chest had gone soft and white and wrinkled from the water. 'Why not?'

'We might have business together yet.'

'You mean, you'll work with him? After what he's done to you?'

'I steal for money. He's my way to maximise cash-flow. I can't handle what I've found: it's too big for me. I need an organisation like his. His will do as well as anyone's. There aren't that many fine-art thieves working with ancient artefacts. It's a specialist trade.'

'You told me you don't know what he wants to know.'

'I don't. Up to a point. But I have a damn good idea. I'd like to confirm it before I do anything else. I can sell a fact, a location, for far more money than I can sell an idea. But I'm damned if I'll give it away because some guy has a hot poker on me. Anyway, he's stolen something of mine and I want a chance to get it back before the police get there. So you stay with me, sister, whether you like it or not.'

'You can't force me up that cliff!'

'Didn't you hear what else I said?'

'What else . . .' Kate's voice faltered. She had heard.

'I want you. I'm crazy for you.' His voice was rough. 'You have to know that. No woman has ever done to me what you've done. I can't stand the idea of you making it with him over there, moaning for him, splitting your legs open for him, kissing his cock, convulsing that gorgeous cunt round his rod. Don't you understand? You've got me totally hooked. I hate you and I want to fuck you in about equal parts. You let all those bastards paddle in your pool. You're sick, lady. But your body is wine and roses, you belong to me like snow belongs on the mountains. But you go with him, the torturing bastard, and I bet you would again.'

She was trembling. They were alone in a grey warm world, steam rising faintly from the surface of the lake and in the distance the diamond sparkle of brilliant light.

'You've got me wrong. I wasn't like this till I met you. It was you who undid something in me.'

She broke off. He was reaching for her, his eyes

150

glittering and his mouth set in a harsh line. Below her was wet grass and fern. He pushed her back, crowding on to her, his lips warm on her face and breast.

This has got to stop, she thought dizzily. I mustn't go with him. He's keeping me prisoner. But she wanted him. Her body adored his and through it all she was exulted that he was trapped as she was; that it worked both ways and that he was the helpless prey of his feelings as she was of hers.

He was pushing into her without style or finesse. The raw need to copulate overcame everything. Kate writhed and lifted to meet each surge of his body. He had never been sweeter. They were both fools to their own sexuality. Mind and intellect and rational thought had all gone out of the window, swept away on a mind-numbing tide of passion as uncontrollable as the sea.

Her body's song lifted with his, sweet in its harmony, elemental in its melody. She was flooded with delight, knowing she would have him again and again. Regardless of everything, this was right. Their bodies knew it was right. He moved superbly, each touch of his flesh a frisson of delight. She lay on lank sodden grass, with small stones and gravel under her. Her hair was in damp wisps about her face. The lake murmured with faint and fading anger to her right. The evil wall of rock towered menacingly over their two joined bodies. The very earth rocked and swayed as he sweetly took her and she felt lifted, upraised, resurrected from fear and doubt into a glowing web of strength and peace.

Her eyes were open as he came and she saw that it was true, that he was as unbearably moved as she was. She was with him, holding him at the point of climax, her own quivering flesh trapping his hot strength within her until he lunged and lunged again so that she fell back, quiet at last, feeling his small after movements as he emptied himself totally into her.

She caught his head and kissed him on the mouth. 'Be kinder to me,' she begged.

He took her wrist and kissed it on the inside. 'I have

to hold out against you,' he said in a strange voice. 'You understand that. Or I'll drown in you.'

They dressed in damp clothes and pulled on their footwear. They ate the bread and the meat they had taken, drinking water from the lake to go with it.

'We have to get up before it gets too dark,' John said, glancing at the sun and the wall above them.

'All the way?' Kate was horrified.

'No, we couldn't. But away from here. It can't be too long before they find us gone.'

'I can't climb it in the dark,' Kate whimpered. 'I don't think I can do it in the light.'

'No, not in the dark. We'll find some crack and jam ourselves in. It's not as sheer as you think. People do climb it for fun, you know. But I sure as hell wish we had a rope. Thank Christ you've got proper shoes on.'

They heard the whine of the outboard simultaneously. 'Shit,' John said explosively. Hastily he picked up every sign that showed they had been there. He looked at Kate's bag measuringly. It was white, dirty now, but definitely white. He dug a hole and buried it, patting the earth over it and then loosening the surface gravel till it didn't show. Then he took Kate's hand and carefully they began to edge their way up through the scree to the foot of the wall.

In an hour the dark came, enough to mask their progress but not enough to stop them from moving slowly upwards. John moved constantly to their right away from where the wall ended in steep scrubby slopes and small gnarled woods. Kate thought this nonsensical, but he deigned eventually to explain. If their route was detected, it would be assumed they had gone over to the shelter of the wooded slopes. He was always choosing the least likely option. If anyone got seriously on to their trail, he hoped they would lose it among these silent rocks.

Their progress was slow, and for Kate at least, terrifying. Mostly they walked and edged along tiny paths, rubble-strewn from the frost-cracked walls above them and occasionally thick with animal droppings.

'What comes here?' Kate gasped, when she had forced John to stop for a moment.

'Ibex.'

They went on. The face was wet, often dripping from the recent rains and high-up streams, but it was rough rock and afforded a decent grip. Sometimes they climbed properly, John making her obey the rule of three fixed holds and only one hand or foot moving at a time. She didn't look down at any time. She knew that if she did she would be finished.

There were periods of respite when the rock took a great step in and Kate could lie down and pretend she was on proper ground. It was on one of these that John proposed they stop for the night. It was getting too dark to see.

Kate looked up. As far as she could tell, they were no nearer the top than an hour previously. She wasn't going to look down and check, though. Once stopped, the wind and cold began to get to her. The nights had been cool at lake level. Up here it was plain damned cold.

They huddled together in a deep crack in the rock. John pushed her hair back and laid his cheek against hers. Her body knew a safety and a contentment with him, but her mind was far from easy.

She had refused to do this, to come up here with him. He did not have the ability to force her unless he used a knife or gun and he had neither, as far as she knew. When she rebelled, he had admitted his infatuation with her, he had ravished her with his words, his admission of weakness, and he had ravished her with his body as he made love to her.

Kate knew he knew she could not control her response to him. 'You've got it really bad,' he had said early on in their acquaintance, and he had proceeded to use her strange infatuation with him ever since, to his advantage.

Had he used it again, quite cynically, down there by the side of the lake? She had wanted to go off, she had meant to, and this had been a threat to him, or at least to his possible income. He had stopped her with words of love and the body of a magician. He was too clever to soft-talk her. He had abused her too thoroughly to make a sudden change of tune realistic. But that harsh confession, almost a confession of love, had been eminently believable. Kate had wanted to believe it. Even now, with her brain telling her she was being suckered, her body adored his resting tight against her. She felt his breathing, the thump of his heart, the close strength of his arms.

'What is it?' he murmured.

'I wish I could be sure you were telling me the truth.'

He moved his face and rubbed noses with her gently. He kissed her mouth, opening it slightly under his and letting her feel his tongue.

That's what he would do, of course. Any doubt she expressed would be met by a display of affection, of lust, of need, as the occasion suggested.

His safest bet would be to kill her, she thought suddenly. She was no use to him, she was merely a hindrance. Well, he hadn't killed her. For whatever reason, he wanted her along.

In the circumstances, it was a cheering thought, and she tried to let the comfort of it lull her to sleep.

If the night was haunted, the day was a nightmare. Kate woke with a jerk that cricked her neck and hit her head on the rock by it. Something had cracked sharply and a tiny fragment of rock had struck her cheek.

It was a pale opalescent daylight, very early in the cool dew-wet morning. Below, the world lay cob-webbed grey and dusky. Only up here in the air was there any real light from the mist-swathed brilliance of the sky.

John was cold beside her, his skin grey and dark with

fatigue. His developing beard gave him the air of a pirate. His sunken eyes gleamed.

There was a strange high whine and another sharp cracking noise.

'Shit,' John said softly.

'What is it? An avalanche?' Kate's voice was hoarse.

'Worse, lady. They've found us.'

'What do you mean?'

John grinned suddenly. 'We're being shot at,' he said. 'Ouch!'

There had been another shot and this one had been so close to John that chips of rock had hurt him. 'Move,' he said urgently. 'The bastards'll kill us.'

They crabbed sideways along the wide rock shelf where they had spent the night. Kate felt like a fly on the wall. A kind of fatalistic calm descended on her. The main thing was, she didn't like heights. She had never wanted to be up here. Being shot at was a minor considersation. Part of her wondered just how good Lucien was. Very good, she suspected.

She felt a mild euphoric urge to sing. 'Keep down,' John snapped.

'There's no need to be rude,' Kate said with dignity. Really, the man had no manners.

'If I didn't know better, I'd say you were drunk.'

'Since we are about to die and it is entirely your fault,' Kate said in an awful voice, 'You might at least be civilised in your behaviour to me.'

'You've gone mad,' John said with conviction. 'That's all I need. Shut up and do what I say or I'll smack you over the chops.'

'I'll push you off this cliff,' Kate said and giggled.

John pressed his body hard into hers, his lips in her hair, her ear. 'Don't, sweetheart,' he said. 'I can't bear it. I know what I've done to you.'

A bullet sang by them and smacked into the rock.

'Tell me you love me,' Kate said. 'I know it won't be true, like everything else, but say it all the same'

He found her mouth and pressed his to it. 'I love

you, Kate,' he whispered and Kate felt the glow warm and hearten her. 'You lie superbly,' she said. 'I love you, darling.'

They moved fast across an open area and then John tried to go up. A bullet hit the rock above them, almost smashing his fingers. They went sideways and then were forced down a little where the shelf narrowed and all but disappeared.

Several minutes later, Kate said: 'He lets us go down and to the left. He won't let us go up or to the right.'

'I know,' John said grimly. 'We're being driven off the wall.'

'What if we call their bluff?'

'I knew from the start you were braver than me. I don't have the kind of optimism. You can freelance, Kate, but I guess I'm going to do what they say.'

Occasionally, a chastening shot was fired just to let them know they were still in the sights, but as long as they kept on moving down and to the left, they were not seriously threatened.

'They'll be waiting for us,' Kate observed.

'Yup.'

'Remember what I said about the tower, in case we're separated.'

'Look out for yourself, Kate. Do whatever you have to do.'

Gradually, the angle of the wall softened and more vegetation clung to its ramparts. 'Separate and run for it,' John said. 'They want me more than you.'

Kate found she was scrabbling on earth and grass. Small bushes grew in the thin, steeply sloping soil rooted in the rock. She hunched herself and began to make her way quickly up the slope.

There was a noise ahead of her. She looked up and saw Emil, grinning. She swerved to the right and plunged into the trees.

It was hopeless. They were all around her. One of them laughed and she knew she was sport for them. She saw John suddenly being held at gunpoint by

Lucien. Pierre loomed in front. She stopped, at bay: sweating, exhausted, filthy and afraid.

John ran at her and hit her. She gave a squawk of surprise and fell over. He grabbed at her, hauled her up and hit her again and again.

'You bitch,' he yelled. 'You did this. You led them to me . . .' He was hauled off and Kate lay on the ground in shock.

She became aware of Raoul crouched over her, his handsome face alive with amusement. 'Oh dear, Kate,' he said reproachfully. 'What is all this? I'm glad to see you, of course, but in such company!'

She said faintly, 'Raoul. He is mad.'

'Then why were you with him, my sweet child?'

She shut her eyes, exhausted and dizzy. 'I was frightened of you,' she said. 'I didn't understand.'

'Understand what?'

She opened her eyes wide. 'He told me what you are.'

'Did he, now.'

'You should have told me. You might have know I wouldn't be shocked. You knew about me in other ways. Why didn't you trust me in this?' He frowned, watching her with dark suspicious eyes. Kate grinned faintly. 'Thief,' she said. 'You think I care?'

Raoul helped her up. They had tied John's wrists behind his back and Lucien stood with the rifle slack in his arms, watching Kate with bright curiosity. She limped over to John and spat at him. 'I held you up. I slowed you down,' she said cruelly. 'Now they have you again.' She turned back to Raoul. 'He knows,' she said coldly. 'That is, he has a very good idea. He wants to verify it so he can sell you the information.'

Jean-Marc minced deliberately up to Kate, placing his elegantly shod feet with care on the wet slippery ground. Birds sang around them; it was late spring, not long past dawn, and life was going on.

'You have changed,' he said in cold tones.

'Nobody told me anything before. Now I know,' Kate

said. Suddenly, she did know. She had met John in Corfu being chased by the police. He had told her was a smuggler and he had something on him, something she knew to be small and heavy. He had told her Raoul was into smuggling stolen archaeological treasures. That fitted. Raoul was clearly a crook, if a remarkably refined one. Then there was that article torn out of *Time Magazine*. 'Albania,' she said. 'You're all stealing stuff out of Albania.'

She had everyone's attention now. They were a strange group, here in the primaeval woods. She wiped her bloody, muddy face and grinned at them. 'I was hiding in the house after I escaped from the terrace. I stole the key to the tower and released him. He told me things last night. I didn't know what to do. I thought if I stuck with him there might be something in it for me. He goes for me, you see.' She pushed her hair back in a grotesque parody of coquettishness. 'You might not think so, but he does, poor fool. So he told me about Albania and he would have told me more, only you found us. I was slowing him down to give me time to think, you see. You've got me wrong, Raoul. Sure, I was bored sexually when you met me. That's why I went off with you so readily. But I was bored with everything. I don't have a job in England anymore. I don't have anything I care about. So why don't you let me help? You don't dislike me entirely, Raoul, do you? It wasn't all an act.'

She saw his face change and knew a flash of incredulous triumph. He had a weakness and she knew what it was and how to exploit it.

'I know how he feels about you,' Raoul said slowly. 'That was why we took you. He had the apple and we wanted it and we thought that if we had you, he would come. And he did. No, my English Miss, it was not an act. It was a pleasure, to do what we did together. I salute you. Evidently you are a woman of enterprise and I have seriously underestimated you.'

'Can we go back to the house?' Kate asked. 'I want a

bath and a change of clothes. I need sleep and food. I can't think straight just now. Let me catch my breath, Raoul, and I'll see what I can come up with.'

She went over to John. His face was inscrutable. 'Pillow talk,' she said softly and laughed. 'You knew all along and you still couldn't stop yourself.' She ran a hand down his body, smiling into his eyes. 'Mmmm,' she said fruitily. Her hand was in his groin. 'Nice.'

Lucien gave a shout of laughter. John made a sudden stiff movement and Lucien hit him, a casual swipe from behind with the gun butt. Kate laughed and turned away.

They took John to the tower. Kate was allowed to go to her room. Anna brought her food, and she bathed and went to bed. She knew Emil stood guard outside her door but it didn't worry her. It would take more than her declaration in the woods to convince them that she was with them. Only Raoul and Jean-Marc mattered, she was sure. The rest were henchmen – including the delectable Lucien – and would do as Raoul said. But Jean-Marc was a force to be reckoned with, and he did not have Raoul's fatal weakness. At least, Kate didn't think he did. She would have to find out.

Chapter Nine

*S*he dressed with exquisite care. Her hair shone burnished in the lamplight. Her nails were filed and painted, her lips a reddened sensual gleam. She chose a simple dress, one that clung and outlined her figure. She had lost weight, her waist had narrowed, and the consequence was that her hips and breasts were more voluptuous by comparison. Inside she shivered, but her deep eyes gave nothing away. She perfumed herself, touched herself, aroused herself, until she felt ready to meet the company below.

Emil guided her down the stairs to where the men sat in the drawing room with drinks, waiting for her before they went in to dinner. She made an entrance, standing in the doorway till they had all turned their heads, but it was to Raoul alone she looked.

His eyes lit up in appreciation. He came forward. 'Such a transformation. I congratulate you.' He took one of her hands and kissed the back of it.

Kate smiled. 'At last I have a chance to be myself,' she said.

Jean-Marc cut across them. He lounged against the mantelpiece, drink in one hand, a thin cigarillo in the other. 'The transformation is incredible,' he said dryly.

Kate looked at him. 'And what is your plan for getting

your prisoner to divulge the information he holds?' she asked. 'Or are you prepared simply to pay for it?'

'My plan is that we threaten your life. I think that if we hurt you, he will tell us what he knows.'

'This was his plan from the first,' Raoul said.

Kate moved across the room, the slight swish of her silky dress accompanying her movements. 'How would you hurt me, Jean-Marc?' she murmured. 'Perhaps I might like it. You never know. Unfortunately however, it will have no effect on the man you are holding. He began our acquaintance by using me to keep the police at bay and he has done little but hit and abuse me ever since, though I command his body. He will not tell you anything, whatever you do to him. Indeed, he is indifferent to my pain. The only way I touch him is here.' She touched the front of Jean-Marc's trousers. He stiffened and Raoul laughed. 'Make love to me before his eyes and he will be hurt. But I don't think he will say anything, because you have him in fear of his life and the information he holds is his surety that he will be kept alive.'

She turned back to Raoul. 'A mismanagement, surely.' She smiled and looked at him under her lashes. 'You have achieved the opposite of what you want. I have two suggestions to offer.'

'Why did he come, if not for you?' Jean-Marc asked.

'To sell his knowledge. He wants to strike a bargain. He knows he doesn't have the resources to exploit what he may have found, and you do.'

'Why did you release him and go with him?'

'I didn't know what was going on here. Suddenly you used me as a prostitute and you locked me up. Naturally I fled. Any girl of spirit would. When I saw him, I knew I could use him to help me get away; I needed a man's strength.' Kate looked Raoul in the eye to emphasise this point. 'A man's strength,' she murmured languidly again. She must be careful not to overdo it, but Raoul was very gullible where sex was concerned. Jean-Marc, the colder fish by comparison, needed more subtle handling.

'What two suggestions?' Raoul asked.

Kate sipped the drink she had been given. Deliberately she went over to a chair and sat herself comfortably in it. She surveyed the room. Each man watched her.

'You let him go.'

Jean-Marc snorted.

'Why?' Raoul asked.

'And follow him. He will lead you to Albania. To the treasure. He is a clever man, a determined man. A greedy man. He will not be able to leave it where he thinks it is.'

'Your other suggestion?'

Kate purred. 'You let me extract the information from him on your behalf.'

'How?' Pierre asked.

Raoul laughed. 'You think he will tell you, *chérie*?'

'So far he has told me much, unlike you. However, I take your point. I rather burnt my boats out there on the hill. He knows I want to work with you; he knows that I betrayed him and he was caught like a fly on the wall because of me.'

'I tracked him,' Lucien said indignantly.

'I slowed him,' Kate said sweetly. 'Once I understood what you were all about here, I knew where I would rather be. But I needed to bring you a prize to prove my allegiance. I did the best I could in the circumstances.'

Raoul bowed. 'But do you think he will tell you anything else now?'

'I think he is clever, though his body will tend to betray him. I think he might tell me lies. Maybe I can persuade him I was play-acting on the hill.'

'Were you?' Jean-Marc asked.

'How can you know?' Kate smiled. 'I must not be too clever or neither of you will trust me, not him and not you. But you can watch me. Guard me. I am one woman against five men. You cannot fear me.' Her tone mocked but she knew her point was valid and would be taken. They could not see her as a serious threat. 'Meanwhile,' she said to Raoul, 'I must write to my friends so that they don't begin to make enquiries about me.'

Again Raoul gave that little nod of acknowledgement. 'I think we should eat,' he said. 'I must not make Anna any more angry than she already is. Come, children. I will investigate this lady more thoroughly later on. We must try her allegiance and see where it really lies.'

Kate shivered inside her sleek dress. She must place every foot precisely. There would not be room for mistakes. She had no doubts whatsoever that she was fighting for her life.

'Make love to me,' Kate whispered. She kissed Raoul's hand, kneeling at his feet. He sat in his chair, caressing his brandy glass with one hand. The other had been appropriated by Kate.

'What if I don't trust you, *chérie*?'

'Won't that add to the piquancy?'

He sat forward. 'You are adorable in this mood, Kate. But I think Jean-Marc is right not to trust you.'

'There is a factor he fails to take into consideration,' Kate said.

'And that is?'

Kate touched his sleeve. The tiny gesture made her shiver. She looked up again into the hawk face above hers. 'You.'

'Me?'

'A woman who has been with you does not lightly forget the experience.'

'But you left me.'

'You frightened me. You gave me to the others. You interfered with your maid. Is it any wonder that I ran when I could?'

'You did not like it with the others?'

'Lucien is a dear boy, too pretty not to be enjoyed. But you did not ask me or consult me concerning the

163

others. I do not want the pig Pierre in me, nor that horrible Emil.'

Raoul laughed. 'Emil does not like girls. He is a guard dog who does not like meat. So useful, when it is me that is guarded.'

'I thought you were done with me,' Kate said directly. 'That was insupportable.'

'Oh no, not done with you.' Raoul's voice was caressing. The other men had left them and were in the billiards room. Kate could hear the snick of the balls and the occasional voice raised in conversation. 'But I am not done with Anna, either. She belongs to my family. It would be cruel to ignore her. Besides, she has her ways. She knows how to please me.'

'Perhaps we can please you together. Then she might not dislike me so much. I have no desire to own you, Raoul, nor will I submit to being owned. But I think you and I have unfinished business.'

Kate could see his excitement. His lips had thinned a little and she caught the occasional gleam of his teeth. His eyes were glittering. Truly, he was deviant. She must exploit his deviance, play up to it, lead him further in and so become mistress of him. Only in that way would she be safe.

He kissed her. His mouth had the old skill, the ability to arouse, to sensitise, to promise the white blaze of excitement that would come in surrender to lust. To be with him, in his arms, sharing the excitement when it came, to be his partner in lust, was both his promise and his desire. Kate would do it. She knew he was superb, terrifying in his commitment to pleasure, but now she must go with him, lead him until he acknowledged her his equal.

With her lips brushing his, she said: 'Sorrell.'

'What of him?'

'Don't mess him up.'

'Why not?'

She drew back slightly and smiles. 'I might want him,' she said simply. 'As you might want a pretty

164

female prisoner. It excites me, that he is there to be played with. I wonder if I could arouse him, even though he hates me.'

'He wants your body.'

'I want his. And it might be useful. Will he believe as he makes love with me that I would betray him at the flick of a finger? Your finger, Raoul.'

'I find it entertaining that though he knows you help me, he might yet be made to please you. And I agree,' Raoul said, sublimely unaware of the irony of the situation, 'that in his arrogance he will not understand how little you mean to him, how it is just his body that appeals.'

Kate began to undo Raoul's shirt buttons. 'Make love to me,' she said again, an urgent pleading in her voice. 'I need you. Now.'

He carried her upstairs. His physical strength was impressive. Kate held him round his neck and kissed his face and his throat. They went to her room. He lowered her on to her bed, but immediately she sank to the floor. She knelt before the standing man and began to open his clothes.

'Let me drink from the fountain of youth,' she said. Raoul didn't laugh. Kate knew already that he was singularly humourless where sex was converned. She took out his penis and held it for a moment.

Men were honey. Truly this experience, if she survived it, would teach her that. There was honey in men's bodies to extract, to exploit, to savour, and she should let no dim and changeable morality affect that realisation. In future, she must plot her path through life quietly, stealing this special joy from those around her, so that they did not realise she fed on them vampire-fashion, satisfying her lust, her adoration of the male sex, before passing on to the next man. It was the only way to stay safe, to remain intact, to preserve her liberty and independence.

Raoul hardened in her hands. She looked up at him towering above her. 'I adore you,' she said. 'I adore this. I own this at this moment. You will pleasure me until I am satisfied and when you are drained, I will take someone else.'

In a swift smooth gesture she slid the sheath of her dress over her head, feeling the heavy silkiness of her hair fall back into place. Now she knelt naked but for a black slip of lace at her sex, and the garter belt and stockings she wore. Her body was pale in the lamplight, smooth, satin-skinned, and from it a faint perfume arose.

'Raoul,' she whispered. 'Prepare to die.'

She kissed his sex, little tender sucky kisses that tugged his penis now this way, now that. She licked the glistening tip, her red lips parted, and she let her white sharp teeth rest against the hard engorged length of him.

Now she kissed the eye, squeezing it gently, kissing it with pursed lips and reddening it slightly with her lip gloss. Again her tongue snaked out and she ran it round, wetting and lubricating the weapon she caressed so fervently.

She stood up very slowly, stroking her breasts as she rose with Raoul's elastic hardness. When she was fully up, still wearing her high heels, she put his penis between her rounded smooth thighs. She held him there against the slight roughness of her stockings. His pale flesh contrasted with the blackness of her stockings, and the milkiness of her naked thighs above.

'Is this what men do together?' she whispered, pushing his jacket back and off, opening his white shirt and baring his chest so she could bend and kiss it. Her hands went into his trouser belt, to release it. He would not need any clothes now. There must be no barrier between them.

'Men?' he said.

'Men. When they are together.' Her hand came round and felt the hard curve of his buttocks. 'Or is it always this?'

She stabbed him so that her finger went into the cleft

and she felt the tightness of his arse. He jerked where she held him but made no move to escape.

'I have used boys but I prefer women,' Raoul said. His forehead had sweat on it.

Kate released his penis. She slid his trousers down so that her breasts rubbed across his stomach and went into his groin. 'Do you like women with women,' she murmured, her hair falling all over his stiff member. She used one hand to grasp him and she gently frotted him, using her hair as a mild abrasive.

'Katya,' he said with difficulty.

She helped him to step out of his remaining clothing and led him to the bed.

'It is a fit thing to worship,' she said huskily. She made him lie on his back on the bed. She climbed on to it herself and crouched over him, still in her high heels and wearing her black stockings. Now she removed her panties. She crouched so that her knees were wide apart as she straddled him. His head was slightly raised on her pillows. He looked down the length of his own body into her sex, seeing his own raised before it.

Kate reached for her bag. Still kneeling over him, feeling the soft bounce of his hardness against the front of her vulva, she rummaged for her lipstick. When she had the gold tube in her hands, she opened it. Now she drew a fat red waxed line around his column. She put the lipstick to one side. She rocked forward on to one knee and began to insert his stiffness of sex into her velvet pouch. She looked in his face as she did so. He stared down at himself being swallowed into her moist warm squeezing flesh.

She held him part-way in. Her fingers stirred the hair, crisp and curling in his groin. She felt for and teased his balls. She squeezed the stalk she held trapped, and then lifted herself slightly so he could see her labia tight against his flesh, kissing it, sucking it, holding it. She grasped his sex and masturbated him even as he penetrated her. Then she released him with her hand and engulfed him with her sex. She swallowed him entirely. She sucked his whole long length deep into her and arched her back, thrusting her breasts forward as she felt the exquisite pressure inside her. Her flesh bubbled with desire. She felt her vagina ripple of its own accord and strove to control it. He mustn't come yet. She wasn't nearly ready to be done with him.

She felt his hands begin to caress her nipples and a low sigh of pleasure came from deep in her throat. She reached again for the lipstick and curving forward, she now outlined her nipples in red. She bent right into him and gave him her breasts to suck. He took the softened, lengthened things and sucked each in turn, his eyes shut, his face a mask of desire.

She moved on his penis, stroking it with her internal flesh, pressing on him, masturbating him inside her with magical secret fingers so that his dizzy mind couldn't know what she did with him, the sensation was so extraordinary. She folded his desire into her being, took it into her own lust, fed it, inflamed it and brought him slowly and gently towards the inevitable moment.

His mouth came open in a wordless shout of pleasure carried almost to the extremity of pain. Kate drew back and began to rock on him so that she rode his penis and at the same time stroked his thighs with her buttocks on every forward swing. She moved harder and faster. His own body jerked in response. His fingers dug deep into her flesh. Kate cried out, shouting, and she slid one shoe off and began to beat him with it on his thigh, as though she rode a horse.

Raoul shouted hoarsely. He lifted his body, carrying Kate's weight with his own. She felt his spurt, so vigorous it was, and knew her own flesh crumbled and melted and liquified into a vortex of lust fulfilled.

She took each hard thrust of his climaxing body, glorying in her own satisfied urge and her power over the man beneath her. She had never known the triumph of the courtesan, to move a man's mind by moving his body. Her own age dismissed it, but here was something timeless, calling down all the ages, when women had made men bend to their will not by proving themselves equal, something so self-evident it hardly needed proving, but by manipulating against them to women's own advantage the greater sexual drive of the male of the species.

She climbed off the man and lay with her head at the foot of the bed. She felt him move and sit up.

'Katya,' he said. 'What a feast.'

'Eat me,' she said faintly, looking at the ceiling.

'I beg your pardon?'

'Where I am red from you. Eat me.'

She opened her legs. Her sexflesh throbbed from his onslaught. She knew some of the lipstick with which she had decorated his organ would have rubbed off on her. 'Kiss my lips,' she moaned. 'Taste me.'

He came forward on to his knees, between her legs. Kate shivered as he stroked her inner thigh above the top of her stockings. As he bent to obey her, Kate said: 'I will have myself pierced.'

'Comment?'

'I will wear jewellery there. Don't you think it is a good idea?'

'May I buy you the jewellery? I feel it is something that should be a present from a man.'

'A gold ring,' Kate murmured. 'A diamond stud.'

She felt the man's head between her thighs. She felt his tongue, his lips. She opened her legs still wider, her head slipping back over the end of the bed.

Raoul lifted his head. 'You are dazzling, my darling. It would be good to know if this is the real you.'

'Kiss me,' she said. 'What would you like me to do to prove that this is how I am?'

'I will have them bring in Sorrell,' Raoul said. He sucked her labia and stretched them in his mouth. His tongue flickered and she felt it touch her anus. She sighed. 'Like this?' she queried gently.

'Why not?'

'So be it. Only I will not have Pierre and Emil see me like this.'

'Lucien, then.'

'And his gun,' Kate said, and laughed. 'We must not forget the gun.'

Chapter Ten

*H*e was ragged and filthy still. Evidently they had not taken her at her word when she had asked for him to be decently treated. His wrists were bound and Kate saw fresh marks on his face. Lucien brought him in, the rifle slung negligently over one shoulder. They knew he could not escape.

Lucien absorbed the scene before him, the two of them naked save for Kate's stockings and high heels. He smiled.

'We have the apple,' Raoul said. 'I have your woman. Why hold out on us in this distressing way, Sorrell? Can't you see you have lost?' He put one hand over Kate's naked shoulder and stroked her breast absently as he spoke. She arched slightly and touched his throat with her lips.

'She's not my woman,' John said. Kate saw his lips were cracked. She wondered if he had been fed and given anything to drink.

'No,' Raoul agreed. He turned to Kate. His eyes were brilliant and cruel. 'Prove to me, my sweet, who it is you care for.'

'None of you,' Kate said. 'It is this that I want.' She touched Raoul's softened sex. Then she crawled up the bed on hands and knees. When she reached the top she rolled half over and laughed.

Raoul followed her. Delicately, he lifted one of her legs, allowing her sex to be exposed before him. He bent his dark and handsome head till his lips touched hers, her sexual lips. He kissed her, again and again, murmuring at her sweetness, at the musk of her, at the fragrance of their past lust.

Kate lay smiling, accepting what he did. Lucien moved the gun from one shoulder to the other and eased his clothes slightly.

Gently Raoul rocked Kate over on to her face again. He began to kiss her buttocks, caressing their soft rounded contours, dividing them with his strong hands and kissing her anus, penetrating it with his tongue.

'Sorrell tells me,' Kate said, her head comfortably sideways on her pillow, 'that there was a people in Latin America who made pottery of sexual positions. They really liked it where you are now.'

'Do you?' Raoul asked.

Kate rolled over. 'Do you?' she said, looking into his eyes.

She could smell his rearousal. She kissed his chest, licking his hair as if she were a cat. She looked up into his face. 'I'll have to find out,' she whispered. Even as she spoke, her hands came round, seeking under him, seeking that entrance to his body that made her feel cruel.

She felt her own breathing shorten with excitement. Her chest lifted and her lips drew slightly back. A dizziness threatened her. She kept her eyes away from John even as she had not looked down when he had taken her on that awful cliff. If she looked, she would be lost.

Instead she looked directly into Raoul's face, so close to her as her hands reached behind and under him. The tightness of his buttocks inflamed her. She clawed into them, between them, and felt his muscles give before her onslaught.

172

'Raoul,' she whispered, aware that he shared her excitement; it was contagious.

Now she could feel the strange crinkled skin sunk in there, hidden, protected. She withdrew one hand and licked her fingers till they were wet. She put them back and began to touch him, more and more firmly.

His chest was against her breast. Gradually he moved his knees apart, opening the way for her as she sought to enter him. Now she pressed longer, more persistently, remembering that he said he had been with his own sex. Had he permitted this? Had he felt a man thrusting here where she was so delicate? Or had he been content to be the ravager, feeling a man's tight place satisfy him in the way that a woman should.

She slipped a finger in him. His penis lifted and butted her. She put one hand between their bodies and began to toy with him, to stroke and caress his hardness. With the other she entered him and began to simulate sex itself.

He grunted softly as she ravished so gently and carefully at his rear. She clasped his urgent sex hard with other hand, masturbating backwards and forwards over the rigid member.

Suddenly she released him. She went round behind him and pushed so that he fell forward on the bed exposing his rear to her hot gaze. He knelt with his knees wide apart, his face forward and down on her pillows. She reached under him and found his swinging sex. With her other hand she now deeply penetrated his rear, forcing him to squirm and moan as she transfixed him. At the same time she worked his penis to bring him to climax.

He was jerking in her hands and she felt the warm rush of wetness. His balls swung against her curled fist. When she was sure he was done, she released him. She bent right forward and kissed his puckered anus, holding his buttocks apart and kissing him as she kissed his mouth, passionately, full of sensual desire.

When she sat up he rolled on to his back. His face

was blurred and he smiled slackly at her. His eyes hardly focused. It was as she thought. He was a slave to his own sensuality and would explore it beyond thought, beyond reason, beyond sense.

She turned and looked at the other two men in the room.

Lucien watch her with a lively alertness, clearly hoping that his turn would come. John was stiff as stone, his dark face a mask.

She stretched her length against Raoul. 'Hot and cold,' she murmured.

'*Chérie?*' He might have been drugged.

'Sweet and sour. Rough and gentle.' She made almost no noise, shaping her lips against his ear so that each word was a kiss as much as a sound. 'Sorrell,' she said. 'You harsh, me gentle. Yes?'

Raoul stirred and turned his head on the pillow, his eyes alive and intelligent once more. His mouth curved into a cruel smile. There was no way the two across the room could have heard her. He nodded slightly. 'As you say.'

'What about Lucien?' Kate asked out loud.

'Lucien?'

'I think he is excited, Raoul. This seems hard on him.'

'Hey, you want her, Lucien?'

The young man almost danced on the spot. Raoul stood up and came over to him, taking the gun. John's head never turned. He simply stared woodenly forward.

Kate took the man quickly. He was very excited and she made sure she controlled the act between them. She refused to let him enter her body and instead, to Raoul's intense amusement, she made him stand naked while she stood at his back with her arms around him. She pressed her breasts into his back; she grasped his sex and masturbated him; and she pumped her body so that his was forced to move as she did.

He came, shooting across the room. He turned to grab Kate but she ducked and laughed playfully. 'Not 'this time, my sweet,' she carolled. 'I am mistress here. Out of this room we do as you say, but this is my room and I command the performance.'

Raoul had brought the brandy with him and the three of them now drank. 'Raoul,' Kate said in a pretty, pleading voice.

'My dear?'

'Leave me alone with Sorrell.'

'Why should I do any such thing?'

'I don't think he will play with me with you here. If Lucien guards outside the door, he cannot escape.'

'What if he hurts you?'

Kate considered. She smiled. 'What would you do if he did, Raoul? He told me you played games with him in the cellar. He told me you threatened to let Anna choose the games. Would you do that, if you found that he had hurt me?'

'I think I would.' Raoul put his head to one side. 'What a delicious mind you have, dear Katya. You never fail to amaze me.'

Kate smiled archly. 'I've hardly started. I amaze myself, Raoul.' She stretched again and ran her hands down her body. 'I find out something new about myself all the time. I have so much to thank you for.'

'We will go,' Raoul agreed, 'but Lucien will be outside the door at all times, until he is relieved on guard. You understand?'

'I understand,' said Kate who did. She was being guarded too, though Raoul didn't say as much.

'Don't go,' John said harshly.

Raoul tittered. 'Perhaps you overestimate your powers, *chérie*.'

'I'll kill her,' John said. He looked directly at Kate.

Raoul began to untie his wrists. 'She seems willing to take the risk.'

'Anna will be pleased,' Lucien said.

'Bring some food,' Kate said. 'He is no use to me if he faints from hunger.'

* * *

All the while he had been in the room, John had been forced to stand. Now he sank wearily into the armchair and Kate gave him a glass of brandy. His hand trembled as he drank it.

She could smell him, smell the dirt and the sweat and the fear he had felt. No hero, this man, but vulnerable flesh like herself. It would be hard to imagine that smooth creature Raoul in such a state. Even at the peak of excitement he retained an elegance of manner. His cruelties were never coarse.

She said nothing while he drank the brandy. She slid off her shoes and stockings and put on a négligé to cover her nakedness. Anna brought in a tray of cold meats, salad, wine and bread. Kate left it with John while she showered, tying her hair back to make herself look younger and more innocent.

She was shocked by her appearance in the mirror. She had never considered herself a beauty, having tolerable looks but no better. Now she saw her lips were fuller and redder, her eyes enlarged and brilliant, the hollows in her cheeks deepened, adding prominence to the bones above. Her hair was lush with health, and shining. The indulgence, the glut of sex, was having an extraordinary effect on her. She was becoming beautiful. She was recreating herself, making herself over and the results were startling and a little frightening.

She went back through to John. He had finished eating and drinking and lay with his head back in exhaustion.

'Coming into the bathroom,' she said quietly.

'Leave me alone. If I wake up I'll murder you.'

'Come into the bathroom. You've fed and had something to drink. Now you need to be clean. I'll make them find you fresh clothes. And you must shave.'

He lifted his head heavily and looked at her with sunken eyes. 'Don't you believe me?' he said with menace.

'Don't be such a fool,' Kate said bitingly.

He blinked. 'This is your revenge, is it, for that

business in Corfu? Or is it because I dumped you in Paris? A woman scorned and all that.'

'Whatever you say it is. So come into the bathroom.'

She tuned and went in, turning on the taps and filling the bath with fragrant petals, aromatic and soothing.

She heard him come in behind her where she knelt, stirring the water and testing its temperature. When she was satisfied she stood up.

He leant against the wall, too tired to support his own weight. Kate reached for his shirt buttons and started to undo them.

'I hate you, you bitch,' he said, his voice trembling.

'I know. Let me get you clean. Then I'll let you rest. You'll feel better then.'

'So they can torture me again?'

'Not if I can stop them. I've pointed out that you will hardly sign your own death warrant by telling them what they want to know. I've explained they are going about this the wrong way.'

'What's the right way?'

'Kindness in a harsh world.'

'This, you mean.' Kate took his shirt off him. 'Yes,' she said calmly. 'This. I'm your friend here, you know.'

'With friends like you . . .'

'Don't worry about that. Nobody's asking you anything right now, except to step in the bath and feel better. I'm going to take your trousers off.'

She knelt to remove his boots and socks. Then her long fingers slid under his waistband and she opened his trousers. He made no effort to resist her and she slid the remainder of his clothes down and off his slack exhausted body. Then she took his hand and led him to the bath.

He stepped into the tub and slid slowly down into the scented embrace of oiled water. He closed his eyes, leaning back, almost submerged. His skin shuddered as the water enfolded it in its hot depths. Kate pushed up her sleeves and began to wash him.

She was infinitely slow and gentle, her mind suspended, webbed in time, even as the water held him weightless. She must take each moment as it came and not think beyond, except in so far as she must plan their getaway. It was her emotions, her feelings, that she must control. If she thought too much about what she was doing, she would not be able to do it.

Her belief in her femininity, in her own essential decentness, warred with the revelations that had come to her during her love-making with Raoul. Sex was like heroin. It was a fix. It was a fix she needed and she didn't have to love the drug, or who supplied it. It was the fix itself she was in love with.

If she ever made it back into the normal world, she would retain this knowledge of herself. She could suppress it. She could ignore it. She could deny it. But she could not change it nor make it go away. She was in love with the erect penis, the act of copulation, her own seesawing response. Amid fear and violence, from men she despised, she had drawn the honey and never again would she confuse the donor with the gift.

Her hands went over the man's body, all over it. He made no move to stop her as she soaped and sponged his tired flesh. His eyes were closed, his breathing slow and regular. Probably he was asleep. Kate stroked and soothed and cleansed in a private passion, going everywhere she wanted.

He really did sleep for a while and she supported his head when he threatened to slip and wake himself as his face went under. As the water cooled, she moved him and his eyes flickered open.

He looked at her stonily, like a lizard. Kate eased him down into the water until his hair was wet. She shampooed it, and then she helped him out of the bath.

He was frighteningly weak. She took him over to the shower and cleaned him down. Then she towelled his clean wet body and hair. She sat him down on the bathroom chair and broke the seals on the shaving equipment supplied in every bathroom in the Maison du Lac.

He closed his eyes again and let his head fall back as she shaved him, drawing the blade across his throat in steady sweeps. When she was done she rummaged in her own things and then opened the towels she had swathed him in. She applied salve to the sore parts of his body and face. She brushed his hair and led him into her bedroom. She sat him in the armchair and carefully dried his hair using her own hairdrier and adaptor. She finished and put it away. She came back with more brandy.

'What now?' he said carefully. 'Am I expected to pay my way?'

'You must come to bed and sleep.'

'Sleep?'

'You need it.'

'I need more than sleep.' His voice had a dangerous edge to it.

'I know. But for now, you must sleep.'

He lay taut beside her for a brief while. She forced her own breathing to sound regular and relaxed. They lay like knight and lady in the chivalric ideal, perfect love, perfectly spiritual, having no recourse to the body's gross desires.

It was just that she did desire him grossly. Her body wanted to mingle itself with his, feel the fire of his lust, feel his strength against her vulnerability.

He couldn't hold out for long and she felt rather than heard him relax and slip into sleep. She had spent most of the day in bed and was hardly tired herself. For a long time she lay, just knowing he was there, naked beside her nakedness. She smelt him but she didn't touch him. He hated her. The one thing she felt she could not face was that instinctive withdrawal brought about by unintentional physical contact with a loathly thing. If she touched him and he reacted as if she were a slug who slimed him, then she might not any longer be able to play the part that she must.

* * *

'Kate.'

'Yes.'

'What's happened to you?'

'Perhaps I was always like this.'

'A whore.'

'To have sex for pleasure? Don't you? Or are all people who enjoy it whores?'

'You know what I mean.'

'No. No, I don't know what you mean at all.'

There was a silence. His voice stroked her in the dark. 'You're so beautiful.'

She didn't respond. She had nothing to say.

'I want you,' he said presently. 'Despite everything. You know that.'

The satisfaction was sweet and thrilling.

'I can see why men drowned women as witches.'

'That's stupid. They drowned old ugly women, not sexy young numbers. Men have always found a use for them.'

'Why do I want you against my will, then?'

'Because you're stupid,' Kate said bitterly. 'Because you think your own rational processes must be right even when they're wrong. Because you don't understand what sex is, and you try to blame me for that.'

'What is it?'

'Chemistry.'

'That's all? No love. No companionship. Nothing of the mind. No kindness.'

'They might come after. The chemistry comes first. And sometimes it's all that comes. Men like you won't admit it. That is, you can screw around, but if a woman does it, she has to be a whore or a witch.'

'No difference between us, then.' John stirred slightly in the bed. Kate's heart began to beat in an irregular fashion.

'I guess we fool ourselves and each other about in equal doses. I don't underestimate women's capacity for self-deception any more than I do men's.'

John touched her on the hip. Kate held still. His hand

came up and over her flat belly. He let it rest there for a moment. Then he slid it down. Now it was over her sexual mound.

'I can have you if I want. That's it, is it? You're there for the asking. I mean, for the taking.'

'Yes.' Kate could not control the huskiness in her voice. He was on his side, his head up and resting on his hand, the other hand over her body. He squeezed slightly. 'What are your feelings in the matter?'

'Do you care?'

'Oddly enough, I do. I mean, are you doing this to please Raoul? Or to spite him?'

'Perhaps he doesn't come into it.'

'He comes into you.' John's fingers slid over her mound and sank into the cleft within. He touched her clitoris and she felt speared by desire. She reached out gently in the dark and touched his chest. Then she remembered it might be sore and let it be.

'It's like a peach,' he murmured. 'The way you divide here, the velvet feel of you. Why do you have to be the way you are, Kate? Why couldn't you have this body, this appeal, and be what I thought you were at first?'

Kate closed herself to what he said. He had always hurt her and no doubt he always would, so long as their strange association lasted. However things worked out, she didn't have much longer with him. She must take what she so earnestly desired and be grateful he wasn't what she wanted him to be. Then it would have been unbearable.

She moved on to her side facing him in the quiet warm darkness. She found his face and reached hers to it so she could kiss him.

It was as though he sought to prove he wasn't what he said. He kissed her with such tenderness, such desire, that tears slipped from the corners of her eyes. She sighed and arched into him, stroking him tenderly and kissing him, bringing her body to his to let him know it was open and ready for him.

He moved on top of her, using his elbows to keep his

weight from pressing too hard. She wrapped her arms tightly round him and held him as close as she could, pressing herself ardently into him, kissing him passionately, feeling his sex aroused and firm where he lay against her.

They clung like adolescent children hardly able to control the passions they unleashed. He was trembling, his lips brushed her, and when she touched his brow she knew he frowned in concentration as the wind of desire swept them both up and whirled them dizzily into its embrace.

Their bodies twisted and writhed as they ached to feel each separate part of each other. Kate's hands were on his back, on his buttocks, on his thighs, anywhere where she could touch him and adore him. The smell of his skin filled her nostrils. She was beside herself with the joy of him, and when he became more urgent, more insistent, she hardly knew how much time had passed in their exquisite exploration of each other's arousal.

He slid into her and she closed round him in ecstasy. He was moving, taking them both together up through the layers of tension and need to the moment of sweating agony, just before orgasm, when pleasure was at its peak but everything must burst and be fulfilled. Kate controlled her desire to shout; it was all the control she had but there was no way she could forget that outside her door was a man with a gun and no way did she want him to hear her excess of passion. This was private. This was for the two of them. It might never happen again, probably it would never happen again, but that made it all the more important that it was right.

It *was* right, too. She felt his muscle ripple and expand, flower open and shoot its hot load deep into her. Her own sex was writhing around his, rippling, convulsing, extending his orgasm by the length and strength of its own.

They were on their sides, arms twined together, bodies heaving and sweating but close, as close as they could get. He was rubbing his face against her, murmuring blind words in her ear, kissing her hair, and if he could feel the wetness that came from her eyes he didn't say anything.

After a while they were quiet. 'Thank you,' said Kate.

'Why are you thanking me?'

Because you treated me like a human being, was the answer, but she wouldn't give it. 'I know you don't like me. But you made that as much pleasure for me as you could.'

'For me. I made it a pleasure for me. I pretended you were someone else.'

'A useful technique,' Kate said in a level voice. She was astonished at her own pain.

'What now?'

'Sleep.'

'And tomorrow?'

'I don't know,' Kate said. 'I've told them it's no use torturing you. I've told them to let you go and to follow you. I've told them to keep you in good condition so I can play sex games with you.'

'Oh,' John said blankly.

'But I don't know how much they'll listen to me. Raoul is a fool over sex, he can't control it, but Jean-Marc is a really cold customer and he doesn't trust me an inch. The others don't matter. They'll do what Raoul says.'

'Will you?'

'Do what Raoul says? Of course I will, if I think it'll help.'

'Help who?'

'Me.'

'And what do you want?'

'To get safely away from here. I wonder if they would let me escape with you and so keep an eye on you while they followed you back to Albania.'

'Who told you about Albania?'

'I worked it out. But why bring something from

183

Albania into Greece? I thought Greece really protected its borders against the smuggling of ancient remains.'

'They do, but there aren't any antiquities in Corfu, so really they only protect the mainland. I was hopping to Italy from Albania.'

'With an apple? I heard Raoul mention it.'

'Yes, an apple. Raoul has it now. I'd like it back.'

'Will you tell me about the apple?'

'I love pillow talk with you, Kate. It serves to keep in my mind that you are a treacherous bitch, even if you are an irresistible one.'

'The apple.'

'The apple. The golden apple. The apple of discord as given to Aphrodite by Paris.'

'You mean you had an apple of gold?'

'Solid gold. Raoul has it now.'

Kate was silent. Her mind turned over what she had heard. 'I hadn't quite appreciated how high the stakes were,' she said. 'And there's more treasure, is there? I mean, this came from Albania?'

'It came from Albania. Yes, I think there is a lot more treasure. Specifically, the statue of Paris the apple came from. And Aphrodite herself. Life-size, gold and ivory. Worth a few deaths, eh?'

Kate shivered. 'No. Not to me. I don't like statues. Did you ever read that story of Prosper Mérimée's? At least, I think it was his. About the people who dug up a statue of Venus in their garden or something. In the night it comes alive and goes up the stairs and gets into bed with someone, killing their partner by crushing them to death. I mean, I can't remember the story properly, whether it's a wife or a husband who's killed and why. Maybe it was a mistress. I've forgotten everything except the horror of waking to the stone thing in bed with you, and the body crushed beneath it. You see, they knew it must have walked. There was no other way for it to get where it was found.'

John said: 'This is the part where you ask me if I know exactly where the statue is. And how I know.

And if I don't know, how much do I know and how do I intend to find out.'

Kate smiled in the dark and put her arms round him. She rubbed noses and touched his lips with hers. 'Stay alive,' she said. 'That's all I want. I don't give a damn about gold and ivory statues. I'm an insurance assessor from west London, not a thief. Antiquities should be in a museum, not hoiked round the world by people like you and sold to collectors who hide them away from everyone so they can't be seen and enjoyed and marvelled over. But all through this, John Sorrell, I've done my damnedest to keep you alive, in one piece and on the loose and I haven't changed a bit. I'm screwing Raoul to stop him from thinking too hard and because I'd rather screw him than be beaten or murdered by him. I'm going to screw him upside-down and back to front till he doesn't know how to think any longer, and if I can think of some way of getting to Jean-Marc, I'll have a go at him too.'

'Why do you help me all the time, if you do, when you don't approve of what I do?'

'I find you utterly irresistible. Haven't you realised that?' Kate wanted to laugh, she was so happy.

'You're too clever,' John whispered. 'You have this uncanny knack of saying what I want to hear. I just don't believe it. You're fooling me like you're fooling Raoul.'

'I love you,' she said.

'No.'

Kate laughed again. 'Go to sleep. Tomorrow will be horrible. Let's hold to tonight for now.'

She rolled over in his arms so that she lay on her side with her knees drawn up. He lay tight against her back, so that his body was the same shape as hers. His arms were round her. Secure, happy and satisfied, Kate slept.

Things were very different in the morning. They came for John when the two of them were deeply asleep and totally off guard, curled together and nestling in obvious amity. Raoul was altogether less pliant when Kate appeared downstairs for breakfast, though she took it as a good sign that she was allowed out of her room. She found it hard to look cheerful and to eat. She wanted to know what they were doing to John.

'So, my dear Kate,' said Raoul, purring with malice. 'What do you have to report after your night's efforts?'

Kate reached for the toast. 'He's too clever,' she said briefly. 'He told me about Paris and Aphrodite and about the statue, but that's all. I don't know where it is or how well he knows or even how he knows. He was expecting me to probe, Raoul. The man isn't that stupid.'

'We want the statue,' Jean-Marc said.

'He can't cope with it, he knows that,' Kate said. 'Stop roughing him up and work with him. Then you'll get it. The damn thing's life-size. It's going to take a lot of smuggle it out. What will you do? Go by sea?'

She gathered by the electrified silence that she had ventured too far.

'Or through Yugoslavia and the war zone,' she enquired politely. 'Or by air? Or tunnelling under the Adriatic. How about irradiating it with something like caesium with a short half-life. Your buyer can keep it in lead until the thirty years are up.'

'This is not funny,' Raould said frostily.

'Or you could find out what Sorrell's ideas might be. He's an ingenious man. You can double-cross him later. Push him too far and he'll never tell you. He'll find a competitor or set up his own organisation. You're a fool, Raoul,' said Kate, eyeing him sternly. 'And you are advised by fools.' She looked at Jean-Marc and suddenly realised what his perversion was.

'I see the night has refreshed you,' Jean-Marc said.

'Sex clears the mind,' Kate said brutally. 'You should try it. That's why Raoul is top dog here.'

Lucien sniggered. They were all at the table. No doubt John was in the tower, then. Kate hoped he would not use the water gate yet. It depended on his fear of torture, she thought. This seemed a reasonable fear to her.

'Torture him and kill him afterwards when he has told us all he knows,' said Jean-Marc, watching Kate.

She smiled. 'And if he lies? Or if he hasn't got near enough yet and you cannot work out where it is from what he tells you?'

Jean-Marc shrugged. 'A risk we run.'

Kate looked at Raoul. 'He hates me. You know that. You saw for yourself. But he can't resist me. He wants to believe I am on his side, even though his common sense tells him he is wrong. If you engineer things so that I escape with him convincingly, he will have the proof he needs to trust me. All I have to do is stay with him after that. You hardly have to follow him. I can get in touch with you at intervals. You know he has to go to Albania. I will go with him, and when he has solved the puzzle of the statue's whereabouts, I will call you in. You can then do with him as you wish. He will no longer be necessary.'

'Do you think us complete fools?' Jean-Marc asked angrily.

'He has a point, Kate.' Raoul's tone was very dry. 'Why should we trust you to such an extent?'

Kate looked at Raoul and smiled. 'Sorrell is not the only one hooked in this game,' she said. She licked her lips. 'Besides, you think I can't tell who must be the winners and who the losers in this? I won't willingly range myself where I know I must fail.'

'If you feel as you claim to feel for Raoul,' Jean-Marc said, 'how come you go so readily with this other man? Any other man.'

'Not any man.' Kate was swift and angry. 'That's what caused the trouble before.' She stopped with an effort. Then once more she raised her eyes to meet with Raoul's. 'I cannot resist,' she said in a husky voice. She was totally convincing. Her hands trembled. 'I want to be a slave to you.' She managed a tremulous smile. 'But you see, the irony is that that is how he feels about me.

Oh, he can resist me up to a point. But only up to a point. If I help him, he is lost. And I enjoy my power over him as I enjoy your power over me. You understand, Raoul, don't you? You know what I'm talking about.'

She watched the effect of her words on the vanity of the man. His hawk face glowed and she knew she must play stronger games yet to convince him. There was Jean-Marc to deal with too. She felt her body within her clothes, alien and malleable. She would bend it to her will, and in doing so take Raoul with her and bend him all unknowing to her will too. He would think he did what he wanted to do.

She became aware during the day of tensions within the group. Pierre was sick of hanging around and wanted some action, preferably of a brutal kind. Lucien lusted after her furtively and watched her like a dog might watch a bone. Jean-Marc was angry, disbelieving her presentation of herself but unable to do more than put a doubt into Raoul's mind concerning his own sexual omnipotence.

Worse was to follow. In the afternoon, Raoul put into action what was obviously Jean-Marc's idea, to test Kate's loyalty. That it was lunacy was beside the point. They didn't need Kate; she was a nuisance, and had Raoul been thinking clearly, or listening to advice, he would have disposed of Kate as soon as it was safe to do so. The truth was, it was her personal loyalty to himself that he was testing. He needed to know whether she lied sexually to him or to John. His vanity had been attacked and if Jean-Marc was proved to be right, Kate knew her chances were slender. She had been expecting something like this. But it horrified her when it came.

She was taken to one of the attic rooms. It contained a brass bedstead with nothing but a bare mattress on it. Shockingly, John was tied by his wrists to the bedstead and he had a mask over his face so that he could not see. He was quite naked.

She was going to witness him being tortured. Kate felt her insides melt and coalesce. She wanted to die. She couldn't take this. There would be no more games. She would scream and cry and he would be mutilated and they would both be killed. Of course he would tell them anything he knew. Anyone would. Whatever the long term sense of the situation, under the immediacy of torture he would give them everything they wanted to make it stop. Kate had known it all along, and so evidently had Jean-Marc.

Anna came in. The heavy-set woman was not unattractive, with her slanting dark eyes and mass of rich curling dark hair, but the sturdy frame was unmistakably peasant and the wide full lips too ready to sneer. She looked sideways at Kate and then she studied the man on the bed with interest.

No one said anything. Raoul held Kate's arm and placed his finger to his lips. She wasn't to speak. Now that she had seen John, seen his predicament, Raoul led her out of the room.

'This is a game,' he said gently.

Kate was too breathless to speak.

'The game is that you go in and play with the man. If he cannot resist you as you say, you will have an effect on him despite his bonds. These must not be released, of course. You understand?'

'Yes,' faltered Kate.

'Kiss him. Love him. Make him ready. Then, at the last moment, when he believes it is you because he has heard you and felt you at his body, Anna will take your place and consummate the act. She will say nothing, of course, but you will be there to murmur if the need should arise.' Raoul stopped and put his head on one side. He was smiling. He waited for Kate's reaction.

She licked her lips. If you were a voyeur and a pervert like Raoul, it made a sort of ghastly sense. It fitted with all that she had said, that John could not resist her, that she enjoyed her power over him, that she was a slave to Raoul's wishes, that she enjoyed sexual games as Raoul did, for their own sake.

'Will you watch?' she asked. Her voice cracked slightly. She must be very careful. She was going to give herself away quite badly at any moment now.

'I will watch. I will be in the room. No one else will be there, apart from yourself. And Sorrell. And Anna, of course.'

Kate pinned a horrid smile to her lips. 'I'll do my best, master.'

He put a finger under her chin and lifted her face. 'You will succeed. I get bored so easily. You have not bored me yet, Kate, but it could happen. You understand?'

'I understand.'

Back in the room, she stood for a moment looking down at the bound naked man. On silent feet Raoul entered and stood by Anna. The two of them were quite silent, watching, waiting.

Kate swallowed. 'John,' she said. 'What have they done to you?'

The masked head turned towards her. 'Kate?' said a muffled voice.

She sat on the edge of the bed and touched his hip. 'Have they hurt you?'

'No. Untie me, dammit.'

'I can't.'

'Take the mask off.'

'I can't. They said, they said if I did, they'd take me away.'

'Why are you here then?'

'I'm supposed to be persuading you I'm on your side.'

He fell silent. Kate saw that his chest was healing well. She bent over it so that her hair brushed his skin, and kissed it. 'I wish this was over,' she said.

'Not as much as I do.'

'Why don't you tell them what they want to know? It

190

can't be in their interests to kill you. They'll go to Albania and you'll be out of pocket, sure, but you'll be out of all this.'

'It's been really interesting knowing you.'

She ran her hands over him. 'John. Don't. Not like this.'

'If I live so long, I'll treasure the memory. The memories. You're unique, darling. You know that?'

'We had something. In other circumstances – ' Kate broke off.

'We had one thing,' John said cruelly.

She touched his sex. He jumped slightly and then lay still. 'What does it matter?' he said, and Kate heard the weariness through his mask. 'You look like an ordinary woman, but down below you make music like no one else. A real vampire lady. Packed full of sex and nothing else at all. Blood sucker.'

'You hate me because you want me.' Kate caressed his penis.

'Yeah. Something like that. And because of the company you keep.'

'This is the last, John. They're taking me away. This is goodbye.'

'Away?'

'Raoul said so. I don't think I'll see you again.'

'Good.'

'I know you don't believe me, but it was real between us. For me, at any rate.'

'You want a valedictory one. I get you.'

'I can please you. Let me.'

He laughed. 'They'll never believe this back home.'

She aroused him slowly. She used her hands and her lips and her tongue. She was shocked at how easy it was, how much her hands knew, how her talent had grown. She was shocked because nothing could prevent her from wanting this man even though he loathed her.

He moved on the bed slightly, erect now, and she cradled his balls and teased back the skin over the inflamed head of his sex. She bent her head, her hair

191

brushing his thighs, and felt something on her shoulder.

She looked up. Anna was there, smiling. Slowly Kate drew back. Anna bent her head over the man on the bed and kissed his penis.

Kate withdrew, Anna filling her place. Every nerve in her body trembled and vibrated with emotional pain. No more arguing. No more persuading. She must get away, with or without John. She had done more than was humanly reasonable and she had been driven beyond what she could handle.

She walked backwards until she stod by Raoul, aware that he watched her but unable to remove her fascinated gaze from the bed. Anna was hoisting her skirts and preparing to mount the man that she, Kate, had prepared. The cruel sexual joke was approaching its climax.

When she did turn her head, she saw sweat beading Raoul's brow and upper lip. Her weary mind continued to work. His excitement wasn't from what he saw directly, which was Anna astride his enemy in sexual congress. It was from the situation itself, brought about by him. He, Raoul, controlled the players. All of them, witting and unwitting, did as he wanted. That was the source of his pleasure. He was the puppet-master and they jerked to his strings.

She heard John cry out and saw his savage upward thrust. Anna moved for a moment on him and then stopped. She reached out a hand and stroked his chest, touching him delicately. She touched the hollows of his neck. Kate wanted to scream.

'Satisfied?' he asked. Anna kissed his arms, his shoulders. She removed the mask.

The moment continued, infinitely long. John didn't rage. He said nothing. His eyes stared at the woman on him, then slowly raked the room. He saw Kate with Raoul. One possessive hand lay on her shoulder. Raoul smiled.

John said nothing. But it was as though the stuffing was removed from a toy. He sagged. He sank in on himself. He lost shape and definition. He was a thoroughly beaten man.

Kate took Raoul by the hand and led him out of the room. In the corridor, she smiled at him. 'Tell me,' she said, 'Does Lucien go both ways?'

'Both ways?'

'With both sexes.'

Raoul became guarded. 'He does.'

'And Jean-Marc?'

Raoul shrugged. 'He has little interest. He is cold in that way.'

'I think he goes with women sometimes.'

'Sometimes. But I do not think he really enjoys it. I would not trouble yourself, *petite*, if that is in your mind. You will not persuade him to your cause however clever that delicious body is. He lacks appetite.'

'For me and those like me,' Kate said. 'I know that. But I think his dislike of me is more than mistrust. He is jealous, Raoul, jealous of my influence over you.'

This was a mistake. 'You have no influence,' Raoul said haughtily.

'I know. But Jean-Marc fears me and he doesn't understand the pleasure you get with me. I think he prefers men.'

Raoul smiled incredulously.

'I think he prefers men,' Kate persisted. 'He loves you and hates me. I bet he hates any woman you show much pleasure in.'

Raoul studied her thoughtfully. Kate went desperately on. 'Try him with Lucien, if Lucien will play. He's such a pretty boy and if he goes both ways, then he might entertain Jean-Marc.'

'Why? Why are you so concerned for Jean-Marc, pretty one?'

'He is my enemy. He frightens me. I think he gives you bad advice because it is based on jealousy. If he were satisfied himself he would be a better lieutenant. You could control him more easily and trust him more. And you might enjoy it.'

'How might I enjoy it?'

'Watching him and Lucien.'

Now she had got to him. None of the other arguments worked like this one. The voyeur in him was aroused and Kate saw his mind play over the scenario she had proposed. 'We could watch together,' she said slyly.

'What if he won't play, he isn't interested?' Raoul murmured.

'Try him. Bribe Lucien to seduce him. Lucien is bored and unsatisfied. There is much going on here in the Maison du Lac, but little for him. You would kill two birds with one stone.'

Kate knew she could take no more and made her preparations accordingly. She could hardly appear in jeans and walking boots, but she put on a dress with a full skirt so that movement would not be impeded and she packed the pockets with essentials. She would need money and so she wrapped it in a plastic bag along with her bank card, not daring to take her passport but needing proof of her identity. She wore light sandals since she expected a swim and she went down to the kitchen, ostensibly to get some milk to drink, but in reality to steal a knife. In her room she found a leather belt and she inserted the knife horizontally into its plaiting and fixed the whole thing against her body round her waist where the dress masked it. Food she would have to do without, unless she found anything edible en route, doubtful in spring and with her ignorance of botany, but the Pyrenees hardly lacked water. She would not die of thirst out there, if she made it that far.

She inspected Raoul's library, but it was full of Latin texts and French classics. Nothing told her how to hotwire a car. She did steal some matches, however. She didn't see herself lighting a fire out there in the wild, but if she strayed too far and got herself seriously lost, it might not be a bad idea.

Raoul, Jean-Marc and Lucien were all occupied manipulating and being manipulated by each other. Her sudden freedom to roam the house indicated that her idea was paying off in at least one respect. Emil sat on the terrace and chewed his fingers whilst Pierre snored in the drawing room.

Anna had not reappeared. Kate had no desire to see her and was grateful for her absence, whatever it might mean. She could think of no way of getting a message through to John. No doubt he would be told if she got away successfully. Then he could make his own break for freedom using the water gate. Kate did not delude herself he would want to be with her. He would go hard and fast once he was free. Even if she was shot, Kate decided fatalistically, it was better to die quickly, free, mistress of herself, than it was to continue the lie she had involved herself in in this horrible house. She reckoned they would kill her soon anyway, as soon as she stopped devising sexy scenarios for Raoul to enjoy. They would never trust her. Even their stupidity had limits.

She wouldn't have minded the lie so much if she hadn't been so good at it. If Raoul had failed to excite her, if the sights she witnessed had produced only disgust, she could have carried on. But Lucien's cavortings had not repulsed her. Part of her had liked it. Even as she wallowed in vice, she got a kick out of it. Raoul, for all his vanity, was a superb lover. Depravity didn't stop him being good between her thighs. The murderous Lucien was a lovely specimen of manhood. It entertained her to plot Jean-Marc's sexual downfall, even if she would never see it. Part of her wanted to sit on Raoul's lap, sit with her skirt up and her panties off so she could feel his naked member rouse at what he saw and come up under her. She could picture it: Jean-Marc red and gasping, Lucien laughing, Raoul tight and excited, his hardness up her, her arm round his neck, laughing, drinking . . .

Kate pulled herself together. It was time to go.

195

She went down through the kitchens again. She went through the neglected kitchen garden and out across the green. She pushed through the scrubby vegetation to the shore. The sun stone steadily from a clear soft blue sky. Tears ran down her cheeks. She expected to be caught. She was very afraid. She remembered doing this with John; John whom she now left in this vile place on his own without her frail protection. Perhaps Anna would develop a softness for him. There had been something in the way her solid body had curved over his poor pale bound figure after the false love-making, something plaintive. Poor Anna, emotionally tied to the horrible Raoul. She deserved better.

Kate entered the water in a suicidal frame of mind. Her sandals slid on the slimy stones. The hem of her skirt began to float up. She was close to the edge of the terrace, its square stonework rising to her right. She had determined to swim round under it and repeat what had happened before. In the space under the terrace she would wait out the hours until nightfall, sitting alone in the cold and the wet. John might be above her, but she was beyond plans to go up into the tower and see. She was beyond everything but a primaeval need to get away, to be herself, to be what she was. Alone. Terrified. Friendless. Far from safety and help.

Entering the water was horrible. Kate waded quietly with her skirt all around her. The water suddenly deepened and she was swimming. She kept herself low in the water and as close to the slimy stonework as she could. She swam with a silent breaststroke. As soon as she thought she had reached the arch, she would duck-dive and try to find it.

There was a tiny fountain of water ahead of her. Kate, swimming quietly, wondered what it was. Some little lake-creature, free and going about its business, no doubt.

The second time, she heard the crack of the rifle. She lifted her head.

Emil stood above her on the terrace. He was so close she could see him grin as he levelled the rifle again.

She stopped, treading water. 'Don't shoot,' she said. He didn't speak English, her mind said idiotically. But her meaning should be obvious enough.

'*Ici*,' he said. He gestured along the terrace to the steps.

She could duck under the water and try for the arch, but they would find it this time. Anyway, a bullet could penetrate the water for some distance. Her chances of being shot were very high.

Emil sat himself on the stone rail and watched her as she swam to the steps. When she reached them, Kate found that all sense had left her. She was numbed with shock. She ignored everything and swam on. She had been suicidal indeed. If she had put on a bikini she could at least have pretended to be swimming for pleasure. What on earth had gone through her mind, doing this? She had thrown away all the care, all the suffering of the last few days. She might as well have stood up and shouted that she was going to the police.

She felt a jolt on her shoulder. There was angry shouting. She kept swimming. Raoul had heard the rifle shots and come from wherever he had been. Her shoulder felt rather funny but she kept swimming; steadily, a slow breaststroke, unable to stop, unable to turn, unable to think.

It became peaceful. She disturbed some ducks who flew off with an indignant chatter. They would have young somewhere, it was that time of year.

It wasn't terribly cold, especially on the surface. The sun beat against the rock wall half the day and it reflected heat out. The lake took heat from it as well as the direct sunlight. It was cold at night, she thought. She knew because of her past efforts to get away.

Kate heard the whine of the boat engine as it caught and fired up. It was like an angry wasp, she thought dreamily. One arm was really quite difficult now, the shoulder it was attached to stiff and unresponsive. If she kept swimming like this, with one weakening arm, she would turn in a vast circle and come back safely to Raoul.

She looked at the shore. It looked as far away as ever, yet she had been swimming since time immemorial.

There was a thudding in her ears now. Her arm stopped working altogether. Kate rolled on to her back and looked at her pursuers.

The boat danced under the terrace. Pierre was at the tiller with Emil up front with the rifle. Raoul was climbing in. They would be with her in about five seconds, Kate reckoned. She tittered slightly. She was a winged bird. At least she wouldn't have to pretend any more. That part was all over. She didn't really care what they did to her now. It was all over in every sense for her. And for John. Pity about John. It would be nice to believe in reincarnation right now. Then she could hope that at some other time, in some other place . . .

The boat had set off during these leisurely thoughts and Kate saw it suddenly leap in the air and spill its occupants. They floundered in the water while she idled on her back, an interested though remote spectator. Someone was in the boat and he was steering it across the men wallowing in the water, who dived smartly out of the way of the deadly propellor. Now the boat circled away from the terrace and heeled at an alarming angle. Kate saw with even more interest that a second boat had appeared from the direction of the boathouse. This was a small fat rowing boat being rowed by a small fat person, which thought made Kate titter again. Really, the entertainment was excellent. The only pity of it was that her shoulder felt like lead. Quite literally, like lead. It was bitterly cold right into its inside and it weighed her down, dragging her with its enormous weight so that her chin kept going under the surface. It was becoming an effort to stay afloat.

She looked up into the sky and smiled. Goodbye sky, she thought. I'm dying on a nice day. The Pyrenees are probably nice if you aren't with a crew of deranged and depraved thieves.

The speedboat drew near and danced to a stop. John looked at her, his hair stuck wet to his head.

'Can you climb in?'

'They shot me,' she said cunningly.

'Where?'

'In my shoulder.' He ought to be able to work it out, she thought lazily, skulling with her hands. She was canted right over in the water now as the heavy shoulder tugged remorselessly at her.

John looked over his shoulder. The rowing boat drew steadily nearer, the rower with her back to them. The men in the water were swimming towards the terrace. Lucien had appeared and was aiming a gun at them.

'More than one,' Kate said.

'Boat? I think it's Anna.'

'Gun.'

John looked again. Then he got a hand under her good arm and heaved.

The boat bounced unhappily, its gunwhale tipping over alarmingly. Kate floundered in over the side and rolled into the bottom boards. She was stabbed by a ferocious fiery pain and passed out. It could only have lasted a second or so because when she came round John was heading the boat towards the shore again.

He had got out of the tower at the right moment. By some incredible coincidence he had come up from under the water to knock the boat over. Meanwhile she was soaked, shot and exhausted. Kate lay in agony, her shoulder throbbing and stabbed at intervals with a terrible pain.

They came up to the little wooden jetty where it jutted into the water beside the garage where the Renault was. John tied the painter and turned his attention to Kate.

'You'd better go,' she said dully. 'My shoulder hurts too much. You'll never make it with me along.'

He lifted her and half threw her on to the wooden

planking of the jetty. She screamed at the pain. Then he vaulted lightly up beside her.

'A quitter,' he observed. 'I might have known it.'

Anna arrived in the rowing boat and sedately tied it up. She climbed out and came over to help John lift Kate. She looked at Kate's shoulder – her strappy dress revealed the wound – and bent to tear her own petticoat.

A shot rang out. It was a hand gun and Lucien's aim was not so true. The rifle was in the water somewhere, dropped when Emil had fallen.

Roughly Anna bound Kate's shoulder. John held her. Then they lifted her to her feet.

'The car,' Kate gasped. John was already kicking the lock of the garage in. But he could do nothing with the car. It was locked and there were no keys.

'I can break into it but I can't get it started,' he said desperately. 'Can you?' he asked Anna.

She shook her head. At that moment there was a dull thud. They ran out of the garage.

All looked the same. Anna smiled. Slowly, almost majestically, some black smoke rolled out of the open windows of the Maison du Lac.

John turned to Anna. 'Your doing?' She nodded. 'Good girl. Shall we do the same here? We don't want them swimming over and using it, do we?'

They took the petrol cans stored neatly at the back. They emptied the petrol over everything and John smashed a window of the car to tip some inside as well.

Kate tottered slowly away. She didn't like to think why Anna had changed sides nor did she want to dwell on her own infirmity. They ought to leave her. She needed a hospital bed. They would have to leave her and she would have to hope they got help before the angry men on the island got to her.

There were flames now from the house on the island. Kate could see a lot of activity on the terrace. The house was full of rather lovely things; Raoul had very good taste and the money to indulge it. Kate wondered if they would try to save them.

John joined her. 'We haven't any matches,' he said regretfully. 'I don't think they'll dare use the car, though. The minute the engine starts it'll explode, with all that vapour in there.'

Kate rummaged in her sodden clinging clothes with her good hand. She found the plastic bag with her money in it. 'In there,' she said faintly.

'Good girl.' He was amused. 'Perhaps I won't leave you behind after all. That's only a flesh wound, you know. You can stop camping it up.'

He emptied a can on to the ground, backing away from the garage as he went. At a suitable distance and with both women well away, he lit a match.

They must have been damp. It took him four goes. Then the spilt petrol caught, the flame racing along the vapour above it. It entered the garage and for a second time hung in stasis.

They crouched, turned away. The long moment dragged and then suddenly the sky was split and the ground reverberated. Kate felt the great lash of heat and when she turned round she saw flames shooting high into the sky. The roof had blown off the garage and the smell was indescribable. John was laughing. 'Never say I didn't make the earth move for you,' he said. 'I think it's time to go.'

Chapter Eleven

'*P*aris was a clot, really,' said John.

They were resting, hidden in a small hollow, huddled together. To her chagrin, Kate found that John's callous assessment of her damaged shoulder was quite right. It was a nagging pain, no more, and she found that she forgot about it most of the time as she struggle with inadequate footwear on rough and variable terrain.

'He was?'

'You know about him?'

'No.'

'He was the son of King Priam of Troy, but the Oracle predicted at his birth that he would cause the downfall of Troy, so they left him on a hillside to die.'

'Yuck.'

'*Autre temps, autre moeurs*,' John said tolerantly. 'Anyway, a shepherd took him over and brought him up.'

'He was lucky,' said Kate, nursing her ankle. She wondered what Anna made of all this.

'After he was fed milk by a she-bear.' John gazed mildly at Kate. He seemed in the best of spirits. Kate, by comparison, felt waspish.

'Anyway, there he was, minding his foster-father's

flocks one day, when Hermes appeared. It was a bit like that in those days, gods and lesser gods popping up when you least expected it.' John chewed grass and relaxed with an arm behind his head. 'Hermes had three women with him and he asked Paris to choose the prettiest.' John broke off again to look at Anna and Kate. 'Naive, Paris,' he added. 'He might have known there was a catch.'

'Which was?'

'It was a set-up, of course. The three dames and Hermes had come from a wedding. Peleus was a mortal, a stooge for Zeus, and he was marrying Thetis, a sea-goddess. You see, Zeus was after her – Thetis I mean – the horny old goat, but it had been predicted that her son would be greater than its father. Zeus wasn't having that, so he had her marry Peleus, since it wouldn't matter a damn if Thetis's son was greater than Peleus, the nobody.'

'Was their son greater?'

'Sure. Peleus was king of Phthia. But his son, and this is the joke, was Achilles.'

'I'm not laughing,' Kate said politely.

'You will. Okay, so Peleus the insignificant king is marrying Thetis the sea-nymph. A nereid, to be precise. They haven't invited Eris, goddess of spite, to the beano. Eris is cross and by way of revenge chucks a golden apple in among the guests which is inscribed "To the fairest". Now these ladies aren't modest, and at the feast are Athena, Aphrodite and Hera. Athena is Zeus's daughter, the goddess of wisdom and war. Hera is Zeus's wife, and incidentally his sister, a jealous and malevolent cow if ever there was one, though one admits Zeus played around a lot; and Aphrodite was the goddess of love with the sole mission to be lovely. And Paris chose her.'

'I've got lost.'

'Hermes took the golden apple and the three lovelies to innocent young Paris, gave him the apple since known as the apple of discord, and made him choose the most lovely goddess. The judgment of Paris, as it is known, was for Aphrodite.'

'I guess the other two were furious.'

'Hera and Athena? I should say so. Mind you, they all tried to bribe the lad and it was Aphrodite's bribe that he took.'

'Which was?'

'The love of the most beautiful woman in the world.'

'Wait a minute,' said Kate. 'Does Troy come into this?'

'We're getting there. Paris goes back to Troy and is recognised as Priam's son and the rightful prince. The Oracle is ignored or forgotten. Off at Sparta on business, he sees Helen and falls in love with her. She's the wife of Menelaus, king of Sparta; she's the most beautiful woman in the world, though sadly not the brightest and, of course, she falls in love with Paris. That's his prize for giving Aphrodite the apple. Paris, being a man of action, whisks her off back to Troy, thus precipitating the Trojan war which does indeed bring about Troy's downfall, just like the Oracle said. Needless to say, Hera and Athena preferred the Greek side, having been slighted by Paris. You remember Peleus and Thetis?'

'Er . . .'

'The wedding where Eris chucked the golden apple.'

'Oh yes.'

'Their son Achilles was the principal Greek warrior who fought Paris. Paris killed him, of course. He had that heel.'

'Oh,' Kate said, somewhat blankly.

'And I had the golden apple, the apple of discord,' John said softly.

'I thought we were in myth.'

'From a statue of Paris, as he handed it to Aphrodite. Good-looking boy, nude as a statue though one feels it was improbable he looked after the sheep and goats without a stitch on.'

'Does Raoul have the apple now?'

'He does.'

'*Non*,' Anna said, startling them hideously. Not only had she spoken, she had understood what they had been saying. She delved into the bag she carried and lifted out an object wrapped in a leather bag.

'Sweet Jesus,' whispered John. He reached out very gently and took the pouch from Anna. He opened the drawstrings and took from within a large solid object swathed in silk. He opened the silk wrapping and exposed the dully shining rounded object.

It was an apple, classic in shape, life-size, with one delicately moulded leaf quivering on a stalk.

'You took it?' he said to Anna, his voice soft.

She nodded.

'Do you speak English?'

She pursed her mouth and shrugged.

'A little?'

'A little,' she said.

'You speak French?' he said.

'Of here. Of the mountains. You understand?'

'I understand. I guess it suits Raoul to pretend you don't speak. Why have you come with us, Anna? Don't you like Raoul anymore?' Kate asked.

Anna leant towards John, swaying slightly from the waist as she did so. She held his eyes with her dark slanting glance. She took his hand and raised it to her lips. She kissed the back of it and smiled, a deep slow meaningful smile.

Kate felt stabbed by jealousy. She didn't go for all this sultry stuff. She frankly preferred Anna as the idiot housemaid hunching malevolently round the house, a slave to Raoul's perverted desires. Anna as intelligent and resourceful companion to John, and intent on having recourse to his body now and again, did not suit Kate at all.

It looked as though it suited John a great deal. He held the apple, savouring its cool heavy rounded contours in his palm, and he smiled back at Anna in a way that would have made any susceptible female heart thump with excitement. There was something undeniably attractive about the man. Kate had felt it from the first.

'Well,' he said eventually. 'I guess we can assume that pursuit will be fairly dedicated. I had hoped that what with blowing up their house and car they might just not bother with us any longer. I don't think that'll be the case now.' He put the apple away. Then he took Anna by the chin and kissed her mouth several times. When he let go of her she looked down, smiling and well-satisfied with the effect of her gift. After a moment, her eyes slid round and she looked briefly at Kate who immediately looked away. She understood what was going on. Anna was extracting her man from her grasp and she was enjoying the process.

Fine, thought Kate bitterly. Just fine. He hates me because I went with Raoul for his sake, to keep him alive. He goes with her because she bought him with an apple. 'Hadn't we better get going?' she asked, keeping the rough edge out of her voice. He was not going to have the satisfaction of knowing how she felt. 'Where are we headed, anyway?'

'Spain.'

'Can't we go to Luz? Anna will have friends there.'

'Spain in the first instance. Ça va, Anna?'

'Ça va bien, Sorrell.'

'I think you're crazy,' Kate said thickly. 'I'm going to Luz.'

His gaze was level. Would he tempt her again, she wondered. Would he use his sexual power over her as he had done before when she objected to what he wanted to do?

'I can point you in the right direction,' he said. 'I don't think you'll make it. We have to consider the fact that we have killers after us now. No more games, Kate, bedroom or otherwise. I don't mean to sound insulting, but you mustn't rely on Raoul wanting you again. If they find us, they'll kill us.'

Kate was flaming. 'I don't think for one moment Raoul will refrain from killing me. I'm not so vain or so

206

foolish as to think I was anything other than a distraction for a time. I stopped him thinking clearly because he is a goat over sex and goat-brained when he's at it. But I don't want to go to Spain. I have no passport, no papers. At least I am in France legally and Luz is a damn sight nearer than anywhere in Spain. Anna might be besotted with you. Anna might not care that you are a criminal, a thief, a smuggler. But I do.'

'A low-down ornery critter,' said John. 'Jealous, ducky? I don't remember my being a criminal bothering you before.'

'Things are different now.'

'There's Anna,' John said obligingly.

'I know more of what you are up to, and I think it's disgusting. The fact that you know a lot, I mean you have real archaeological knowledge, makes it worse. And I don't see why I should be your patsy and go to Spain. I needed you before. I don't need you now.'

'They're coming.'

'After you, with the apple. I don't matter.'

'They don't know who has the apple until they search the corpses. You do matter. You're going to the police.'

'I won't tell them about you. You needn't be afraid.' Kate was magnificently scornful.

'That isn't exactly what I'm afraid of. I admit I don't want you dead.'

Anna jerked suddenly, her head up and turned to one side, like an animal in the wild who hears something.

'What is it?' John asked quietly.

'*Ils viennent.*'

Kate felt fear suddenly freeze her heart. She was glad when John took her hand and Anna's and led them quietly up out of the little dell in which they had sheltered. He released their hands and began to make his way swiftly and silently through the feathery birches and rank grass. Equally silently, Anna and Kate followed. Kate had heard nothing but she knew she trusted Anna. For the first time, she was glad she was along. This was no love game. They were running for their lives. Time's winged chariot was certainly at their back – full of thieves and murderers.

She wondered if she could persuade John to leave the apple for them to find. Perhaps they would give up then.

She didn't really believe it.

They ran. They ran up; always up, it seemed to Kate as her shoulder ached and throbbed, her ankles and feet threatened to give way and the breath came harsh in her throat. They didn't see their pursuers but they felt them. It was a driving force, driving them to go on when they needed to rest, driving them blind when they needed to think and plan.

Anna made no complaint, naturally enough. She was strong, far stronger than Kate. Kate suspected she had more stamina than John himself. He was their leader, however, and the two women followed where he led. Kate had no breath to argue, even if she had wanted to.

It grew colder and darker. They climbed through cork oak, beech, silver birch and Scots pine. Then they came above the tree line from out of a gloomy mountain pine forest. John stopped and looked round him.

The air sang with coolness and the onset of night. There was a resinous tang to the air. The upland meadow before them was carpeted with grass and sweet small spring flowers, saxifrages and gentians, narcissi and creeping azalea. They had seen no beasts other than themselves, no lizard, no ibex, no mouflon, no boar, bear or deer. They had heard however the crash of things running through the trees ahead of them or to one side. They had heard the shrill whistle of the marmot warning of their approach. But all these creatures kept out of sight, like their pursuers.

It was a haunted flight.

Above the meadow, raw rock was lifted from the green turf. John led them uneasily across the open ground. High above them a huge bird hung, watching, though whether it was vulture or eagle Kate could not tell.

The rock was pale limestone. John began to hunt along its broken face. 'Here,' he said in quiet triumph. 'We'll spend the night here. Tomorrow we'll be in Spain, safe.'

It was a cave, dry-floored though dungy. Quickly they cleaned the floor, moving the loose stuff to one side. There must be no evidence of their presence from the outside. Anna, not unnaturally, had food in her bag. They all ate cheese and bread.

It was cold and very still in the cave, the air musty. 'We'll have to sleep,' John said. 'We must do the best we can.'

Kate shivered in her strappy dress. It was dry and crumpled from her swim, dirty from her forest flight. The three of them huddled together, John in the middle.

She didn't exactly sleep. She slid into brief shallow oblivion, to rise again into awareness and discomfort, to sink again in muffled dreams.

She came awake to movement. She felt the calmness of resignation. John was stirring, his hard male body making the small movements she understood so well.

He and Anna, of course. This was Anna's payment, her reward for betraying her employer. Kate wondered what it was that had shaken that allegiance. Perhaps it was all right for her to choose to go with his friends, but not all right for him to use her as an instrument of torture on another man. Having commanded her to have sex with another man, Raoul had lost her.

Kate didn't know. She couldn't know. She didn't want to know.

What she did know was what was going on now.

Her mind supplied what she could not see. Anna's skirts up, John's trousers open, the two of them pressing warm bodies together, linked by their engorged genitals.

Perhaps she should move away. But it was so cold

and it was unsafe to go out of the cave. She would look like a sulking child.

His shirt had come slightly out of his loosened waistband. Where she lay stiffly against him, she could feel bare flesh.

It was warm. She could smell his skin. As he moved to service Anna, so he rubbed against Kate.

In the end she gave way. She put her lips to that exposed triangle of living warmth. Every movement now brought his skin against her lips. She let a hand rest lightly on his hip and lay there, smelling him, wanting him, hating herself.

When they were still she rose to her feet and walked deeper into the cave. She lit a match, walking towards the back wall. The pain inside her was enormous. She saw that a crack ran down behind a fold in the rock, and that it was a gap, wide enough for her slender body. She held a match through and saw a larger cavern within. She wriggled through. It was a very long cavern. Kate walked across a soft crumbling floor. It was warmer. Her matches lit leaping shadows. At the far end she stopped.

The air was unpleasant here. The cavern had dropped quite sharply. Kate's match flared oddly. If she walked on bat dung, there might be methane hanging in pockets here. It was explosive; she must go back to the others.

She turned to go back up the slope. As she did so, a shape leapt out at her.

It took her three more matches to make it out. She saw the bison, drawn in what looked like faint rusty blood, following the cracks and shapes of the living rock. She saw the handmarks and, tremblingly, she placed her palm almost over them, comparing hers with that of a man ten thousand, thirty thousand years older than herself.

When she returned and lay down, John turned to her. He touched her cheek in the dark and felt it wet.

'It isn't what you think,' she said quietly.

210

'Good.'

'There's another cave, further in.'

'Is there?'

'It's warmer than this one. It slopes down. I think the air gets bad.'

'Right.'

'It's got prehistoric art on the wall.'

He was very silent. His voice was strained when he spoke. 'Give me the matches, Kate,' he said.

She fumbled in her pocket and gave them to him.

He went away. He was gone a long time. When he came back, he was shaking.

'It moves you too,' said Kate.

'You bet.' His voice was bitter.

'Sorry you can't chisel it off the walls and carry it out of here to sell?'

'If I could see where your face was, I'd slap it.'

'You can't care about it.'

'Can't I?'

'Anyone would think you were a real archaeologist instead of an inept thief.'

They pretended to sleep.

In the morning, he almost died.

They rose early, ate a little of what was left, and set off through the shivery dawn. John wanted to get high enough to orient them, before he made the crossing into Spain. The sweet mountain meadows gave way to a wilder scree-strewn landscape. Water ran down and collected in hollows. Above them the snow melted as spring progressed. Coupled with spring rains, this made the land soggy and tricksy.

They were in a moonscape of broken boulders. The threat to their ankles was real; if one of them broke a bone here they were in serious trouble. It was with relief that they dropped slightly back on to bright green vegetation.

John was in the lead. He gave a small shout as his foot went into the ground without resistance. His body weight carried him helplessly forward. A moment later he was floundering, already in up to his knees and sinking fast.

He was only a few feet from dry land. Kate flung her length on the rock and held out her hand.

His closed over her wrist, her hand tightening round his wrist in its turn. She used her other hand to get a good grip on a projection of rock. She began to pull.

It was hopeless. He leant forward but he could get no purchase for his feet at all. His movements released gusts of foul-smelling vapour. The brilliant green surface wavered slowly and resettled. He couldn't reach the rock and Kate didn't have the strength to haul him loose from the sticky clutch of the mire.

He was down to his armpits now. He didn't speak at all, but his face was greenish grey, mud-spattered from his silent struggle. Kate felt the active malevolent tug of the bog. Her arm felt as if it were coming away from her shoulder. Unthinkingly, she had given him the hand from her injured arm. Her shoulder felt as if a red hot lance were being inserted into it, quite apart from the feeling that her joints were tearing apart. The palm of her hand that gripped the rock was on fire also. She saw the rock was red stained where her skin had worn away.

Anna couln't help. Kate occupied the only piece of hard land from which John could be reached. Kate heard her praying. Then Anna sat on Kate's back and tried to lean forward to get a second grip on John's hand. But her arms were too stubby compared to the long-limbed Kate. She could do nothing.

There was no vegetation of any size, no branches, no wood, nothing to use.

'Ils viennent,' Anna said for the second time.

Kate would have laughed hysterically if the pain hadn't been so awful. As it was, she and John stared into each other's faces, frozen, knowing what was a about to happen. Raoul was irrelevant to the knowledge they both had. In several minutes John would go under and die slowly, horribly, inches away from her.

Kate's vision began to dim. The world became misted and colourless. Even John's loved face began to fade.

The cloud drifted clammy and cold across their tableau. They all but vanished from each other's sight. In seconds they were sodden and bitterly cold. Anna held Kate's waist, pulling back on the terrible thing that was happening in the bog.

They heard Lucien talking. They heard boots striking rocks. Someone swore, Emil maybe. The voices rose and fell. The noise of their passage came and went. They were alone again.

'Anna,' said Kate.

'*Oui.*'

'Under my dress. *Ma jupe.* Round my waist. A belt. *Une ceinture.*'

Anna groped and found the plaited leather belt. She released it while Kate felt the sweat pour cold from her brow. She really couldn't hold on much longer. She could feel their joined hands slipping.

There was no need to say anything else. Anna sat on Kate again, astride her back, and threw one end of the belt towards John.

With a terrible lurch, he grabbed it with his other hand. He wrapped it round his wrist. He was down to his shoulders now. If he let his head down his chin went in. Anna dug her knees into the rock and strained backwards.

Somehow Kate found a last ounce of strength. Somehow she ignored the screaming agony of her arms and shoulders. The two women pulled. John's face went down into the mire. He gave a jerk and moved inches towards them.

Kate renewed her grip on his wrist. The women pulled. There was an appalling sucking noise. John slid further towards them. His hands touched the rock. He let go of Kate and gripped the rock like a lover, his body still trailing in the bog. For a while he hung on, his blackened face against the grey lichened surface of the rock. Kate moved stiffly. She and Anna knelt side by side. They each gripped him under one shoulder. They pulled, he scrabbled, and he was free.

For a long time he lay huddled in a foetal ball of stinking mud, saying nothing, his eyes open and staring. Kate watched him helplessly. He really was no hero. The man was struggling with fear now, even as he had struggled with the bog. Not a brave man at all.

The sun shone dimly, a yellow disc through the cloud.

'They passed us while you were in there,' Kate said. 'They're ahead of us now. The cloud came down and saved us.'

'Yes,' John said. It was a croak, but at least he was talking, responding again. Anna looked at Kate. She nodded. They stood up and lifted John to his feet.

They followed the contour, going east into the morning sun. Only Anna walked with any ease. John shambled in his black wet coat, his shoulders hunched. Kate wanted to weep: her palm was burnt raw and her shoulder hurt so much. It was bleeding again, but that hardly seemed to matter. They had to survive, get over the border, and then everything would be all right.

At last they came to water. The sun was hot now. Anna made them stop. She and Kate stripped John and washed his clothes while he washed his body and hair. Anna took off some petticoats so John could dry himself and rub his cold skin.

He lay dozing in the sun, his skin twitching like an animal's hide when insects landed on it. His clothes steamed faintly. Anna dressed Kate's shoulder. They finished the food she had brought, drank from the stream, and went on.

At last Kate saw where they were. They were high on a wind-blown ridge, just on the north side of a sheer face humped to their right. Ahead was the bowl, the cirque she knew too well.

They were 1400 metres above the Maison du Lac. John had led them to the great wall of rock. Now they had to pass into Spain.

Anna was like a mountain goat, untroubled by the enormity of the plunge to their left. They crabbed along a narrow path out on the rock face itself. They worked up and to their left. Above them the rock whistled and sang. For Kate it was a nightmare without end.

They stopped, crouching together, Kate facing the rock. 'We're almost there,' John said. 'We're going through the Brêche de Roland, Kate. The wind will be very strong. Do you think you can make it?'

She lifted a weary face. 'What does it matter?'

'We've got this far. We're alive. We've almost reached safety. Don't be defeatist.'

She would have laughed if she had still had the energy. 'Will I have to hang on?' she asked. 'My arms aren't so great.' Nor were her hands, one palm being virtually raw.

'I'll help you when we go through. I'll take you one at a time. Anna you first, *comprends*?'

'*Oui.*'

'*Bien*. Now we climb. This is called the Echelle des Sarradets, by the way. It's quite famous.'

As a climb it was easy, the footholds laughably clear and firm. The problem was that they were 1400 metres up and one mistake was all it would need to finish this thing.

The whistling got louder. Kate realised that it was the wind coming through the hole in the wall, the hole they were going through. The wind would be a real force up here, she suddenly realised. She wasn't sure she would have the strength. She mustn't pull John with her if she started to go. Naturally he would get Anna through first. He wasn't likely to lose her, or risk being pulled to his death, plucked off the rock by a fool.

'Okay.' He had stopped again. They were on a comparatively wide platform that miraculously had a handrail. Kate remembered that climbers came here for fun. The thought made her feel sick.

Anna and John were talking. Then they went away. Kate sat huddled against the rock with her eyes closed, resting, not thinking. Time passed. She slept briefly. Then he was by her side.

'I'm not a thief, Kate,' he said.

'What?'

'Before we do this thing. I'm working for Interpol, trying to get evidence to jail Martineau and his gang. You weren't meant to be involved.'

'Corfu,' she said weakly.

'A bluff. I wouldn't have hurt you any more than I did. You were unlucky. The police there didn't know I was working with Interpol. Raoul was on my heels. He had to believe I was for real. I'm sorry, Kate. Obviously he followed you after Paris and found some way to ingratiate himself with you. How did he do it?'

'He rescued me from a car careering down the road.'

'Driven by Pierre or Lucien, no doubt.'

'You're a policeman, then.'

'Temporarily. I'm an archaeologist really. Look, if anything goes wrong and you get through and I don't, go to the Spanish police and ask to speak to Interpol. You want Jean-Mari Duprès, Rue Gambetta, Paris. He knows all about me.'

'Why didn't you want me to go to the police before?'

'The local police don't know what's going on. If you had gone to them, Raoul would have made off. I still hoped to bring things together then.'

'And now?'

'Yes, and now. Don't let Anna know I intend to put her erstwhile master behind bars for as many years as I can. She might switch loyalties again.'

'Why do you tell me all this now?'

He was silent for a while. He smiled at her. 'Can't you guess?'

'No.'

'Okay. I trust you at last. I'm sure whose side you're on. I wasn't before.'

'I'd dance and cheer but you know where we are. Also, it doesn't seem to matter so very much any more.'

216

His lips touched her forehead. 'Through the Brêche, Kate. The wind is very strong.'

As he said, the wind was very strong. It tore Kate, lifting her bodily off the rock. She felt John behind her, holding her by main force. She scrabbled with her poor sore hands. Her aching arms screamed in protest. Loose rock fell in tiny landslides. The world roared in her ears, her skirts flying high.

Then she was through.

She stood, eyes closed, her back to the rock, facing south. The sun flooded her body, warming her cold tired limbs. John came up to her. Anna was there. The three of them began to descend.

It was quite different country this side of the watershed. Drier, harsher, it was a land of earth colours compared to the greys and greens of the French side. Though she was thirsty for much of the day, Kate felt only relief. Her pain was manageable, safety was at hand and the sun shone warmly on her grubby skin.

Anna stopped and said goodbye. She had a cousin in a nearby village. She stomped off along a dusty track as if she had been planning this visit from the start, her long black skirts swinging and her basket on her arm. She seemed quite happy for John to have the apple, and it was not clear whether she knew what its value might be or not.

Kate and John went on down in silence. Below them a green valley stretched. Pylons marched along its sides. Green snow-melt water roared along the river at the bottom. Houses with roofs, steep-pitched to shed winter snows, clustered under spired churches. It was pretty.

'I have some French money,' Kate said, 'and my bank card. No passport, of course.'

'Resourceful woman. I suggest we eat and get clean clothes as far as we can with the money. I'll talk to the local fuzz. We should be in funds after twenty or thirty phone calls.'

Their filthy appearance brought no problems, John

217

explained that they had got lost in the heights, they were stupid English, and were their French francs acceptable? Of course they were, at a price.

So two hours later Kate found herself in a cheap cotton skirt and a tee shirt from the local shop with a lammergeyer depicted on it. She faced a large dish of food. They had a carafe of local wine. The dish of stew, the goat's cheese salad, the fresh fruit, the bread had all been ambrosial. The wine was nectar. She had disinfectant on her shoulder which stung pleasantly. Her stiff weary limbs creaked and settled. She had a room with a bed. Kate had every intention of sleeping in it very soon.

They didn't talk much over the food, too tired to do anything but eat. Kate went to bed while John went off to attempt to get through to Interpol.

She never felt him join her between the coarse white sheets. She slept as if dead. It was late the next day when she surfaced. John wasn't there, but she could see where he had been, the depression in the pillows. No doubt he had to see the police again, she thought sleepily.

She dozed in the shadowy room for hours. It was lovely to feel her body clean, her sore limbs rested.

John came back. He sat on the edge of the bed and looked at her.

'Awake at last.'

'Mmm. And hungry.'

'I've had breakfast. About four hours ago.'

'I'll have lunch straight after then, and catch up.'

'How do you feel?'

'Stiff. You?'

'I'm all right. Thanks to you and Anna.'

She looked at him. 'I always knew you weren't a brute.'

'That's encouraging. As for you . . .' His voice tailed off. Kate shut her eyes. 'As for you, you are unique. You make your own rules. I think you did care for me in the Maison du Lac.'

She opened her eyes. 'That terrible place. I'm glad Anna burnt it down. What will Raoul do now?'

'Follow me to Albania.'

She lay watching him. His face was tanned and rugged, his hazel eyes long-lashed and private.

'Does the statue exist?'

'I think so. I'd love to find it. However, the plan remains in place. They follow me and are caught in the act.'

'Why did you come to the Pyrenees? What part of the plan was that?'

'No part, foolish wench. I came because they had you. They took you to hook me. They said they would swap you for the apple. I had kind of leaked it on the grapevine that I had the apple and was going for the statue.'

'You came to rescue me.' Kate felt smugly content.

'But as it happened, you held all the cards,' John said. 'Of course, I wasn't trusting you at that stage. I mean, you could have been a plant in Corfu. You were unnaturally handy, being where you were at that particular time. Then you lured me to France. You can see I had a right to be suspicious of the part you were playing.'

'You did rescue me. I was drowning.'

'I saw your fatuous attempt to get away. It lacked the subtlety I had come to expect from you. However, I came out through your water gate and upset their applecart. That was a very nasty way out of the tower.'

'I just couldn't take any more. Something snapped.'

'That business with Anna.'

'And my part in it.' Tears rolled fat and warm down Kate's cheeks.

He leant over her on the bed. She felt him kiss her cheeks, her eyes. She put stiff arms round his neck and caressed where his hair ended. He moved the covers off her and lay on the naked sleepwarm body. He kissed her and shed his clothing. He felt wonderful. His sex was hard already. It slipped easily into her body.

219

She closed her eyes and rocked to the rhythm of his loving. She felt high above the world again, up on the wind-scoured dizzy heights. It was as if she would fall off if she weren't careful.

He took her up gently through slow waves, dropping back and moving up again and again, each time a little higher, a little nearer to her breaking point. She allowed him to have absolute command of her, making little or no effort herself. He had begun in her gently, but as he continued he hardened and grew more urgent. His swollen member began to force pleasure with each thrust, take pleasure, create pleasure. She felt his attention leave her as he moved into the country of climax where each of us is alone. Yet their bodies had harmony. They were reaching the heights together, each in their passionate bubble of feeling.

She felt her vagina swell and burst, the warm wet flow surging in ripples around his enormous shaft. It too flowered open and filled her. He thrust hard, very hard. Then he was done, hanging over her, his heart thumping strong in his chest, his breath short, the smell of his coming strong between them.

The warm room was very quiet. A fly buzzed, caught in the shutters. Somewhere outside a car went by like an angry wasp.

He moved stiffly off her. 'The police are going to write you a pass,' he said, 'so you can get back to England without your passport. They will confirm it was burnt in a house fire and you'll be able to apply for a replacement. I don't know what the bank will do about any travellers cheques you might have lost. Then there are your clothes.'

'When do you leave?' she asked directly.

'This afternoon. This is goodbye, Kate.'

She stroked his hair and smiled. 'Goodbye,' she said softly. His leaving present was contained within her body. There was nothing more to say.

Chapter Twelve

*H*e was thin-faced. He looked to be a lean, intelligent man and his looks didn't lie. There was sensitivity in the line of his lip and sadness in his eyes.

He was proposing marriage.

Kate was aghast. She had loved this man for three long bitter years, been starved of his company, wept with grief in the night, and longed passionately for circumstances that would make him hers.

Now she had the lot. He would leave his wife. He would marry her. He was desolate without her. He wanted her to forgive the delay. He would tell Francine immediately, move in with Kate and set the divorce in train.

Kate didn't want him to move in. She had been aware of a pang of sad lost lust when she opened her door to him and saw him standing there, but now she didn't feel even that. She wanted desperately for him to go.

Somewhere recently she had found herself. In the muddle, the fear, the sex and the fury, was the woman she wanted to be. The woman she was. Never had she felt so truly independent. The world was hers, her playground. Her nature had liberated itself from the cultural baggage that had so weighed her down. She felt light and free. She had been given wings. She was just getting ready to fly.

The very last thing she wanted was a stale love freshly packaged. Marriage appealed to her like living inside razor wire. Was it worth explaining this to Paul?

She didn't think so. He wouldn't understand and it didn't matter to her that he should. So she told him it was over. She had broken it off too completely to resurrect it. She didn't want to resurrect it. Francine could have him.

'There's someone else,' Paul said acutely, watching her.

'No. Not in the sense you mean.'

He raised his eyebrows incredulously. 'There's more than one sense.'

'Yes. Certainly I've been with other men since we split up. Paul, I like it. I don't want to belong. I enjoy sex. I don't want marriage.'

'But you felt so bitter about Francine. You always told me how you would love it if I could stay. I don't understand, Kate. Were you playing with me?'

'No. I meant it. But since we parted I've changed. I know now that marriage wouldn't work for me. Not with you, not with anyone. I like men for company, for companionship, for sex. I don't want a husband. I don't want to live with anyone, male or female.'

'You sound very hard all of a sudden.'

'I guess I am very hard,' Kate said quietly. 'So no regrets, Paul. This is what I'm really like, only I didn't know it. We would have gone sour together. We've had a lucky release. Go back to Francine and decide what you want to do in relation to her, but leave me out of the equation. As far as your marriage is concerned, I don't exist.'

'You'll sleep with me but not marry me, is that it?'

'You hypocritical bastard. You've just spent three years doing that to me.'

'So this is revenge.'

'Go away, Paul. Get out of my life. No, I won't sleep with you. Find some other patsy. I've got a life to live.'

She flew to Corfu and made her way by taxi and by bus to the far north-east of the island. She wanted to reach Ágios Stéfanos and by the time she had succeeded, she was hot and tired and dusty.

To her left the hillside rose dry and bleached under the sun. Apart from a few cypresses, only a thin green scrub of juniper and thistles veiled the naked bones of the mountainside. On her right the land dropped sharply below the road to the sea. It was cultivated with olives and lemons and vegetable patches scraped out of the red crumbling earth. Below, the sea was an unbearable blue, so beautiful it hurt. Tiny boats with rust-red sails plied the channel. Fishing boats worked. Across from them, hazed and mysterious in the heat, lay Albania. She could just see Lake Butrinto, the vast marshy inland sea. Corfu was homely by comparison.

The village was a collection of red-roofed white houses jammed together on the steep hillside. Apart from the one precipitous road that the bus tumbled alarmingly down, there were only narrow lanes and steps between the houses. Pots of flowers stood on the steps. Washing hung out of windows. Though the plaster crumbled in the heat, so the houses had a scabby look, in total it was charming.

It was a working fishing village. On the shoreside, nets were strung, tainting the air with the smell of rotting seaweed and old fish. Boats were pulled up. Following directions, Kate made her way to the house of Spirídon Liapádes.

He was a big man with a heavy belly and a vast beard. He welcomed Kate like a conspirator and took her into his house.

She hadn't known what to expect. Certainly her Western arrogance had failed to prepare her for shady rooms tiled in cool pastel colours, heavy with the weight of flowering plants, bright with the weaving of rugs and cushions. The house was beautiful inside. Spiri fetched her wine and fruit. John Sorrell came into the room.

She saw his body as a totality. He was of medium height, quite compact and muscular, a man who gave the impression of being entire of himself. A man who knew his own boundaries, had come to terms with them. A man without room for someone else.

If he realised she was studying him, he gave no sign of it. His eyes were bright with secret intelligence, his voice light and amused.

'Good journey?'

'Yes. I could do with a shower. I'm very dusty.'

'Seeing you clean'll be a new experience.'

'It won't last,' Kate said dryly. 'Being in your company somehow means mud and blood and lack of sanitation.'

She caught the gleam of white teeth as he grinned at her. 'You can always go home to Epsom or Richmond or Westway or whatever godawful place you live in.'

'You're not a domestic man in any sense, are you?'

'No. I'm not.'

It hung like a faint challenge between them. Kate laughed. 'It's one of your attractions,' she said maliciously.

'What are the others?'

'Pheromonal.'

That shut him up.

Corfu lies one and a half miles from Albania at its closest point. The armed patrol boats had virtually ceased to operate since the downfall of Ramiz Alia, the Communist successor to Enver Hoxha. The watery border was still guarded but it was a lax business now. It focused more on stopping people leaving Albania than preventing people from entering the country.

Spiri took them across in his fishing boat that night. He had made the run many times. As a younger man he had enjoyed dodging the bullets. Smuggling was a way of life he enjoyed. He almost regretted the failure of the Communist regime. Life had lost some excitement for him.

'Why don't we enter the country legally?' Kate asked. There was a faint feeling of boys' games being played.

'Because we'd have to leave it legally,' John said. 'I don't think they'd like our hand luggage.'

'But we aren't stealing anything.'

'We want to look as though we're stealing something.'

'Wouldn't it be easier if we had them on our side? I'm only worrying about being accidentally shot, you understand.'

'There's nothing to being shot. I'm shot all the time. Don't fuss, woman. The point is, we don't risk our lives on their acting ability. The last thing we want is clumsy local policemen thundering around stopping the donkey traffic so we can pass. This isn't a subtle country, Kate. Not at the bureaucratic level, anyway.'

The landing was quick and quiet. No one met them. John took a moment to orient himself and then he set off inland, Kate meekly following.

They both wore walking boots and carried knapsacks with food and a blanket. Kate had prepared for this, but even so she found it a long night.

Towards dawn they found themselves in a mountainous country seemingly miles from any habitation. Great clefts split the naked stony heights. The clefts were wooded and often at the bottom a thin stream ran. In one of these wooded areas John stopped. They were in a clearing. Between the trees were roughly thatched shelters, mere roofs of woven vegetation. John spread his blanket under one of these.

Kate could see the remains of a considerable hearth. 'Do people live here?' she asked. It was a level of poverty she could hardly imagine.

'The people of the mountains,' John said. 'That's romantic nonsense, of course. The thieves and brigands and outcasts who live out here live a seminomadic life. They stay in the villages sometimes; sometimes they live right out here. There are caves for winter, but in summer these rough shelters are enough. They're tough, and in their way they're free. It's been a hell of a regime under Hoxha, you know.'

He was getting food out of his rucksack. Kate leant gratefully against a tree, the muscles of her legs twanging unpleasantly. 'What made you do all this?' she asked curiously. 'Did you find it too dull down on the dig, or something?'

He stopped what he was doing and looked at her steadily for a moment. Then he continued, breaking a long loaf in two, sorting out meat and cheese and hard-boiled eggs.

'My father got me into it,' he said. 'In a way.'

'Your father?'

'He was out in Greece in the war. He was a British Liaison Officer. His job was to supply the Greek resistance with arms and money. The Greeks had a guerrilla movement under Zervas after the Germans invaded them. The *andartes*. Very brave men.'

He began to eat. He didn't look at Kate. He was telling himself the story, lost in memory. 'The Communists were very active in the movement. After a time ELAS became the main resistance group, but they had a different agenda to the British, and to many Greeks. Their chance came in 1944 when the Germans left. They turned on their own people. They had been keeping back arms and supplies for years. Now they wanted to turn Greece Communist. As it happens, they lost, but that isn't what brought me here.'

He chewed thoughtfully for a while.

'My father died out here in a sense. He was never happy back home afterwards and I remember him as a bitter man, turned in on himself. He loved this part of the world with a passion that far exceeded anything I or my mother ever meant to him in later years. Anyway, he was something of a Classicist and he knew his stuff concerning the history of these parts, including the story of Nero's legion.'

'Nero's legion?'

'Nero was mad. He was also greedy and he antagonised and terrorised in about equal parts. He needed money and he needed to look good, for a variety of reasons. So he collected himself some fancy sculpture from Delphi. They reckon he took something like five hundred bronzes and simply sprinkled them about Rome.'

'Was anything left?'

'Sure. You can hardly exaggerate the importance of Delphi to the Greeks. It symbolised the civilised world to them and they centred their cult of Apollo there. It had the Oracle, of course, and was the base, the centre, for the Amphictyonic League. It was the site of the Pythian games. This was where it was at, in those times. But Rome pillaged it pretty thoroughly. It wasn't just Nero, but he was the worst.'

He lit a cigarette. He had his shirt unbuttoned and the sleeves turned back. Kate could see his throat, his forearms, in the growing light of day. She felt she had never seen anyone so truly alive as this man.

'The first consignments went by sea, naturally enough. It was the easiest means of transport in those days. It's probably still the best. But a ship went down and some really prize pieces were lost. Nero didn't put up with failure so he issued one of those unobeyable commands. He ordered an impossibility. He wanted the next goody to come by land, via Illyria. A Roman legion would protect it from bandits. Everyone knew the Illyrians were pirates: it was about their only claim to fame. But Nero wanted his statue and he was going to have it. Or heads would roll.'

'A particular statue?'

'A particular statue group. Paris giving the golden apple to Aphrodite. Someone – some fool – had told Nero that the statue of Aphrodite resembled Poppaea, his mistress, later his wife. They think she was the hot one; she thought up the worst excesses, by the way. Nero just enjoyed carrying out her ideas. Anyway, his infatuation with the lady meant that getting the statue superceded everything. He had to have it. So it was brought overland.'

'And lost?'

'And lost. There's an account of the men who brought the statue group, what they went through, all in that dry historian's Latin. It's an incredible tale, an epic in its way. But they were attacked once too often and the loot was stolen.'

'What happened to the men, the Romans?'

'Their leader bravely went back to Rome and was crucified for his pains. The men mostly ran away. Anyway, it was assumed that the bandits cut the statues up, melted them down. Aphrodite was gold and ivory, according to legend. Fabulous. Then my father heard rumours.'

'In wartime?'

'People fled into these mountains and out of them. Italy invaded Albania so it was part of the Axis. In 1944 Hoxha the Communist got it. He'd been an anti-Fascist guerrilla fighter and was a founding father of the Albanian Communist Party. The border closed and that was that.'

'What were the rumours?'

'That the group still existed, or part of it anyway. That it had been buried for centuries but recent earth movements had exposed it. This part of the world has earthquakes all the time. Some loot appeared: a corselet with golden embossing, stuff like that.'

'That's all you have to go on? Rumour? Oh, what about the apple?'

'We made that. It's only gold on the outside. When I heard about Interpol and this business about fleecing Albania, I was desperate to get involved. I want the statue group. I want it in a museum, where it belongs. So I had to set myself up to attract the attention of Martineau. He was the one Interpol were after. They were my passport into Albania. To help them, I could legitimately search for the statue. The Albanians can't fund the search; they don't have a bean to spare. The West is too mean and doesn't believe in the group's existence. Only the police have an interest, because they want to get Martineau. I'm just slipping myself in where I fit.'

'How do you know where to look?'

'My father wrote down everything he heard. He talked to people. He made notes. When he died last year I found them in his papers. Clues, if you like.'

'So we are headed where he heard this thing was?'

'That's right. We have to cross the river Dhrin and get into the Nemercke mountains. We're meeting someone there.'

He stopped. His words hung in the cool morning air. Kate was very tired. And dazzled.

'Do you really expect to find it?'

'Come here.'

She looked at him. He was apparently relaxed, watching her. She undid her shirt buttons and came across, sitting facing him.

He reached out and touched her face. Then he put a hand to her warm breasts. He touched them; stroked them. 'Let's worship the old way,' he said. 'These mountains demand it, don't you think?'

'The old way?'

'With our bodies.' He bowed his head and kissed her breasts. She looked down on the top of his bent head, saw his soft bright hair. His lips were soft on her skin. She felt its arousal, felt her breasts ache slightly with the desire to be caressed.

He kissed her nipples, pursing his lips and sucking very slightly, drawing them through his lips so they lengthened. His hand came up and slipped inside her shirt. She felt the slightly rough palm against her ribs, at her back.

Gently, she pulled the shirt off. Now he kissed her shoulders, her throat. Above them a bird sang. She could smell myrtle on the air, juniper, basil. She put her head back as he felt for her belt buckle and released it. She moved to let him strip her. Soon she lay naked on his blanket, the sky bright above her, the trees clustering round.

He undressed himself. He kissed her belly. He allowed a finger to come up between her thighs. She parted her legs slightly. He touched her clitoris.

Desire lanced her. She felt her face flush. His own was impassive. Gently, he pushed her legs further apart. He lowered his head and she felt his hair on the skin of her legs.

She drew up her knees and opened them. He tongued her sticky flesh apart. She felt him tug gently at her labia. She felt his tongue walk up and down her sex, dance up and down its valleys and ridges. She felt it swell like a bud, and then flower open. He caressed it open, erect and vulnerable. He kissed it sweetly. His tongue ran up and down. Then he slid his tongue into her entrance. The tip teased her inner flesh. He ran it round, stirring, tantalising, enticing her to want more.

She did. She lay passive while he moved up her body. He kissed her navel, the undercurve of her breasts, the nipples, her throat, her lips. She felt his body press on hers. He moved – his sex was big – and she helped him so that the enlarged tip of him began to slide into her.

He did it very slowly, drawing out the moment so that she was able to feel every exquisite sensation. The swollen end of him pressed her vagina open. He increased the pressure against her slight resistance. He began to pass into her body. She felt her flesh yield. She felt his pressure in her. She felt the fullness as he entered her more completely. She felt the richness of his body at hers, in hers, filling hers. Her whole body became merely an extension of her organ of pleasure. She fell into the sensual abyss, drowning in sweetness. He moved, long slow strokes. She couldn't see, couldn't hear anything, couldn't feel anything apart from this glory in her body, the bigness of him filling her empty spaces. He moved and she moved with him, one beast, one sexual beast.

He moved faster in her now, more urgent as his own need began to carry him up. She was with him, her inner flesh beginning to ripple independent of her movements, in tune with his thrusting. She gasped: there wasn't enough air. The smell of sex was in her nostrils, it was unbearably exciting. She thrust up hard and felt herself burst and become a wet hot vortex, all foaming lust, all explosions of climax, and in the middle of her frenzy he came, bursting open in her and filling her with his divine gift.

So alone were they that they slept in their tangle of sweat and sex-soaked limbs. There was no need to cover themselves or hide what they did. There was no one here; they were alone in all the world and quite apart from humanity. The sun rose high in the sky and kept them warm. They might have been Adam and Eve in the first garden.

They woke and Kate felt John at her. There was something delicious about lying here open to him, allowing him to plunder her body as he wanted. The treasure was equally hers. As he took, he gave. She lay slack and let him do as he wished, and he did, satisfying his lust as it came on him without ceremony, as if they were beasts on the mountain and had no need of words.

She felt she could do this for ever: lie warm and fed, allowing the beautiful male to rut with her as he felt inclined. Her body felt luminous and light, floating as he filled it with his seed and as her own orgasms were drawn from her simply, continuously, easily. All the strain of partnering was gone. All the stressful need to be something she wasn't. She laughed with the pleasure of it. What woman could ask for more in the sensual world? Food, sun, and coupling with the male of her choice. He was a fountain of strength and seed. Somehow he too was released by their circumstances. The rules didn't apply. There was no commitment beyond the commitment to pleasuring each other.

So they worshipped in the old way, with sleep and wine and sun on naked skin, and the day-long hours to use as they wished.

In the evening, they set off again. They walked all night, and when Kate protested that the mountains were so empty they could move by day, John pointed out that the sun was too hot and there were shepherds in the daytime, even in these very remote parts, high on hilltops. To the north was a richer valley with villages in it. They no longer had high mountains between themselves and the north. Their isolation was coming to an end.

The next morning they met with the men John was coming to see; the men who had promised to help him.

They were extraordinary people. They wore linen shirts embroidered at the hems and sleeves, with stout leather belts around them. Over these tunic shirts, they wore goatskin waistcoats, open sleeveless jackets in hairy hide. Their trousers were bound below the knee and their footwear was a curious mixture of peasant sandal and western shoe.

They were tall, mostly bearded, with heavy bull-like shoulders and curling hair growing densely to frame their rounded Greek faces.

They were a race apart, neither Albanian nor Greek. They had lived in these mountains since before recorded time, a tribal people making their living from robbery and the animals they herded. They owed no allegiance except to each other.

Women, Kate felt, were plainly insignificant. They spoke a bastardised Greek with John while she sat quietly by. They ate together. After a while, John came over to her.

'These people,' he said. He had a hard-edged glittery look, his eyes dancing and cold.

'Yes.' Kate felt her spine creep. The tension in him was unmistakable.

'They have customs. Not our customs.'

'No. Of course.'

'Phormis's woman. She's in the tents over there. He offers her to me.'

'Like Eskimos.'

'Yes. If you think about it, it's a survival trick for any people on the edge of extinction, with a narrow gene pool.' His voice was suddenly dry and academic, the contrast startling as his mind took over momentarily from his body. 'They let strangers fertilise their women. It serves to establish trust, brotherhood, temporary membership of the group. And it increases the genetic diversity of the group. It has survival value. There aren't many of these people left. They won't survive long, either. The Communists didn't get them, but democracy will. They can't hold out.'

'It's all right.' Kate said edgily. 'You don't need my permission. You know that. I can handle this, John. You're insulting me.'

'No, listen.' The glittering look was back. 'It works both ways.'

The silence was absolute. She wasn't stupid. After a while, she said: 'I go with him. You go with her.'

'That's it.'

'If I don't?'

John shrugged. 'Work it out.'

She stood up suddenly and looked down at him, crouched on the ground. 'Now?'

'Yes, now.' He stood up, too. They looked at each other. Then they walked over to Phormis, the head of the band. Together the three of them walked to the tents.

It was very goaty. The tents must be made of goatskin. It wasn't horrible, but it was pervasive. Inside the largest tent were bright rugs and cushions. A small oil lamp burned. It smelled very sweet; it must have been burning olive oil. The bottom of the tents were rolled up so that air moved in as the day's heat built up. As she got used to the goat smell, Kate saw that the tent was a pleasant place: clean, aromatic with cooking smells and herbs, brightly coloured in its shadows.

Thin mattresses with cloths flung over them and cushions heaped on them stood around the walls. One of them was occupied.

Phormis's woman was astonishing. She lay on one of the mattresses braiding her hair. She was Minoan; a pure Minoan. Her red crimped hair hung to her waist, where it was unbraided. It smelled of lemon and myrtle. Her face was long with a large nose. Her huge eyes were oval, on the slant, her cheekbones high. It was a face out of antiquity, as pure a racial type as ever Kate had seen. Breaking all the rules of western beauty, she was amazing. She was stunningly beautiful. The only thing lacking was the tight Minoan bodice exposing the breasts; the flaring layers of floor-length skirt.

John spoke rapidly to Phormis who laughed and slapped him on the back. Then plainly John said something about Kate. She saw the robber leader's eyes move over her thoughtfully. Then John moved over to the girl and crouched before her.

'It depends whether she accepts me,' he said to Kate without turning his head. 'If either of you rejects the man offered, the deal's off.'

The girl looked John over appraisingly, as if he were a horse. She touched his cheek, his straight hair. She said something to Phormis, who laughed. He spoke to John, who undid his shirt and pulled it back.

She inspected his chest. Then she looked at Phormis and said two words.

Immediately his attention switched to Kate. For the first time she realised that the coupling would occur here, simultaneously, in each other's company.

He stood in front of her, waiting. She realised that in a way she held the cards. It was up to her to call the shots. This was an exchange of politeness, not a brutal assault.

She let her mind curl over the business, over the

man. He was a fine male specimen, that much was true. He must have been well over six feet tall and built broad to match, though it was hard to tell under his flowing clothes.

The head was primitive but noble in its way. There was nothing mean or sly about him. He was a proud beast, a strong beast, one used to command. A thinker. A man of action. She could do worse.

She took off her shirt and gestured for him to do the same.

He stripped his top half quickly, looking at her breasts. Alone of his band, he wore boots. Standing in linen trousers tucked into boots, he still looked very fine.

His chest was covered in curls almost as dense as those on his head. The hair was black, streaked with grey. Kate moved towards him. She reached out and touched his arm, his shoulder where the muscle bulged smooth and shining. His skin was stretched tight, the muscle hard beneath it. Kate sat on the mattress and took her boots off.

Phormis knelt and began to undo her belt.

Across from them she saw that the girl was touching John with her hair, stroking his naked chest and back with it. She leant into him and rubbed her head like a cat against him. She drew down the neckline of her blouse and allowed her breasts to thrust free. For a minute her hands were slack at her sides where she knelt. Her breasts were rounded and firm, jutting out to John. The illusion was complete. She looked exactly like a Cretan figurine: bulging breasts, narrow waist, flounced skirt.

John placed his two hands on her waist and bent to kiss her breasts. Kate turned back to Phormis. She held his eyes with hers and removed her trousers. For a moment he looked down her body. Then he nodded as if in satisfaction with what he saw. He spoke two words and smiled, his eyes dark and corrupt and ancient. Kate lay back, spreading her hair, lifting her arms to display herself better. She knew her breasts were full, her waist was narrow, and that her hips had a womanly swell to them. She had long legs, slim-thighed and sweetly made. The activities of her recent life had slimmed and strengthened her. She looked the healthy animal she was.

She heard John's voice. 'He says you have been well-used. It's a compliment. He means your body is used to loving and able for it.'

Phormis removed his trousers. She saw his heavy genitals swing free, the riot of curling black hair making her think briefly of Pan. His legs were very muscular, very hairy. He had an Attic godliness, a robust hairy sensuality, devil and god combined in a man with a man's humour and tastes.

She reached out and caught the swinging shaft. Phormis grunted. She brought in her other hand cupped the heavy balls. They felt full and ripe.

He said something again to her and looked across at John. The girl was leaning back, pulling up her skirts with her knees open, displaying her naked sex for him to look at. She heard John make a noise, a stifled sound, at the same time as his head whipped round to stare at Phormis.

The two men locked eyes. Phormis laughed and spoke. He got up from Kate quite casually, his sex swinging as he moved. He went over to John and crouched beside him, looking into his woman's sex.

'Come here, Kate,' John said, his voice not quite steady. 'Come here and learn something.'

Kate came across. She was quite naked, but no one took any notice of her. All eyes were on Phormis's girl.

She was grinning, letting them all look at her. Kate gasped.

All down the length of her vulva were little gold rings. They pierced the labia either side of the girl's sex, and effectively held it shut against intruders.

Phormis spoke at length. John replied angrily. Phormis laughed and called out in a bellowing voice. The doorflap to the tent moved. An old woman came in.

Bickering and twittering, she approached the group. She pushed back her black enveloping peasant dress and knelt in front of the girl. John began to explain in a low voice.

'They do this to girls. Phormis says it's to protect them from being raped, either by their own man or anyone else. Only the women can release the rings. For this girl to have sex, an older woman has to permit it. It's protection, he says.'

The older woman had her hands in the girl's vagina. The girl was laughing, watching the men from under long thick dark lashes, flirting with them while her body was made ready. The old woman gathered up the rings, said something salty enough to make the girl laugh and Phormis blush, and went out of the tent clutching her skirts.

'I thought she was going to stay and watch too,' Kate said with relief.

'No,' John said, his attention on the dark flower in front of him. He reached in a hand and tentatively touched the soft flesh. The girl made a slight sexual noise and Kate saw her clitoris move.

She went back to her own mattress and lay down. Phormis came by her. He slid a fat thumb into his mouth and sucked it wet. Then he placed it between Kate's legs. A second later it entered her body.

She arched over the little invader, clenching with her muscles. She felt the thumb explore her internally, as if to grasp her dimensions. Then he knelt between her legs. Without ceremony, he picked up his mighty sex. He leant forward and Kate felt herself impaled.

As rides went, it was a simple one. He put it in and he moved it about. The quality of the experience, its uniqueness, came from the man himself; who he was and why he was in her. As a reason for congress, it was a new experience for Kate.

He was also massively endowed. The big heavy

member swung in and out with primaeval vigour, with raw strength. He had no subtlety. He had grace, he had strength, he had a superb and virile organ. Kate thoroughly enjoyed what he did to her.

It was a very ripe experience.

When he was done he sat calmly beside her; lighting an evil little cigar which he smoked with evident pleasure. He inspected his penis happily. It lay slack and wet-looking, a solid lump of flesh. He patted Kate's thigh approvingly and smiled at her. He evidently felt that following custom was no penance as far as she was concerned.

Her body felt replete. It was an altogether interesting thing, this business with Phormis. Idly she looked over at John.

The girl was bent double, her back high off the ground and arched like a cat. She was raised on her feet and hands in the position of the crab. John knelt at her with his sex inside her, thumping hard into her sprung and swinging body.

She cried out sharply and a torrent of words poured out of her. John thrust with extra vigour and then he relaxed. She stayed as she was for a few moments, then she lowered herself so that she lay on the floor. The instant her back touched the floor, she sprang up in a liquid flow of movement and fastened herself on John's sex. He gave a shout of surprise and pain. Phormis laughed, bellowing with laughter. Obviously he was aware of this trick she played. She was fastened like a ferret to John's penis. She shook her head from side to side, worrying him like a dog might. Her hair flew around her, across his belly and thighs, in a dark red fountain. Then she released him and sat up proudly, stroking her breasts and preening.

The four of them were fairly quiet for a while. Then the girl spoke. She and Phormis spoke back and forth for a while. Then he switched to Greek and spoke to John.

The conversation was grave. After a while Phormis

got up and went over to his woman. She took a hold of his sex and began to play with it. He lay back, still talking to John while she bent over his lap, toying with his sex, kissing it and stroking it with her hair. John came over to Kate.

'This is what normally happens,' he said. The tone of his voice gave nothing away. He gave the information neutrally.

'After each man has exhibited his strength and worthiness to be considered as temporary brother, he goes back to his own woman. As a test of his virility, he now repeats what he has just done with his own woman. This proves his seed is worth the business, because he is properly vigorous in sexual matters.

'Oh,' Kate said blankly.

'There's a catch. I didn't know about this, by the way. This particular bit of it, I mean.'

'You knew about the other bit?'

'The exchange. Oh yes. I thought it might happen, but I wasn't sure.'

'You didn't think to warn me.'

'Did you need warning?'

'I guess not,' Kate said in a low voice.

'However, this next bit is somewhat different as I'm sure you'll agree.'

'I go with you in front of them.'

'That's part of it. Look, they're getting going. You can see the other part.'

The girl was on her knees, facing away from Phormis. She hiked up her long skirt and bent right forward so that her backside stuck up in the air. She put her forehead on the floor. Phormis entered her with a finger in a leisurely fashion and moved it about. In the restricted light of the tent, it was a moment before Kate saw precisely what he was doing.

He was invading her anus. It wasn't her vagina. He was proposing to penetrate her anally.

'Why?' Kate said in a strangled voice.

'My seed is my gift to her and to the group. He won't

239

sully it with his at this stage. The idea is that I impregnate her, you see. My loins are the ones that matter here. He has to prove his virility though, to make you want to keep his seed and wish it well in your body. He will prove it by fucking her straight after fucking you, to show you what a bull of a man he is, how sons by him will be vigorous creamy lovers and daughter will be strong and welcoming lovers. He goes in her back passage so his seed won't muddle with mine. I have to do the same with you.'

Kate tried to speak and failed.

'Are you game?' She saw his expression was lopsided. He was both attracted and appalled. The civilised man in him was outraged. The libertine, the primitive man, was entranced.

She looked again. Phormis was putting his huge member into the girl's rear. He called over his shoulder to them.

'He wants us to help,' John said. 'He says he's big for her. He needs help to get it in.'

'Dear heaven,' Kate said faintly. 'I don't believe this.'

They went over. John took one of her buttocks, Kate took the other. They pulled her open and Phormis grunted and pushed.

His vast flesh slid into the tight passage. Kate saw it crush as it went in. She felt the bottom convulse and grasped against at the buttock she hauled back on. Sweat stood out on Phormis's brow. For a moment she reached under him and held his balls. They were the size of lemons: huge, fat with sperm. Phormis cried out softly and thrust home. He said something to John, who released the girl, then he bent down to where her face was crushed into the floor. He stroked her hair back and found her face. He pressed his lips to hers and murmured wordlessly to her. She managed a faint smile and then Phormis began to thrust.

John was pale. 'Did he hurt you?' he asked.

Kate felt the wickedness rise in her. 'No. He's big, but I took him.'

'Oh shit,' said John. 'I'm getting out of my depth here.'

'Think of the statue. And penetrate me. Ravish me. Do it, Sorrell. Do it.'

She bent like the girl with her forehead on the floor as if she worshipped. Her rear poked up. She felt John's fingers fumble in her vagina and then, they slid with slippery ease into her rear.

It was ravishing. The pleasure was so acute she couldn't bear it. She stuffed a fist in her mouth so only the odd muffled sob could escape. She felt his cock enter her. She had meant to play with him, to arouse him, but their activity with Phormis had done the job for her. He was hard erect.

He took her with quick stabbing blows. Her vagina went into orgasm immediately. It fluttered and convulsed and tremors shook it. She felt it oozing as John thudded into her; she felt her own come and Phormis's dribble down her thighs. She was all liquid fire in there, boiling as lust shook her and made her stomach muscles hurt.

He did it as quickly as he could. Kate ignored him afterwards, ignored everything. She slumped naked on the mattress with the seed of two men oozing from her body, and she slept.

She woke much later. Someone was at her body. She stirred, trying to remember why she felt so odd, why her limbs were so heavy. She didn't know where she was, who she was with, what she was doing.

There were hands at her. Water. Voices. She opened her eyes.

Two women encased in robes were touching her. They were washing her and chatting to each other as they went about their work. She felt them open her legs and pry open her sex. 'What?' she said, beginning to resist.

John's voice cut across her bewilderment. 'They are looking after you,' he said quietly. 'Don't worry. They make sure you aren't torn or hurt in any way. Apparently, if a man makes a girl bleed or hurts her, he is forbidden to have sex for a certain amount of time till he learns better manners. They've already dealt with Phormis's woman. They've replaced her rings.'

Kate lay on her back as the women's hands went over her, inspecting her, washing her, checking her. 'It's some system,' she said shakily.

'It has its points,' agreed John. 'I'll help you dress afterwards. They'll feed us. Then they'll take us to the statue.'

Chapter Thirteen

They ate pieces of lamb skewered on thin sticks and roasted over an open fire. There were bowls of basil and rosemary sauce into which they all dipped their meat. There were little spicy rice balls, huge tomatoes, and fruit. They drank a resinous wine, crude and coarse. Kate felt the heart go into her. It was as if she became part of the mountains, part of the ribs of harsh sun-blasted rock on which they sat. She felt powerful.

She felt sensual too. Having Phormis's great sex in her body had stretched it. She could feel the after-image of his size in her sexual muscles. It was delicious, teasing. Her rear felt most odd. She had to try not to wriggle. The women had greased it, to her considerable embarrassment, but she appreciated their wisdom now. It was slippery and sly, faintly tingling.

She lusted for John. They had business to do, but her body was awake and interfering with her thoughts. She wanted another of those long steamy sun-drenched sessions with him, where she fell in and out of sleep so that his sex was woven into the fabric of her dreams.

They began to walk afterwards; her, John, Phormis, and two of his men.

It was deep in the night. The day had been spent in sex and sleep and food. A great moon hung high in the sky and they walked in its cold light. Kate didn't like it. She felt it was ominous. Which of those two rejected goddesses was symbolised by the moon? If she were abroad tonight, she would not be pleased by their errand; to bring her hated rival to the eyes of the world, depicted at the moment the mortal Paris selected her, at the moment of her rival's humiliation.

They walked long and hard.

'Imagine that legion,' John said quietly. He had been walking in a glow of patriarchal splendour with Phormis, but for a moment he had dropped back to accompany Kate who was trotting quietly in the rear.

'They had to cart that damned statue group from Delphi across this terrain, heading west and north through the Pindus mountains and into Illyria. Then they would have gone up to Epirus and so taken ship to Italy. Even Nero didn't expect them to cart it all the way up and round via Venice.'

He stopped for a moment. 'What a hell of a job. How could they protect the thing? They must have spent most of their time hauling to help the oxen.'

'Did anyone record the journey?'

'The official historians mentioned it, notably Tacitus. You know what official Latin prose is like. "Since that Nero, as was his habitual practice, ordered that the goddess should be brought with all haste and good care, safe into his keeping, it was entrusted that the noblest of his legions should undertake the task, notwithstanding the difficulties that might arise in that the Illyrians were known to be . . ." Etcetera, etcetera.'

Kate didn't actually know what official Latin prose was like, but she took the point. 'Did anyone who made the journey keep a diary or anything?'

'If they did, we've lost it. They didn't exactly carry reams of paper around with them, so it's unlikely. Keeping a diary on clay or wax tablets is tricky.'

'There's no first-hand account then?' Kate ignored his irony.

'No. Several contemporary accounts mention Nero's

244

statue or Nero's legion in terms that obviously mean asking for the impossible. You know, like "Pyrrhic victory" means you lose more than you gain. You can tell these were loaded phrases. It's a story waiting to be told. I'm surprised Hollywood never got its hands on it.'

They rested and ate some food, dried chewy meat mostly. Kate suspected it was goat. She found it surprisingly restorative. They went on until dawn. Finally, they arrived.

They squatted together, shivering a little in the damp grey air. A high valley, fairly flat-bottomed, lay below them. On its flanks was a mass of loose rubble and scree. White limestone cliffs reared above them. The first rays of the rising sun caught these cliffs and they began to glow. Kate stared in amazement and Phormis, seeing her face, spoke to John.

'He says they call the cliffs the Shining Ones,' he said. 'It's like Delphi itself. The cliffs flame in the sun. They're riddled with caves, too. That's the point, of course.'

'This is where the legion was attacked?' asked Kate.

'The bandits came out of the caves. They'd been living in them. They waited till the legion had reached the neck of the valley, about a mile up that way, then they attacked. It was a grisly business.'

'And it's in these caves that armaments have been found?'

'That's right.'

'Why haven't they been pillaged? What makes you think that anything is left?'

John looked at her. 'This is Phormis's story,' he said. 'What happened was this. Two years ago his band was coming through this valley. A little boy aged about five wandered off into the caves and got lost. They value their young highly and they hunted for him for five days. They were frightened of getting lost themselves in the endless tunnels and caverns, and eventually they decided the child must have died. They stayed here, mourning him, when one day he reappeared from the hillside up there. He was all right. He was a bit skinnier than usual, but otherwise fine. And he had a story to tell.'

John stopped and rolled himself a cigarette. He didn't look at Kate. 'His story was this. He wandered about in the dark for some time and got very frightened. Then he heard the lady singing so he knew it was okay. He followed the sound of the lady's voice till he found her. The lady looked after him, fed him, told him stories and played with him. She was very beautiful and she shone, the child said. She was a golden lady. Eventually she said it was time he went home and she helped him out on to the hillside and pointed him in the direction of his people.'

There was a long silence. 'You mean,' said Kate in an ominous voice, 'that we are here risking our lives following up the tale of a lost child about a talking statue that you think is evidence of Aphrodite?'

'Yes,' said John. 'That's what I mean.' He grinned at her. 'It's a hell of a tale.'

'It seemes to me that every story from these parts has that epic nonsense feel,' Kate said robustly.

'It's an epic country,' said John. 'Very old, in terms of humanity. Very haunted.'

They rejoined the others and discovered that Phormis and the three men with him would wait for them. They would make camp in the valley while Kate and John investigated the caves.

'Why won't they come with us?' asked Kate.

'Superstition,' John said briefly. 'They think it will bring them bad luck.'

'But they help us?'

'Sure. They have this very pragmatic approach. If we plunder the caves, we get the bad luck. If they help us after the deed is done, they get a share of the loot. But no bad luck sticks to them.'

'Is this bad luck specific or general?' Kate asked icily.

'Specific. You aren't superstitious, are you?'

'Just as well I'm not, it seems. What is it, the local equivalent of the curse of the Pharaohs?'

'I guess so. You know, usual sort of thing. Death, woe unto the seventh generation and all that.'

'I don't have any children.'

'Neither do I. So we don't have a problem, do we?'

They had torches, spare batteries, food and water, a compass and a pot of luminous paint to mark their way. They set off almost immediately. There was little point in waiting.

Kate had never been caving. Initially she found she was filled with a childish sense of wonder and she kept wanting to waste the torches by staring round them in the larger caverns. The whole hillside was honeycombed. Some were vast cathedrals of stone filled with natural pillars. The rock was often wet and mineral-stained so that it shone rosy pink and deep red, green and brown in the flicker of their light. Every time they stopped to rest, John put out the torch they shared, but when they ate he lit a candle so that they could see.

The air temperature was very steady, mild and comfortable. the floor was rough and dry with broken material on it. The quietness was absolute and after a while Kate felt the air press thickly against her face, a blanket that muffled sound and sense and vision.

She told John. He let her light a candle and walk round for a little, exploring where they were till she recovered her sense of what was around them, her feeling of space.

They left the series of vast vaulted caverns and squeezed through cracks and along narrow places, grunting with effort. Much of this was done totally in the dark; John leading, working by feel and only occasionally using a torch to check ahead.

Kate had the sensation that they were going down. The floors, when she could see them, sloped away, rubble strewn, rough. The walls were always closer now. She grazed her knuckles, banged her head, scraped her hips as she worked her way deeper and deeper into the heart of the mountain.

They didn't talk much. Her thoughts became thunderous. She had no sense of time.

They came to water. John investigated the running stream carefully. Then he removed his boots and trousers and waded out into it. Kate sat watching him with the small light going deeper and deeper into the moving water. He came up and out the other side.

'I'll come back,' he called. 'I'll get the stuff across. It's pretty cold.'

He did as he had said. He left the torch he was using with Kate and carried his clothes and his haversack across, Kate playing the light so he could see. She then stripped, stuffed her clothes into her knapsack and set off.

He waited, watching her. 'Feel with your feet,' he said.

She got to midstream. The water swirled round her waist, tugging her feet. She could hardly bear the feel of the bottom and it was in her mind that blind fish with sharp teeth could live here.

The cold was intense. She concentrated on not dropping the precious torch. She put a foot forward and almost slipped.

She gave a sob. She was suddenly held. John had come back for her.

They arrived safely on the far shore and sat down.

'Okay?' John asked in an impersonal voice.

Kate swore with savagery.

'I've done this kind of thing before,' said John. 'You get used to it. We're marvellously adaptive creatures, you know. We get used to anything if we don't fight it.'

He lit a candle to save the torches. Kate looked at him. His shirt was open and his wet lower limbs were still naked. He had a sturdy strength, a kind of compact resilience about him. He wasn't bad to have around in a crisis, she thought. She thought, he's mine, too. I don't own him. I don't have to keep him. I don't have to stay faithful to him. I don't have to give anything up for him. But I have him as well as everything else. And for now, he's mine. He's chosen to have me along. He didn't need me, but I'm here. I'm not assessing insurance.

'I need you,' said John uncannily echoing her thoughts.

'How?'

'I don't think I could do this alone. And I'm not done with you, woman.'

The candle flickered, though there should be no draught. Shadows leapt. He stirred slightly and Kate saw his sex swell.

'I read a book once,' she said quietly. 'It was about this couple; their marriage was on the rocks and they went to Austria or somewhere equally decadent on holiday. She began an affair with a sort of ex-Nazi count. They all went caving together – I think the husband was a speleologist or something – and they got lost. Anyway, they went on and on trying to find a way out, with days passing, you understand. And all the time the husband investigated ahead and the count and the wife screwed like rabbits every time he was round a corner or in the next cavern or negotiating a waterfall or something. The count swore if ever they got free he'd marry her. She swore she wouldn't waste any more time with the complacent boring toad she'd married but would abandon all and marry the count. He was up her more times than a lift in the Empire State Building.'

John chuckled. His sex was very big now. Kate was sitting cross-legged, watching him as she spoke.

'So eventually, when they are getting up or down some ferociously dangerous bit, someone slips and the wife has her husband and the count dangling on each of the two ends of the one rope. Neither can rescue himself. She is holding both and can't hang on. If one goes, the other will be safe.'

'She has to make the decision between them?' asked John. 'Life for one and death for the other?'

249

'That's it.'

'So what does she decide?'

'Read the book,' said Kate and kissed his sex.

He lay back, his arms behind his head, her dark head bent over him.

'I love it when you do that,' he said quietly.

'I adore your cock,' said Kate. She kissed it again, feeling it lift and stir against her lips. 'I can worship it,' she said quietly. 'It's my personal household god, my *lares* and *penates*.'

'Worship it?'

'For now. I can bend over to it. Kiss it. Tongue it. Suck it. I can take it into my body. I can bring it up and take it down again. It blesses me.'

She had his foreskin back. She was sucking and kissing the swollen tip even as she spoke.

'It's just sex,' said John, struggling to keep control of himself.

'No, it's not. It's my toy. My pleasure. My plaything. My comforter. My master.'

John hips lifted and he thrust into her mouth. 'It's not just you,' Kate crooned and laughed suddenly. 'Wonderful, magical men. Full of honey. Full of sweetness.' She moved up his body and kissed his mouth, opening it with hers. She dropped her body on to his and groaned with the glory of his penetration. He was moving into her. She was dazed with pleasure, with the ease of it and the intensity. Why had it been so screwed up all her life? Why was it this simple now, when it had been so complicated before?

She felt a whole person. This largesse, the act of penetration, was her birthright.

The candle guttered and went out. In the velvet darkness, John exploded upwards. She saw light, splintered and full of rainbow colour. Her whole body was flooded with peace. She stretched out on him, savouring his skin rubbing against hers. An insane, intense happiness filled her.

'You crazy bitch,' said John. His voice shook slightly.

Kate wiped the tears from the corners of her eyes. She kissed him: his face, his ears, his hair, his mouth. 'You know,' she said presently, sniffing and wiping her nose, 'I can see a bit.'

John looked round. The cave walls had a greenish glow, very faint and edge of vision. 'Bioluminescence,' he said. 'Great. It'll save on the torches. We'll still need to mark our way, though. I don't want to be lost down here.'

'Maybe the golden lady will help us,' Kate teased.

'I've got mine along,' said John and slapped her on the rump.

They found the bones next.

Kate was jumpy. The bones glowed slightly as did everything organic now. 'What animal are they?' she asked.

John crouched professionally over them lighting a candle. 'I'm no anatomist,' he said vaguely. His forehead was creased in thought.

He had long fingers, clever fingers, Kate thought, who evaluated intelligence with length in this matter. He turned the bones over and over with gentleness. They were slender and curving. He lit a torch and started to search the area. Kate sat down and waited.

When he finally stopped she asked him what he had found. 'Ribs.'

'Do you know what they are ribs of?'

'People,' he said briefly. 'I can't age them, of course.'

They went on. They were on a long downward-sloping ramp. Kate sincerely hoped there was no water at the bottom. She hadn't liked that part at all. Looking back, it was reassuring to see the odd blob of paint, securely marking their way out of this labyrinth. She didn't think she could bear to be down here without knowing escape was easy.

John stopped again. Now he searched intently with a torch. 'Here,' he said quietly.

Kate had never seen anything so poignant in all her

251

life, as this evidence of an old death. 'Look.' John pointed the torch beam. In among the ribcage something gleamed

'What is it?'

'A sword hilt. He died by the sword. The blade has gone, look, but here are the oxidised remains. But the bone hilt is here. No crosspiece, see. This was the legionary's principal weapon, the *gladius*. A short sword for thrusting. See?'

He plucked the thing carefully out from the pathetic cage of ribs and turned it over in his hands. 'The bandits must have followed them in. They must have retreated through the dark until here they turned and faced their pursuers. They had already abandoned the statue group. They knew they had nothing beyond their personal pride as fighting men, as Romans.'

'When did all this happen?'

'AD sixty-five. Poor sods.'

'Dying in the dark, unburied?'

'They are buried, Kate. We are in the kingdom of the underworld, remember. Pluto's kingdom.'

'I am not buried alive,' Kate said forcefully. 'If you go on like this, I'm going home.'

John laughed. 'Sorry. It's a professional disease, feeling history come alive. Ignore me.'

They began to search the area. John told Kate not to touch things, just to call to him if she found anything. The dry temperate atmosphere had preserved things very well. It needed a professionally equipped team to investigate properly. They should observe and record only, take a few suitable artefacts for proof, and leave the rest as undisturbed as possible.

Thus chastised, Kate worked meekly. It was, she admitted to herself, unpleasant. She became quite widely separated from John and she had a craven desire to stay as close to him as possible. It was no use castigating herself for this weak feminine longing. She found him protective and reassuring and she liked it.

The cave they were in was the stuff of nightmare.

The floor sloped more and more steeply so that at times Kate actually slid on loose rubble and once or twice she found herself grabbing for a support. After a while she went down deliberately. It had come into her mind that at its bottom there might be some horrid underground sea or lake. She had no desire to plummet fully dressed into this unknown buried water and for some inscrutable male reason John refused to allow her take off her knapsack.

She was using her torch all the time. John used the other one. Since they might well have achieved their object, they could afford to be more free in the matter.

It became so steep that Kate sat on her backside and edged herself down using her boots as a brake. She dislodged little stones; she could hear them as they chinked in the distance.

It was a while before she noticed that the roof was coming down even more steeply than the floor. She was edging her way into what was an increasingly vertical slit in the floor. She stopped. That is, she tried to stop but she slid on a little way. Only jamming herself with her hands against the roof stopped her.

Several things happened at once. In grabbing for the roof she hit it with the torch. The bulb went out. She heard the little avalanche she had created trickle away round her. She spent a second in absolute silence and absolute darkness. Then she heard stones hitting some far-off floor.

A pit. She was on the edge of a pit. The stones had gone over the edge and fallen clear and silent until they struck bottom. Kate gave a little sob.

'John,' she shouted. Her voice echoed only dully. The low roof, now a few inches above her head, seemed to reflect the sound she made and bounce it down into the unseen pit.

'John,' she shouted again. At the same time she braced herself carefully and tried to wriggle backwards up the slope.

More stones fell. She went up a couple of inches and

slid a foot or two further back down. She dropped the torch, clinging to the roof in terror, trying to jam herself solid. She heard the torch roll. The silence came. Then she heard a distant crash.

Sweat poured from her brow, stinging her eyes. Dear heavens, it had been several seconds before the torch hit bottom. The drop must be enormous.

'John,' she shouted, her voice breaking in the middle of a sob.

'Hello. Kate.' She nearly fainted with relief.

'Don't come down.' She didn't need a large male thumping into her and sending them both over the edge.

'What have you found?'

John's voice sounded odd. Panic must be affecting her ears. 'I've slipped,' she said. Her voice had cracked again and the fear in it was naked. 'There's an edge a little below me. It's very steep here. I'm jammed under the roof. I've dropped the torch.'

It seemed to her she could hear muttering. I must remember this, she thought feverishly. I hallucinate when I'm terrified.

He had a rope. She knew he had a rope. Why didn't he tie it to something and sling it down?

'Kate, dear,' called someone. Something.

'John!'

'He can't answer just now. How are you, my sweet one? Whom do you betray now?'

Raoul. Kate sobbed quietly and felt the tears run down her dirt-streaked cheeks. Naturally the point of this exercise had always been to capture Raoul in flagrante so he could be put inside, preferably by the Albanians. She had known she was bait. They had not intended this level of staggering success, however. They had thought to get out with some booty before he caught up with them, and provision had been made for that eventuality. Not for this one. Her life hung by a thread and Raoul, not her beloved John, held the other end.

'Get me up,' she called hoarsely. 'John has a rope. Throw it down so I can grab it and crawl back up.'

'We've used the rope, Katya. It is wrapped very securely round your boyfriend.'

So he was alive. Lucky him. 'Raoul, I can't hang on much longer. Surely you'd rather see me die than let me just slip over this edge out of sight. There isn't much fun for you in me dying by myself down here.'

'It is very entertaining talking to you and watching your boyfriend's face.'

Kate fell silent. Her arms were a burning agony. The moment she tried to relieve the strain, her bottom slid another couple of inches downhill.

She closed her mind and her eyes, shutting off the pain in her arms. There was nothing now. It was a pity, because she had only just started to live. Since that strange moment in Corfu when she had all but raped a man she had just tried to kill, circumstances had conspired to give her a new liberty. With it had come power; power to understand herself and power to be herself and enjoy it. It was such a shame it would last no longer than the few weeks she had had.

John. Her partner in crime. Her partner in a superb sexual adventure which should not have ended just yet. The perfect man: unpossessive, sexy, and having no desire to belong to her. They weren't exactly ships that passed in the night. They were ships that had chosen to steam alongside for a while.

She slid another few inches. A roaring had started in her ears through which she heard Raoul calling to her faintly. Someone shouted; perhaps John was cracking under the strain.

The roaring increased. Very horribly, the floor shook. Detritus on the grand scale poured by her. Kate gave a helpless scream and fell with it.

Very cautiously, Kate moved. She was on rubble which was unstable, but fairly flat. It was under her rather

255

than against her. This small fact was infinitely reassuring. Gravity, at least, was on her side.

She didn't seem to be hurt. She could twitch all her toes, wriggle her bottom, lift her head, and scrunch her fingers into the loose stuff on which she lay. Nothing very obviously hurt and all her limbs seemed to work. She could breathe, though it was a bit dusty. Not even a rib snapped, and she had plenty of ribs, after all. One or two wouldn't matter, as long as nothing punctured her lung.

Kate lay and quite calmly thought what a pass she had been brought to. A couple of broken ribs would be a light escape from this particular adventure. She didn't even have that.

Escape. She might be in one piece, but she was in one piece in the dark, alone. Not only did she have no one to help her, she had active antagonists between herself and the way out.

The way out. Up a cliff, presumably. Kate got on to her knees.

There was some shifting and settling, but she seemed to be on safish ground. Kate reach blindly round her.

Several horrible minutes followed where she groped into empty space. Then she started thinking and picked up some of the millions of pebbles she sat on. Carefully, systematically, she began throwing them in all the directions round her.

Carefully, systematically, Kate worked out she was on a ledge. The it-might-as-well-be bottomless pit was behind her. The cliff face was in front of her. Kate stood up, her hands against it, and felt up as far as she could.

It was quite broken and ledgy. It would probably be an easy climb on a summer's day with grass or sand a few feet below. Kate was in the dark, alone, on a loose footing and with a deep rocky pit behind her.

No one called down to her from above. Maybe they had their own troubles, though frankly Kate was damned if she could imagine them worse off then herself. And they had each other. She was alone.

Going down was hopeless. The lower she went, the worse her troubles were. The hill rose above her and for every foot into the bowels of this damned mountain she descended, the mountain added another couple going up.

If she wasn't going to climb down, she would climb up. She couldn't stay where she was, where no one would come to rescue her. Kate began to climb.

Deprived of sight, it was quite easy. Her fingers and toes had a tremendous sensitivity, even through the stout caps to her boots. Kate shinned up the face in a few minutes flat. She had not, of course, fallen far, hence her lack of injury.

At the top there was a flat area and then the steep slope that she had slithered so disastrously down. Now she was belly-down to it, could she wriggle up using her boots on the roof?

Kate began to do this. Very soon she managed to dislodge a vast amount of loose matter into her face. Choking and sliding, she stopped and had a think.

It must have been either an earthquake or Raoul playing with dynamite. Either way, the narrow slit she had come through was blocked. She could not get up.

Kate lay by herself in the dark. She stroked her hair out of her eyes and smiled. She put her dirty thumb in her mouth and sucked. She fell asleep.

Chapter Fourteen

*T*o wake in darkness is not nice. To know that darkness will last for ever is terrible. Kate faced the most terrible wakening of her life.

She didn't even know what time it was. Her watch had been ripped from her wrist along with its frail and friendly light. She was alone, out of space and time and all that was light in the world.

She began to explore. She avoided the loose foot of the landslip and worked to one side. Here a wall of rock came out. Her ledge stopped, becoming part of a face. There was no way but down.

She worked her way back to the other side. She could see things now: shapes, phantasms, eyeblinks. Her light-starved retinas were playing her tricks.

She had better luck here. The rock face receded as it went up in rough-and-ready steps. Kate climbed.

Eventually she bumped her head on the roof. She scouted systematically, first to one side and then to the other. She found a slit and began to wriggle through it.

She stuck. She tried to go backwards and couldn't. At this point she reached her nadir of misery. It was one thing to die alone, starving, thirsty, in the dark, but where you could stretch out your arms. It was another to lie jammed, crushed, claustrophobically stuck between vast unimaginable tons of rock.

The EarthMover might play games with her and turn again in his long sleep. A couple of inches of rock movement would crush her ribs into her lungs, fracture her skull, snap her spine.

She couldn't even scratch her itching nose.

She began to dig the toes of her boots in. After a while she shoved forward, ignoring the pain. Perhaps she had shed a couple of ounces of weight in that time. Perspiration poured off her; she was not cold. Whatever it was, she suddenly became free, emerging into a larger space.

Kate spent some time wiping her nose and getting her breathing under control. Then she noticed several things.

There must be water not too far away. She could see the rock walls phosphorescing slightly. What had John called it? Bioluminescence. She wasn't in total darkness any more.

She could hear something, too. Very quietly, Kate got to her feet. It seemed a terribly long time since she had stood up like a bipedal human being, and she felt odd and wobbly. She ignored this and began to creep about the cavern she was in.

She found a skull. She found some gold coins. She found some remains of weaons. She found the source of the noise.

She backtracked and worked her way carefully round the chamber she was in. There were two exits, not counting the ghastly slit she had entered by. Then she went back to the source of the noise.

Sometime during her recent hideous experiences a certain steel had entered her soul. Her primitive urge was for human company and having tracked it down against impossible odds, she wanted nothing better than to rush into its arms.

The problem was, it had just attemped to murder her. What she now dearly wished was to escape, first and foremost, and if possible do for the bastards who had tried to do for her.

Her own savagery amazed her. She considered herself a cultured and humane person, essentially decent. Something profound had happened to her when Raoul had allowed her to die rather than throwing her a rope. The very beastliness of the death he had been content for her to suffer, raised a beastliness in her attitude towards him and his henchmen. Somewhere, absurdly, under it all was her profound belief that society didn't work at all unless on the whole the stronger cared for the weaker. Raoul was a man. She was a woman. Shooting her in hot blood was one thing. Strangling her to save his own skin was one thing. But allowing her to die in miserable body-smashing seclusion just for the fun of it, that was quite another. The simple truth was, she wanted him dead and would be happy to help the process along.

They were close to her and they were digging themselves out. There must be a hole, however small, between her cavern and theirs. They were trapped as she had been, she could tell that much. They were digging the rubble away so they could get out from under this terrifying mountain.

She was so very thirsty. She could smell water but she couldn't find it. They would have water, though. And they would have John. She wanted John. He was hers and she would have him back.

She was frightened of making a noise they might hear and it took her a long time to find the hole. When she did, she realised with a kind of malicious triumph that she could get through. She had the feeling that the EarthMover had only just made this particular gap. She sent some silent thank-yous and settled down to listen.

There were four of them. She could hear Raoul, Pierre and Emil. There was also, of course, John. He was helping to dig them out. They all appeared to take turns but they kept John at it continuously. It occurred to Kate he probably didn't feel too good about things.

However, she could hardly sing out she was fine, so she kept silent.

They had lit candles and she could see the central part of the cave and where they worked quite well. She was up in the roof, herself. She could see their careful collection of artefacts. Nothing very valuable there, she thought.

Then she saw the chests. Raoul was sitting by them watching the others work. Now he opened one and shone his torch in. Gold gleamed dully back. Kate nodded to herself. He would not kill John just yet. They needed four men because there were two chests and if her memory served her right, gold weighed almost twice as much as lead. It was fearsomely heavy stuff. They would need muscle to get it to the surface. To sunlight. To the real world, not this realm of Pluto.

After a while Raoul took his place with the rubble-movers and Emil came back to rest. He stretched himself out and appeared to go to sleep. Kate moved into their cavern trying not to scrape her boots. Now she sat in darkness on a high ledge.

Emil noticed nothing. Kate began to descend.

John's knapsack lay invitingly to hand, its contents spilled out. Her own had been torn off her back when she fell down the ramp and over the edge. Delicately, Kate replaced the spare torch, the spare batteries, the food and the water bottle in it. She eased it on to her back and went up the wall like a monkey. The noise made by shifting rock and rubble and the noise made by the shifters as they cursed and swore covered up her small contribution. Emil never stirred.

She drank greedily. Then she investigated the exits she had found.

Very soon she found the water. It had cut deep into the limestone and must have run at different levels in different times. The walkway beside it was as good as a towpath. She felt brave enough to set off alone like this because she also had the luminous paint. She was marking her way. If she got nowhere, she could backtrack and find the men again. If they succeeded in escaping, she could follow them. John and she had marked their way in. When the men broke through the rubble, they could find their way out. Meanwhile, she wanted to know if this water was the same underground stream that she and John had crossed on their way in.

She stopped and washed. It made her feel considerably better. The rubble in her hair had been irritating.

The noise steadily increased. The water speeded up. Kate rounded a corner and found she was above falls. She climbed down and turned another corner. The water ran swift and silent again. On one wall a greenish glow lifted and shimmered faintly at her. Luminous paint. Kate chuckled. She was on their route in and hopefully back out from under the mountain. It was time to go back and get John.

The torch began to get weak on her way back. She didn't like to manage without it because although there was that very faint glow from the walls, it was not enough to let her see obstacles at her feet. She didn't fancy falling into the water and being swept down over the falls.

She left the river where she had marked and came back to the cave she had found. She went quietly across it and listened.

The men were still at work.

She felt uplifted. Selected. Empowered. Everything worked to her advantage. John must have collapsed on the job because at last they had given him a rest. The three of them were in what was in effect a passage leading out of the cave, shifting rubble. John was alone, tied up. His eyes were shut.

Kate climbed down. She crept over to John, collecting a few ribs on the way. His eyes flickered open when she touched him.

She had no time for emotional reunions. She took the knife from her belt and sawed through his ropes. She helped him to his feet and put the ribs where he had

262

been laying. She would have liked to leave the rope as an artistic gesture but they might need it so she put it in the knapsack. Then she crept back over the cave and went up the wall.

John followed her noisily. Once through he tried to speak but she hustled him over to the exit. Only when they were safely by the river, did she stop.

His hands were in a bad way. She helped him wash them and then she washed his face. There was no need to say anything. He knew what she was thinking and she knew what he was thinking.

They stopped to eat. 'How did you get away?' he asked.

'I don't know. Someone down here is on my side. I don't want to probe too deeply in case I offend him. Or her.'

He had trouble descending the falls because his hands were so torn and bloody. Once down they went with great care. They didn't know whether Raoul would find the way they had gone and be following them, or whether he was still attempting to break out through the landslip. If he succeeded, they would meet him shortly.

'Why are you carrying the skull?' John asked at one point.

'I like it,' said Kate.

They came to their own crossing point over the underground river. They could see what the landslip had done, how huge blocks had shifted and released the piles of rock Raoul was digging through. They could hear how he had nearly succeeded.

Kate got busy with the paint. John forded the water and got busy with Kate's knife. Raoul had taken his own away.

Eventually Kate was satisfied. She arranged the freshly painted skull so that Raoul would see it when he finally broke through. Meanwhile John had scraped away their luminous marker so that Raoul would not have it to guide him. She stripped and waded across the water. It seemed to her that the tug of the current was stronger, the water wider and deeper than before. Maybe she was weaker. John had helped her last time but she didn't need help this time, she had toughened up.

Once across, she looked back to admire her handiwork. The luminous skull was nasty from the back view. Hopefully Raoul would have a heart attack when he saw it. By the noises he was making it wouldn't be long before he broke through.

Kate's shirt was open, its bottom knotted up to keep it out of the water. Her lower half was quite naked. She went over to John. He too had not yet dressed, allowing his skin to dry a little before he pulled his clothes back on.

'How do you feel?' Kate murmured.

He was silent a moment. 'You want to do it now, you crazy bitch? We could do with being well in advance of them.'

Kate touched him, touched his sex. Her lips brushed his jawline. 'I've come back from the grave,' she said. 'I have an urge to celebrate.'

'How did you survive?' His fingers came up between her thighs.

'I fell, not very far. I climbed up in the dark. I found I couldn't get back the way I had come. I slept for a while. Then I found a way up.'

'In the dark?'

'In the dark. Oh, John, that's very good.'

'Your sex is velvet. Did I ever tell you that?'

'No. I don't think you did.'

'Your thighs are always cool, always smooth. Like jade.'

'Not hard?'

'No, not hard. Like jade gates. They open and welcome in.'

'Welcome in.'

'Your flesh curls, as if to beckon. I wish I could see it.'

264

'Shine the torch there.'

'I could die inside you, Kate. You take me in and I don't ever want to leave.'

'I won't let you. I won't let you. Only for a little while, now and again. And you must taste other women. I'll taste other men. Then I'll know how good you are in me. Oh Christ.'

He moved sweetly, her whole inner self fused with pleasure.

She could feel his sex in her, every part of it, the wholeness of it, the pressure of it, the sweetness of his movements and the effortless way he carried her up with him to the peak of pleasure, the explosion of joy that they made together every time. They had begun in a cave. Now they continued in a cave. The ground was gritty under her. She lay on her clothes, quite naked, feeling his strong body along the length of her, ignoring the growing noise from their enemies, sublimely happy and sure of what she was at.

Afterwards they crouched together by the water and washed each other's sex. They dressed carefully and turned to go.

'How are we going to repossess that gold?' asked Kate. 'I can't bear for them to have it.'

'Let them carry it out. They won't get far. They need to be caught actually stealing. That, with my testimony, will put them away. You can put in your thrupenny-worth if you like.'

'Repeated attempts to kill me?'

'That's right. That sort of thing.'

A hundred yards later they came up against more evidence of what the quake had achieved. Their way out was blocked. They stared at each other aghast. Kate had been so high it had not occurred to her things might still go wrong. She was sure she was being looked after. Now, it seemed, they were trapped underground and they had murderers right behind them.

* * *

'The first thing is not to fall into their hands,' muttered John. 'We've got to get back to the river, where there's another way.'

'We don't know it leads out.'

'No. But once we're behind Raoul we can let him dig us out. He's done it once. He can do it again. But he mustn't catch us.'

They hurried back. Hastily they stripped and crossed, hand in hand.

The water seemed even deeper and stronger to Kate and she was glad of John's strength, helping her. Just as they reached halfway, when there was no possibility that they could get themselves hidden, the filthy snarling face of Pierre appeared in front of them.

John's torch wavered and caught him full in its beam. He yelled hoarsely and vanished.

They moved forward as fast as they could. 'Maybe he won't have realised it was us,' panted Kate.

'Maybe he didn't see us, just the torch.' John's voice was grim.

The water swirled and pulled at their slipping cold feet. Kate stumbled and was righted by John, else she would have gone under. They blundered forward and it was too late. Pierre was through like a beast of the pit, filthy, furious, and behind him came Raoul and Emil.

Emil, whose mind was perhaps the weakest of the three, saw the glowing luminous skull and the two pale naked figures emerging from the deep. He gave a high scream and fell on his face, babbling. Neither Pierre nor Raoul was such easy meat. Pierre started forward and was restrained by his master. Raoul, with his lips curled back and his teeth bared, was pointing a gun.

John shone his torch full in his face. This was a mistake. Raoul shot him. They were thigh deep in the black river and they both stumbled backwards. John dropped his torch. It fell into the water and for a moment it would be seen turning and twisting as it aligned with the flow. Then it went out. Raoul seemed no longer to care that they were potential packhorses and that he had to get the gold out. He was transfigured with hate, his shaking bloody hands clutching the gun and pointing it at them.

He began to laugh crazily. 'I 'ave you now,' he said, his smooth accent collapsing under the strain of the moment. 'I kill you.'

'We'll carry the gold,' said John. His hand tightened on Kate's. She didn't mind. Dying this way was positively cheery compared to her recent brushes with the Grim Reaper.

'No,' said Raoul, advancing. Rubble and filth fell from his clothes. He was a terrible figure. He held the gun with both hands, his arms stretched straight in front of him. The barrel wavered and shook but most of the time it pointed at them.

'I just hurt you first,' said Raoul. 'When you beg, when the pain is terrible, when you bleed, then I kill you.'

'Look out behind you,' Kate shouted.

Raoul laughed. 'Always you take me for a fool.' He squeezed the trigger. The explosion was enormous. Rock debris showered down.

Kate helped John back to his feet. Raoul sniggered and shot again.

Pierre made a curious whining noise in his throat. '*Patron*,' he said. The wall of water hit them all.

The EarthMover had done his work. The rocks shifted and settled. Water found a new way to go. The river, hardly more than a fat stream before the quake, had been swollen as a breach began to appear in rock between it and another underground waterway. Now the rock burst before the remorseless pressure of water. The released waterflow travelled like a wall down its new course, over the falls, to sweep round the corner and hit them full force.

Raoul's third shot went wide. Kate and John were picked up by a mighty hand and swept downstream.

Behind them, also washed into the water, came Emil, Pierre and Raoul.

The business of staying alive occupied them totally. Kate caught her breath, choked, surfaced again, coughed, went under – and so it went on. She span round and round. She had lost John's hand and she never felt the knapsack as it was ripped off her back. Her shirt banished though again she never felt it go.

What mind she had left was praying to the Chthonic gods. She wanted to be struck on the head by the inevitably lowering roof and knocked out before she was drowned. There was no way this water wasn't going to enter a passage or tunnel it totally filled. That was when she would drown.

She didn't remember the next bit, not ever in her life. Simply, she came to on a beach. It would have been a beach above ground, that is. As it was, she lay on cold pebbles, a shingle shore, and heard the diminishing waters rushing past her.

It was very cold indeed. After a while she lifted her exhausted battered body and attempted to take stock of her surroundings.

She could see. It wasn't the greenish organic glow of creatures making their own light. She could see because very faintly some natural light was seeping in.

Her eyes gobbled the light hungrily. She could see the surface of the water swirling by. The light came from under it.

Her mind was very tired but she worked it out. The river went through a tunnel, a short tunnel. The other end was outside. In sunlight. In the fresh air. Free. At the moment the naked body of a man went by her in the water. His head was up, his hair plastered round his face. One arm lifted and dropped again. Then he was by.

She didn't hesitate. She stepped back into the flow, took breath and dived.

She was in a pool. Above her, natural light poured in so brilliantly she couldn't see. There was a small flow of water out. The rest of the water seemed to go back down into the depths of the mountain. Only its exceptional height, swollen by the changing course of the underground river, had brought it to the surface.

The man in the pool with her wasn't John. It was Raoul.

Kate swam to the edge, warily watching him. There was an unpleasant downward sucking force. Raoul smiled. His teeth in his dark face were very white. He had a big graze on his temple.

'Kate,' he said, his voice rough as if someone had abraded his throat. 'Always you survive.'

'We can get out,' said Kate. 'You can't kill me now. We've escaped to safety.'

'I want to kill you.'

'We had something going once,' Kate said rapidly. 'I only betrayed you because you ill-treated me. You know I don't mind you being a criminal. John Sorrell is a criminal. But he treats me better.'

'You are his woman. We knew it from the first, from Corfu. We had just to dangle you and he would come.'

'Your English is very good,' Kate said admiringly. Her hand groped behind her back, looking for a loose rock, anything she might use as a weapon. But the stream had washed everything loose away.

'You are beautiful, you know? Even now, with your hair all wet against your head. I see your naked breasts and I desire them. But more I desire you dead.'

'The water tears all our clothes off,' Kate said idiotically. She smiled and moved towards him. 'Have me now,' she invited. 'Then kill me. You'll enjoy killing a woman you've just made love to. And I will die in your arms, happy. You are a superb lover, Raoul. The best I've ever had.'

He caught hold of her breasts. 'I want you,' he said harshly. 'I do not want to kill you, pretty Kate, but I must. Always you betray me.'

Her hand went under the water. 'You can't make love

269

to me in this cold,' she said. 'We'll have to go up into the sun.'

Raoul laughed. Her hand was on his sex. She grasped it firmly and pulled with all her might.

It was very gratifying. He went over backwards with a scream cut off by his submergence under the surface. Kate gripped and pulled. His head came up and she hit him with her free hand. It hurt amazingly. Then he got her with one of his hands. He had tremendous strength. He had her off her feet immediately.

Now he had her hair and was pulling her under. Her hand slid off his sex. She gasped and spluttered. He held her down and she knew she was going to drown.

A terrific blow hit her. She came up like a cork. John had arrived fighting fit, it seemed. Raoul rolled over backwards and was sucked down by the undertow.

They climbed up into the sun. They lay wearily, feeling its warmth beat into their aching exhausted bodies. All around them the mountain stretched in glory, up on one side, down on the other. They could see nothing except mountain and sky, distant trees, undergrowth parched by the sun. They could see each other.

They slept. They were woken by the arrival of Pierre.

He was very much alive and very furious. A horrible naked battle ensued. They had only just got him out cold and were considering dropping him down into the water again, when over the horizon came Lucien and Jean-Marc.

John took Kate's hand and they began to run. They were in no fit state to fight again: John had one arm badly sprained, and the two after them were probably armed. The mountainside was not smooth, but had countless bumps and dips. Huge blocks of rock were separated from the living mountain, scattered carelessly on its flanks. They could play a gruesome game of hide-and-seek and get away when it fell dark.

It wasn't a bad idea, but Jean-Marc and Lucien were

fresh and fit and, above all else, shod. Kate and John were in bare feet, their boots long since lost.

It was at the point that she reared sharply backwards, seeing an adder curled on a stone, that Kate knew they would be caught. Her feet would hardly carry her. She was so tired she was beginning not to care if she was caught. John was stumbling badly because one of Raoul's underground shots had grazed his ribs and the wound had opened in the fight and was bleeding copiously.

Ahead of them was a totally bare stretch of sunny mountain with one rock in the middle. Jean-Marc and Lucien were getting close. Kate and John reached the rock and went to the far side of it.

They leant against it, panting. 'Bloody Interpol,' said John. 'They should have been here. Sorry, Kate.'

Kate turned to face the rock, putting her arms round it, letting her cheek and breasts feel its rough caress. She smiled at John and disappeared.

She fell down a sloping earth tunnel, aware that John was falling on top of her. Above them the rock pivoted slightly and settled back, looking as firmly planted as it had to Kate.

She felt like Alice in Wonderland. She went down a long sloping shoot and came out at the bottom. John landed on top of her. Holding his arm and groaning he crawled to his feet. 'Run,' he said feebly. 'Hide. Before they get here.'

They scuttled forward virtually on all fours. It wasn't totally dark but the light was ahead of them, not behind. It was a while before Kate realised why. There was a slight crack in the soil and vegetation above them. Between coarse grass stems and scrubby bushes a little light filtered. From above, the ground had looked continuous. They were experiencing another freak of this changeable living moving mountain.

They walked more slowly now, dusting soil and earth off their bodies. They both limped. John's side was smeared with blood. They held hands and became quiet.

There was a slab blocking the way forward. They squeezed round it and found themselves in a bowl of green light.

It was a tiny rocky amphitheatre open to the sky. Plants trailed above, filtering the sunlight and giving everything a dim and gorgeous glow. To their left, water trickled. A short stone column had been erected by the spring. On it a bronze faun smiled deliciously slyly at them. His slanting eyes danced in the green light. It slid across his shining breast. Riotous curls were at his head and his groin. His penis was erect.

The faun smiled at them. His pointed ears lay neat and flat to his head. His sharp little horns poked through his curls. His tail was up, like his sex.

They turned. There she was, six foot tall, gold and white in the nimbus of light. Aphrodite, impossibly beautiful, smiled her remote and mysterious smile.

There was Paris. His muscles bulged. His veins were lovingly detailed His buttocks were clenched. His thighs and calves were alive and full of tendony strength. One arm was extended with the apple.

John said: 'They didn't melt it down.'

'No.'

'Those Greeks. How they could model the human body.'

'And perfect it and call it divine.' Kate's voice shook.

John sat down. 'I don't feel very well,' he said uncertainly.

'I'll wash your wound. Perhaps we could rest here. I don't know whether they'll mind or not.' Kate looked at their companions.

'This is a sanctuary,' said John. 'We need one. I don't think they'll mind.'

Kate washed his ribs. They both washed their faces and their bodies, as much as they could. The water felt good to torn skin and raw feet.

The floor of the sanctuary was a thin soft grass. It was

warm, the sunlight filtering down and captured in the green place. They slept.

Kate woke and saw Paris looking at her. She admired his splendid nakedness. Then she noticed that he too had a magnificent erection. This was no little business, like that of the nimble pint-sized faun. Paris was modelled on a full grown adult male and his sex had been proudly displayed.

'You loved Helen, not Aphrodite,' she said. She felt very comfortable, her stomach particularly light and empty. Her bones were soft and relaxed, the pain gone out of them. She was warm.

She looked at Aphrodite. Presumably all men loved her. It was her business to be beautiful and she looked like she was good at it.

Paris came over and knelt by her. 'You were a man, not a god,' she said. That he was a man was very evident. She touched his swollen erect penis and found it warm. Bronze was such a satiny, yielding metal. It suited a man's sex. It felt good.

She lay dreamily caressing the statue's sex. In return, Paris stroked her brow. Her thoughts cleared and became limpid, like water.

She stroke his balls and felt them alive and jumpy in her hands. His hair was crisp and silky. She put a hand under him and ran a finger along from his rear to behind his balls. His seam. She did it again and felt him tremble with pleased laughter.

She looked up into his face. His features were classic. The handsome Greek face smiled down at her. His hair curled, covering much of his skull so that the curls lay against his neck and came down over his forehead. The cap of hair shone bronze and Kate stroked it shyly. It felt very warm and soft.

She stroked the bulging shoulders, feeling the swell of living muscle. She ran her hands down his calves. The man was all magnificent strength.

He moved over her, lowering his huge strong muscular body until she was covered. She put her arms round him gladly. 'Thank you for looking after me down there,' she said into his ear. His skin was perfumed and smelled wonderful. There was nothing modern or sweet in it. Rather it was spiced.

He gave her to understand that Aphrodite had looked after her. 'Thank you for looking after my lover,' she said.

The vast body shook slightly with silent laughter. She felt his sex, impossibly long, begin to slide between her thighs.

She opened her legs as wide as they would go. The great limbs trembled on her. The penis felt alive all of its self. It quested, seeking its way in.

He might have been molten bronze, liquid firelight, gold. Her insides twisted in a fearsome spasm of pain and then everything was fine. All the knots were gone.

It wasn't so much like sex as like purified, rarefied pleasure. It was the essence of sensuality. It was fierce and bright and strong, yet she felt molten all through. Her body blazed. She foamed. His hands on her skin, his weight bearing her down, the thrust of his hips, the golden rod he impaled her with – all came together in a synthesis of feeling and Kate's body exploded in sunbursts of orgasm, feeling the pulse of his sex even as she did so.

She felt him lift himself from her. He was laughing, she was sure.

She slept.

Phormis found them before Interpol. This was a relief. They climbed out of the sanctuary that night and walked down the mountain by the light of the waning moon. When they saw lights, they approached cautiously. Phormis found their nude state very funny but provided them both with clothes.

Interpol, accompanied by Albanian security forces, finally arrived. They collected Jean-Marc and Lucien, whom Phormis had tied up. With some difficulty, they also found Pierre, who was wandering around with a cracked skull after Kate had hit him over the head with a stone while he was fighting John.

They were sitting round in Phormis's camp, Kate and John explaining that everyone was too late and they had only kept alive by the skin of their teeth with no thanks to their friends and aids, when the EarthMover rolled over again.

The mountain shivered, groaned, and rumbled deep in its heart. The ground shook gently, evilly, and came to rest once more. Kate had gone quite white and found her heart was hammering. It was a most unpleasant experience.

Dust vented from cracks in the ground. Later she and John went for a walk.

They didn't discuss it. They had said nothing about it. They walked as best they could till the mountain was swelling all around them in vast and archaic splendour.

There was nothing to recognise. New landslips had erupted on the surface, rock crumbling and falling in long broken slopes of dangerous loose scree.

'Aphrodite,' said Kate.

'Wants to stay put,' finished John.

They sat down and looked at each other. 'You're an archaeologist,' Kate said quietly. 'If you find Aphrodite and Paris and that sensual little faun they have for company, your name will be in the history books.'

John went scarlet, like a teenager. 'She's better where she is,' he said clumsily.

Kate watched him steadily. 'We slept in the sanctuary,' she said presently.

'We were safe. They kept us safe.' John had a miserable doggedness about him.

'Did we do anything for them?' asked Kate.

The silence stretched and stretched. The swift Mediterranean night fell. Far below them their friends prepared for sleep. They would all be on the move the following day, Kate and John accompanying the Interpol men and the Security forces.

Stars spangled in the sky. John said. 'We dream dreams.'

'Yes,' said Kate. Both of them, then, in the sanctuary. Aphrodite and Paris. The gods had not been so keen on separation from mortals in those days. Those Arcadian days.

On their way back down the mountain they found a huge declivity, a vast raw bowl opened out into the mountain's interior. The moon rose and shone on what was at the bottom. They collected torches from the camp and returned.

Aphrodite had thanked them for their reticence, it seemed. The mountain had spewed up what it no longer wanted.

A luminous skull. The dead Emil. Some Roman armour. And two chests of gold.

BLACK
lace

Already published

WEB OF DESIRE
Sophie Danson

High-flying executive Marcie is gradually drawn away from the normality of her married life. Strange messages begin to appear on her computer, summoning her to sinister and fetishistic sexual liaisons with strangers whose identity remains secret. She's given glimpses of the world of The Omega Network, where her every desire is known and fulfilled.

ISBN 0 352 32856 8

BLUE HOTEL
Cherri Pickford

Hotelier Ramon can't understand why best-selling author Floy Pennington has come to stay at his quiet hotel in the rural idyll of the English countryside. Her exhibitionist tendencies are driving him crazy, as are her increasingly wanton encounters with the hotel's other guests.

ISBN 0 352 32858 4

CASSANDRA'S CONFLICT
Fredrica Alleyn

Behind the respectable facade of a house in present-day
Hampstead lies a world of decadent indulgence and darkly
bizarre eroticism. The sternly attractive Baron and his beautiful but cruel wife are playing games with the young Cassan-
dra, employed as a nanny in their sumptuous household.
Games where only the Baron knows the rules, and where
there can only be one winner.

ISBN 0 352 32859 2

Forthcoming publications

THE CAPTIVE FLESH
Cleo Cordell

PLEASURE HUNT
Sophie Danson

OUTLANDIA
Georgia Angelis

BLACK ORCHID
Roxanne Carr

BLACK
lace

WE NEED YOUR HELP . . .
to plan the future of women's erotic fiction –

– and no stamp required!

Yours are the only opinions that matter.
Black Lace is a new and exciting venture: the first series
of books devoted to erotic fiction by women for women.

We're going to do our best to provide the brightest,
best-written, bonk-filled books you can buy. And we'd
like your help in these early stages. Tell us what you
want to read.

THE BLACK LACE QUESTIONNAIRE

SECTION ONE: ABOUT YOU

1.1   Sex *(we presume you are female, but so as not to discriminate)*
       are you?
       Male   ☐   Female   ☐

1.2   Age
       under 21   ☐   21–30   ☐
       31–40   ☐   41–50   ☐
       51–60   ☐   over 60   ☐

1.3   At what age did you leave full-time education?
       still in education   ☐   16 or younger   ☐
       17–19   ☐   20 or older   ☐

1.4   Occupation _____

1.5 Annual household income

        under £10,000 ☐   £10–£20,000 ☐

        £20–£30,000 ☐   £30–£40,000 ☐

        over £40,000 ☐

1.6 We are perfectly happy for you to remain anonymous;
but if you would like us to send you a free booklist of
Nexus books for men and Black Lace books for Women,
please insert your name and address

_____

_____

_____

_____

SECTION TWO: ABOUT BUYING BLACK LACE BOOKS

2.1 How did you acquire this copy of *No Lady*

    I bought it myself ☐   My partner bought it ☐

    I borrowed/found it ☐

2.2 How did you find out about Black Lace books?

    I saw them in a shop ☐

    I saw them advertised in a magazine ☐

    I saw the London Underground posters ☐

    I read about them in _____

    Other _____

2.3 Please tick the following statements you agree with:

    I would be less embarrassed about buying Black
Lace books if the cover pictures were less explicit ☐

    I think that in general the pictures on Black
Lace books are about right ☐

    I think Black Lace cover pictures should be as
explicit as possible ☐

2.4 Would you read a Black Lace book in a public place – on
a train for instance?

    Yes ☐   No ☐

SECTION THREE: ABOUT THIS BLACK LACE BOOK

3.1 Do you think the sex content in this book is:
    Too much   ☐   About right   ☐
    Not enough   ☐

3.2 Do you think the writing style in this book is:
    Too unreal/escapist ☐   About right   ☐
    Too down to earth   ☐

3.3 Do you think the story in this book is:
    Too complicated   ☐   About right   ☐
    Too boring/simple   ☐

3.4 Do you think the cover of this book is:
    Too explicit   ☐   About right   ☐
    Not explicit enough ☐

Here's a space for any other comments:

SECTION FOUR: ABOUT OTHER BLACK LACE BOOKS

4.1 How many Black Lace books have you read?   ☐

4.2 If more than one, which one did you prefer?

4.3 Why?

SECTION FIVE: ABOUT YOUR IDEAL EROTIC NOVEL

We want to publish the books you want to read – so this is your chance to tell us exactly what your ideal erotic novel would be like.

5.1 Using a scale of 1 to 5 (1 = no interest at all, 5 = your ideal), please rate the following possible settings for an erotic novel:

Medieval/barbarian/sword 'n' sorcery ☐
Renaissance/Elizabethan/Restoration ☐
Victorian/Edwardian ☐
1920s & 1930s – the Jazz Age ☐
Present day ☐
Future/Science Fiction ☐

5.2 Using the same scale of 1 to 5, please rate the following themes you may find in an erotic novel:

Submissive male/dominant female ☐
Submissive female/dominant male ☐
Lesbianism ☐
Bondage/fetishism ☐
Romantic love ☐
Experimental sex e.g. anal/watersports/sex toys ☐
Gay male sex ☐
Group sex ☐

Using the same scale of 1 to 5, please rate the following styles in which an erotic novel could be written:

Realistic, down to earth, set in real life ☐
Escapist fantasy, but just about believable ☐
Completely unreal, impressionistic, dreamlike ☐

5.3 Would you prefer your ideal erotic novel to be written from the viewpoint of the main male characters or the main female characters?

Male ☐ Female ☐
Both ☐

5.4 What would your ideal Black Lace heroine be like? Tick
as many as you like:

Dominant	☐	Glamorous	☐
Extroverted	☐	Contemporary	☐
Independent	☐	Bisexual	☐
Adventurous	☐	Naive	☐
Intellectual	☐	Introverted	☐
Professional	☐	Kinky	☐
Submissive	☐	Anything else?	☐
Ordinary	☐	_____	

5.5 What would your ideal male lead character be like?
Again, tick as many as you like:

Rugged	☐		
Athletic	☐	Caring	☐
Sophisticated	☐	Cruel	☐
Retiring	☐	Debonair	☐
Outdoor-type	☐	Naive	☐
Executive-type	☐	Intellectual	☐
Ordinary	☐	Professional	☐
Kinky	☐	Romantic	☐
Hunky	☐		
Sexually dominant	☐	Anything else?	☐
Sexually submissive	☐	_____	

5.6 Is there one particular setting or subject matter that your
ideal erotic novel would contain?

_____

SECTION SIX: LAST WORDS

6.1 What do you like best about Black Lace books?

_____

6.2 What do you most dislike about Black Lace books?

_____

6.3 In what way, if any, would you like to change Black
Lace covers?

_____

6.4 Here's a space for any other comments!

_____

_____

_____

_____

_____

Thank you for completing this questionnaire. Now tear it out of the book – carefully! – put it in an envelope and send it to:

Black Lace
FREEPOST
London
W10 5BR

No stamp is required!